KING OF THIEVES

The True Story of Christian Andreas Kasebier:

Tailor, Smuggler, Spy

By

Kevin Casebier

VININGS
HOUSE PRESS

First published by Vinings House Press 2021

First edition

ISBN: 978-1-7377716-1-6

This book was professionally typeset on Reedsy.

Find out more at reedsy.com

"There is nothing noble in being superior to your fellow man; true nobility is being superior to your former self."

Ernest Hemingway

Contents

Preface

In every conceivable manner, the family is link to our past, bridge to our future.

– Alex Haley

Writing a story about a distant family member is a surreal process but was more rewarding than I imagined. This has been a year and a half project that started with genealogy research that began over ten years ago. This is the true story of Christian Andreas Kasebier, a young Prussian apprentice tailor who later became a smuggler, crime boss and spy. During his dramatic career, he became known as both the King of Thieves and the 'Prussian Robin Hood', often stealing from the rich and giving to the poor.

Christian and Johann Kasebier descended from a generation of tailors who traded cloth and made, repaired and altered garments such as coats and dresses. A merchant tailor was a businessperson who sold materials for the garments he made. Merchant banks or modern investment banking evolved from merchants who traded commodities particularly, cloth. Cloth was extremely expensive and cloth merchants were often very wealthy. Many of the most powerful families in Europe, such as the Italian Medici family, derived their wealth from the textile trade.

The strong demand for textiles and cloth production helped fuel wars in the 18th Century. King Frederick II of Prussia desired the autonomous region of Silesia and plotted to seize it from the Austrians for its flourishing textile industries. He deceived young Maria Theresa of Austria when she allowed his troops to occupy the rich province for protection. Instead, King Frederick captured Silesia, which sparked the Silesian Wars (1740-42; 1744-45; 1756-63 aka Seven Years War) and set the stage for the War of Austrian Succession (1740-48). The global Seven Years War (1756-63) was the first world war involving all great powers of Europe where France, Austria, Saxony, Sweden and Russian aligned against Prussia, Hanover and Great Britain.

King Frederick II became popular throughout the German speaking territories and Prussia became one of the preeminent powers in Europe, which led to the rise of Germany. By the end of King Frederick II's reign, textiles accounted for two-thirds of Prussia's national production and the textile industry employed ninety percent of the industrial labor force.

Johann Georg Kasebier (born August 6, 1693), my sixth great grandfather and his youngest brother, Christian Andreas Kasebier together with the rest of the Kasebier family lived and worked at #18 Fleishergasse Strasse later renamed Mittelgasse Strasse in Halle (Saale), Sachsen Anhalt Germany.

Many of the villagers including the Kasebier family were religious and belonged to an unpopular faith known as the Schwarzenau Brethren (organized 1708) later to be known as the Church of the Brethren or "German Baptists" (1908). They rejected established liturgy, including infant baptism and popular Eucharistic practices in favor of following New Testament practices. The Brethren were persecuted for their religious beliefs and their leader, Alexander Mack gathered together his followers including Johann and his family, and brought them to America. In the U.S. they became popularly known as the "Dunkers" for their belief in full-immersion baptisms.

Count Casimir granted Johann permission to leave Wittgenstein and Johann described his arduous voyage in his journal to the Count. Johann, his wife, Maria and their two sons,

Gottfried and Gottlieb arrived in Philadelphia on October 29, 1724, and proceeded to the village of Roxborough PA.

Johann died a young father shortly after his arrival to America. His eldest son, Gottfried 'Godfrey' Kasebier (1718-1774) was forced to move east to Sussex, New Jersey after Indian attacks, including one which killed his younger brother Gottlieb. It was at this time that the Kasebiers changed their religious view, refusing to be pacifists. Subsequently, descendants of the family have participated and fought in every American war.

Gottfried's children spelled their surname differently, with the letter C rather than the German K and sometimes as Casebeer or Casbeer. According to Dr. Josef Brechenmacher, the surname, Casebier, was used to describe a person who could forecast the weather. In an agricultural economy where weather could be the difference between sufficiency and famine one who could accurately predict weather was highly regarded.

Gottfried's son, William, was born (1756-1788) in Pennsylvania, the British Colonies of North America, and later moved to Kentucky. William had a son, Jacob (1781-1865) born in Somerset Pennsylvania, who had a son, Walter born (1822-1885) who had a son, Edward (1859-1924) who had a son, Edwin Foster Casebier (1902-1984), born in Central City (Muhlenberg County), KY who had a son, Edwin Wayne Casebier born in Central City, KY (1934-2007) who had a son, Kevin Casebier born in Louisville, KY, residing in Atlanta, GA and part-time in Seagrove Beach, Fl.

Acknowledgement

This book would not have been possible had it not been for the encouragement of others. My sincere thanks to Stan Foster, Hollywood film actor, producer and director, who first encouraged me to write this story. I owe a debt of gratitude to Lora Mirza, Michael Ludden and Solange Warner for their constructive advice and keen insight. Many thanks to Rob who helped with the book cover design and Nick for his research and assistance, which helped to bring the story to life. I'd like to give a very special thanks along with my love and appreciation to both my daughter, Stephanie who enthusiastically supported this project from concept to completion and my wife, Stacy for her ongoing support; reading early drafts, giving advice on the cover and her amazing editorial skills.

Chapter One

Prague, 1757

Breathing hard from my climb up the hill, I gaze down upon the besieged city. It is a bright, cloudless day and sunlight sparkles on the steely waters of the Vltava. Beyond the river, behind the walls, are fifty thousand soldiers of the Austrian army and their allies. Upon the gatehouse I see the assorted standards of the defenders. On the near side of the bridges stand ranks clad in the red, white and blue of Prussia.

My king, Frederick, won a decisive victory only days ago and his force of one hundred thousand now surrounds the city. He led his army across hundreds of miles and through mountain passes to bring war to his enemy. Ever impatient, he aims to defeat the Austrians, now under the command of Prince Charles of Lorraine. But Charles will not negotiate and reinforcements are on the way. King Frederick needs a way in. And he wants me to find it.

I am Christian Andreas Kasebier, until recently a prisoner residing at the king's pleasure. If I do not succeed, I will be sent back to the filthy, dangerous hell where I have spent the last nine years.

The king considers me useful because I was once a king too. Every man, woman and child in Prussia knew me as the 'King of

Thieves'. I was born a tailor's son but I traveled all over Europe and became as rich as a lord. My band and I robbed whoever we wished, thumbed our noses at our 'superiors' and evaded capture for years. I was known for my cunning, leadership and resourcefulness.

When I was finally put on trial, the king took a great interest. The articulacy of my pleas persuaded him to spare me the hangman's noose. Now he holds my life in his hands for a second time.

I will not live the rest of my days behind bars. I must find a way into the city; give my king what he wants. I will escape death again. I will be free.

Chapter Two

Halle, 1727

'I would simply like a little freedom. Is that so much to ask?'

As we walked along the busy street carrying roped bundles of cloth, my brother Lucian offered a cynical glance.

'Freedom, Christian? The word is meaningless. Who possesses it?' Two years older than me at nineteen, Lucian was shorter and weaker and rather struggling with his load. He nodded towards a bakery. 'Master Gotze, who must rise in the middle of the night to start work when most are abed?'

Beside the bakery was a livery stable. 'Or young Master Neuer, who spends more time with horses and donkeys than people?'

We passed a squad of spearmen clad in the king's colors.

'And as for soldiers'

'At least they travel,' I interjected. 'And see something of the world.' 'Perhaps,' replied Lucian, now panting with the effort of carrying the cloth. 'But they spend most of their time being shouted at or struck. And, as we all know, Christian, you are not one to follow orders without complaint'.

'Wait a moment.'

Annoyed by Lucian's arguments, I was amused to see him call a halt. In truth, the cloth was a strain for me too but I took care not to show it. An empty cart had been left outside the stable and we placed our loads there to take a moment's rest.

'Only a minute,' said Lucian. 'Father is in a dark mood today.' Instead of responding, I simply enjoyed being away from the four walls of my father's shop: the place where I had labored since my earliest years.

Among the sights that caught my eye were a group of young ladies, sitting outside the coffeehouse across the street. The drink was still quite rare in Prussia and it was known that the king did not approve of importation because of the profits made by English merchants. I had never tasted it myself. Father and indeed Mother contended that anything spent on food was money denied to the accounts of the tailor's shop. As a result, meals were adequate but rarely enjoyable. We received little in the way of spending money though clothing at least was no concern; we all made our own.

It was June, nearing midday, and the sugary pastries being consumed by the young ladies had attracted some wasps. Two of them were already flicking gloved hands at the insects and another seemed anxious to move inside.

'We should go,' said Lucian, who had poor eyesight at distance and had not noticed the scene.

'A moment.'

As was often the case in my youth, I acted without thinking. Darting between two passing carriages, I approached the coffeehouse and removed my belt. The proprietor was nowhere to be seen so I stepped inside the low wall that surrounded the establishment. The young ladies were all well attired in colorful gowns with appealingly low necklines. One elegant beauty possessed compelling blue eyes and a lovely head of blonde hair beneath her cap.

Affecting the manner and accent of the noblemen I encountered daily at my father's store, I bowed low. 'Good day to you all, ladies. Might I be of assistance?'

There were four of them and I must admit that three regarded the belt in my hand with confusion, contempt, or a mixture of both.

The blonde lady, however, seemed more curious. 'That rather depends on what you intend.'

Insects – wasps in particular – were a perpetual problem in the summer months. I had become something of an expert at belting flying pests out of the sky and was often summoned by my Mother and siblings to do so. Father was less enthusiastic, largely on account of an incident in which I'd struck his rear end while hunting a particularly evasive mosquito. Needless to say, I suffered considerably more pain.

While bringing down a fly could present a considerable challenge, wasps were easy game. I brandished my belt and took a step forward. 'Allow me to rid you of these troublesome creatures. All I ask is that you remain still. It will not take long.'

'Please,' said the lady. 'They are driving us to distraction.' Despite the disapproving looks of her companions, I set about dispatching the wasps. The first two were swatted away with ease, and I noted an admiring glance from my blonde friend. The third wasp, however, led me a merry dance. I circled the table twice before lashing at it. I caught it well but unfortunately sent it too close to one of the ladies. She cried out, and the proprietor appeared instantly.

Knowing him to be an ill-tempered fellow, I bowed to the ladies and retreated to the welcome sound of applause.

Our tardiness was as much to do with Lucian's spindly arms as my brief detour but it was I who received the blame. Fortunately, my father was dealing with a client, which meant his ire had dimmed by the time he came into the parlor. Our home was situated on Fleishergasse; a large brick house fronted by the shop.

Lucian and I were eating a lunch of cabbage soup and bread. Mother sat in the corner, peeling vegetables above a pail.

Feeling Father's yardstick on my shoulder, I froze.

'The cloth has been unpacked?'

'Yes, Father.'

'And the courtyard has been tidied and cleaned?'

'Yes, Father.'

'Do not tarry next time.'

Happy to escape further sanction, I watched as my father exchanged a silent smile with my mother and refused the offer of soup. He always insisted there be at least two of us in the store and I knew that Mary and Johann would be on duty.

Keen to avoid yet more chores, I decided to engage my Father in conversation. This was always a risk. He sometimes seemed to enjoy the exchanges but on other occasions became annoyed by my tendency towards debate and opinion. We had all undergone some schooling and, though an average tailor, I was a good orator and writer. Father had tried to interest me in the shop accounts but I was far less able with numbers than letters.

'Another visit from Count Casimir, I see, Father?'

'Indeed.'

He sat beside Mother, close to the window. She passed him a newly peeled carrot, which he took a bite of before continuing.

'Johann is clearly his favorite now. He has ordered two capes and another cloak. Apparently, Draxler has not seen a single coin from him since winter.'

Draxler was a rival tailor with a shop just two streets away. The two acted civilly towards each other in public but I had on occasion heard Father curse the man. Though pious, he was a fierce competitor.

'Another cloak,' I said, largely to keep the conversation going. 'Why, he must have one for every day of the month.'

Father turned to Mother. 'The Count is attending a gathering in Potsdam next week. He assured me that he will wear one of Johann's waistcoats.'

Much to do with tailoring bored me but it had always been evident that Johann had a good eye for design. My father – and his before him – had built a reputation based on quality and durability. This is what Kasebiers was known for. But Johann had decided to concentrate on one type of garment, and his highly decorated and unique waistcoats were now in considerable demand. It seemed fitting that the eldest son led the way; he would after all eventually inherit the family business.

'Specialization,' remarked Father. 'I'll admit I was not convinced to start with but this could be the way forward for you younger boys too. Christian, I asked you to give some thought to the matter.'

I glanced at my mother, whose expression suggested I at least try to give a reasonable answer.

Unfortunately, I had not given the subject a moment's thought since the question had been posed.

'Er ...gowns?'

'You're more interested in what's inside the gowns,' quipped Lucian. This was unusually witty for him and I couldn't help laughing. Father did not like such talk and he kicked the bench we were sitting on, bringing an abrupt end to the merriment. Mother looked down as she continued to peel.

'It is a specialty,' I countered.

Father glowered at me, carrot in hand. 'Never easy with you, is it, boy?'

I was the only one he still referred to in this way. Had my mother not been present, I might have mentioned the fact. But ours was generally a peaceful household and I did not like to see her upset.

'Sorry, Father. I will think of another specialty, I promise.'

'You can think of it while you pick up the thread.'

This may not sound like an onerous task but it was one I dreaded. The floor of our workroom was perpetually covered by off-cuts. Father insisted that nothing be wasted. Recovering and sorting every last piece was a horrible job.

I looked to Mother for some support but when she looked up, I knew from her expression that I wouldn't get it. 'Answer, Christian.'

I nodded cordially. 'Yes, Father.'

***

Fortunately for me, Father was busy with customers for the rest of the day. An hour spent crawling around the workroom ensured that most of the thread was collected and I spent another hour sorting it.

As evening approached, I was recruited to assist with an urgent order: we were repairing two greatcoats for a pair of brothers, both infantrymen from the local garrison. I was tasked with re-stitching a sleeve and patching a hole that seemed to have been made by a very sharp blade. I imagined some dramatic encounter. Perhaps with an Austrian grenadier or a Russian Cossack! but knew that the soldiers were as often poked by a careless compatriot. My sister Mary described my work as 'fair' but I was glad Father was too busy to check it. He would invariably find fault and clearly considered me the weak link within our little factory. By contrast, Mary was an excellent seamstress but would never earn the title "apprentice" on account of her gender. I felt this was a pity for both of us.

We received another visitor late in the day: the lad Hugo, whose father supplied our household with firewood. When he knocked on the back door, Mother summoned me to help him unload. Emerging onto the courtyard, I found the squares of stone divided by long shadows. As ever, the tangy odor from the nearby dye-works hung heavily in the air. It was not pleasant but did mask far worse smells.

Hugo was three years my junior but very well built for his age. Like me, he worked only as hard as he had to and much preferred to talk.

'All done for the day?' I asked as he climbed up on to the rear of the cart.

His donkey was a docile beast and – unlike most – didn't need to be tethered.

'All done with deliveries,' he replied while handing me the first bundle of wood. 'But I'm sure Father will have us picking apples until dark.'

Their property was on the eastern side of Halle and included a large warehouse for their wood and a small orchard. As regular customers, we received a discount on the cider that they also produced. Hugo and I occasionally shared a mug or two when we could escape our labors.

'Saw Willem this morning,' he added as I dropped the first bundle outside our woodshed. 'His brother is off to Berlin – cadet school. Lucky swine. He could be a corporal before the year is out.'

I knew Willem and his brother; and will admit I felt rather jealous at this news. For a young man who had never been more than twenty miles from Halle, the thought of 'donning the blue' and seeing something – anything – beyond our province of Brandenburg held great appeal.

As the sons of a master artisan in a protected trade, Johann, Lucian and I were exempt from recruitment, even in the event of war. But there was another reason why a military career was not open to me: my family belonged to the Brethren, a Christian sect utterly opposed to violence. Hugo's family were not keen churchgoers and he'd expressed an interest in a soldierly career for several years. I found it impossible to find any certainty in such matters.

'Have you spoken to your father about it?'

Hugo grinned as he passed down the next bundle. 'In a roundabout way. I shall mention it tonight.'

I said nothing for a while, for I was imagining Willem's brother gathering his belongings into his knapsack and beginning the journey north to cadet school in Berlin. What an adventure – like something from a fairy tale or an ancient legend. It was in my nature to romanticize such things but I did understand the darker side of army life.

The Great War had ended sixty years before my birth. It lasted three decades and brought immense suffering to the middle part of Europe. Before his death, my grandfather had told us of the Swedish invaders; of torture and extortion; of deserted villages and piles of burning bodies.

'Willem reckons that we Brandenburgers start off at a disadvantage,' remarked Hugo. 'The king and the officers consider Pomeranians to be the cream of the crop. At least we're not Silesians or Easterners!'

Hugo removed the last bundle and added it to the pile beside the woodshed. He wiped a grimy sleeve across his grimy face.

'If only we had a mug of cider,' I said.

'New batch coming soon. If two young men were to find themselves with a flask on a fine summer night, they might attend the fair and watch the girls dance.'

I matched his grin. 'I suppose they might'.

That night, my older brother Johann joined us with his wife, Maria.

It was a warm evening but Mother insisted on cooking a chicken and I must admit the meat was fine. Due to the unbearable heat within the kitchen, we ate at the courtyard table. With Father, Mother, Mary, Lucian, myself, Maria, and Johann, it was a tight squeeze. Everyone complimented Mother on the chicken and Father spoke at length about the ills of the city. There had been a spate of robberies in Halle, with several men maimed or killed.

The conversation turned to lighter matters but I detected nervousness from Johann and Maria. They had been married for three years and everyone agreed they were an excellent match. I could never conjure any envy for my brother's success; he was a kind, enthusiastic fellow who I'd always admired. Johann seemed to help everyone get on with each other and the house always felt a better place with him around. Though quiet, Maria possessed a similarly agreeable temperament. When she had first shown her pretty, delicate face, I entertained some sinful thoughts but I now viewed her as a sister. Like the Kasebiers, her family were members of the Brethren.

Johann cast a grave look at his wife before speaking up. 'Father, do you recall our discussion in the spring – about Count Casimir's associates in the Americas?'

The courtyard was now cloaked by darkness, my father's grim features illuminated by grainy candlelight.

'I do.'

'It seems there are some opportunities in the region known as Pennsylvania. Dozens of German families have settled there now, many of them Brethren. The count believes that these colonies will grow swiftly. They are in great need of skilled tradesmen, tailors in particular. My friend Christopher is planning to leave in late summer when the weather is still fair.'

I noticed Mother wringing her hands. She was by nature a cautious soul.

Johann continued and, though his voice wavered, I got the impression he had rehearsed this speech.

'As you know, the count is a great supporter of my work and he has offered to go further than most patrons. He is prepared to fund half the cost of our passage along with some money to establish ourselves.' Johann put his hand on his wife's. She looked no more enthusiastic about the prospect than my mother.

I recalled Johann first mentioning the idea. It had seemed almost beyond belief; the idea of traveling not only outside Brandenburg but to the coasts of Europe and across thousands of miles of ocean to the New World. In all my seventeen years, I had met only a handful who had seen the sea, even fewer who had sailed to far-off lands.

'So, if I can raise the other half, we intend to join Christopher. There are ships leaving in late summer, while the weather is still fair.'

My mother was unable to contain herself. She spoke quickly, tears pouring from her eyes. 'Lord, have mercy, Johann – why? Those ships are death-traps; and the Americas full of criminals and savages.'

Mary put a comforting arm around her.

'Please do not cry, Mama,' said Johann.

His wife was vainly trying to stifle her own tears.

Lucian stared at him, wide-eyed, as if unable to take it in.

Johann continued: ‘Father, I know you would prefer for me to stay but I am not doing this only for myself and Maria. Kasebier’s will soon be known in Potsdam. What if we were known beyond the shores of Europe? On both sides of the ocean? In the old world and the new?’

‘You are a man now,’ said Father quietly. ‘You must make your own decisions. You will have to live by them or die by them.’

With that, he stood and left the table.

Chapter Three

During the ensuing days, Father's mood did not improve. He insisted on unusually long prayers at mealtimes and before bed, and it seemed to me that he was punishing his other children for Johann's decision. How I wished that I was twenty-two and able to provide for myself. I knew that without some career or plan I would never achieve independence, yet I could still see no clear road ahead.

I contented myself with helping my mother. Outbursts from her were rare but I'd always felt that I could sense her unhappiness better than anyone else in the household, and I felt it my duty to raise her spirits. When not occupied with my own chores, I assisted her in the kitchen: cleaning the floor, washing crockery, and slicing vegetables. I also tried to distract her with some jests and imitations at the expense of our more eccentric neighbors and customers.

Fortunately, we also received the usual weekly visit from my elder sisters, Dorothea and Katherine. They too were married, both with one child. Katherine had miscarried in the spring but had by now recovered her health and her usual cheerful demeanor. Dorothea brought some orange cake and I spent a pleasant hour in the company of the three women.

Though I did not always find their chatter of interest, I had in recent years taken note of how female conversation differed from male conversation. I found it of use when talking to girls and felt increasingly confident. The previous year I had won kisses from three and was determined to improve my tally. Unfortunately, this year had started slowly. If Hugo and I could attend the summer fair, my chances would improve.

Though I returned to my chores before Father caught me idling, I still incurred his wrath. While clearing out the kitchen hearth, I somehow marked a garment put out to dry. I thought it best to own up immediately, as my crime would inevitably be discovered. When he saw the mark, Father struck me across the head. It was not a hard blow but I was as tall as him now and knew the day would eventually come when I resisted or struck back. It had been several months since he'd last hit me and, on that occasion, I'd made a remark about the pacifist principles we were supposed to follow as The Brethren. I resisted the temptation this time.

'Get out of my sight, boy.'

I duly obliged but his repeated use of that word cut me deeper than the blow. Of course, I was his youngest; but I was also now old enough to marry or fight for the king.

Gripped by anger, I left the house via the courtyard. Mother called after me but I was in no mood to talk. Circling around to the street, I hid myself within a shadowy alleyway and gazed at the front of our shop. Kasebier – Tailor was rendered in expensive yellow, though some of the paint had peeled away. Through the glass frontage, I could see Father talking to a well-attired customer, hands clasped behind his back. His manner with his esteemed clients always irritated me. Servile and complimentary, he felt it necessary to indulge their every wish, so determined was he to outdo his competitors.

The truth was that the king's tariffs had affected everyone in the clothing business. I had heard enough and seen enough of the accounts to know that Father was struggling. Perhaps it was wrong to judge a hard-working man so harshly but familiarity had bred contempt, and it seemed the feeling was mutual.

With a low bow, my father bade farewell to his visitor. I shrunk further into the shadows as he held the door open for the nobleman and his attendant. I recognized the man as the nephew of a local margrave. He was clad in a fine red jacket and sported both cane and three-cornered hat. As his manservant hurried along behind him, they passed a pitiful sight: widow Hartmann, whose husband had perished while fighting in Riga, and was now reduced to begging on the streets. The nobleman strode past her.

As members of the Brethren, my family had often contributed to charity. Even in these difficult times, I knew Father gave a few thalers to the church; and there was no shortage of worthy causes within the city. I knew also that a select few of the nobles contributed to such causes. Most did not.

Wandering the streets of central Halle, I would normally have expected to see a few familiar faces but my city seemed a strange, alien place. I might have cheered myself by purchasing a cake or a piece of fruit but I'd already spent my meager earnings for that month. Despite my many grievances, I did not begrudge the minimal wages that myself and my siblings received. I had seen enough of life to know that I was fortunate to have been provided with shelter and food – and education until my fourteenth year.

Passing the offices of a well-known lawyer, I wondered –not for the first time – about such a profession. Ideally, I would have already been an apprentice at my age but perhaps such a vocation was still possible. My academic skills had been neglected but my teachers had always considered me a speedy learner and I was the most able linguist in our household. My proudest moments within the shop were spent liaising with those clients who spoke only French or Russian. Once or twice, I had even heard Father boasting about my abilities. These skills had also lapsed but surely there were organizations and companies who could make use of me? After all, why be a middling tailor when I might flourish as something else?

I was in the midst of these ruminations when a hand landed on my right shoulder. I was greatly relieved to find that the assailant was my brother Johann.

'Well, well – time to wander the streets, Christian? You must have been kicked out by Father.'

'Very perceptive,' I countered, moving aside as a muttering fellow with a handcart approached. 'Though the fault lies with you. As usual, I am the one paying for your misdeeds.'

With a ready grin, Johann led the way along Geiststrasse. We were close to the timber market: one of the busiest areas of Halle.

'I thought it best to give him a few days to calm down,' said Johann. 'I've been working at home – getting under Maria's feet.'

'Made any progress with your plans?'

'Hopefully. I'm on my way to The White Hart. I've a meeting with a possible investor.'

I was always happy to spend time with my older brother and a trip to a beer tavern constituted a rare pleasure. Though I always found such places lively and exciting, my parents viewed them as dens of gambling and alcoholism. Johann was the most devout of we three sons but rather more pragmatic than Mother and Father. He had always been one to seek out new places, people, and ideas.

'Can I come with you?' I asked.

Johann narrowed his eyes. 'I wouldn't want to be blamed for leading you astray.'

'Father did tell me to get out of his sight.'

'Very well, but not a word to anyone. Come, I can hear the bells tolling the five o'clock. I'm late.'

The White Hart was a beer tavern situated close to the town hall. I followed Johann down a steep stone staircase and into the dingy establishment. Stale with pipe smoke and sweat, it nonetheless possessed the curious, vibrant atmosphere that I'd previously noted in such places. And despite the warm early evening outside, the underground location kept the place cool.

As Johann and I made our way towards the bar through the closely packed tables, I observed the disparate patrons: In one corner, some tough-looking soldiers, easily identified by their hard faces and well-kept mustaches. In another, a group of musicians cradled their instruments and spoke in gentle tones. Lined up against one wall, chattering young men not much older than myself. There seemed to be only three women present; all with their hair uncovered and their faces made up.

I held back while Johann squeezed his way to the bar. Jostled by a big fellow with a livid scar across his cheek, I found a little space between two tables. Those gathered around erupted into laughter when a man threw down his hand of cards and stormed away towards the steps. One of those remaining scooped up a handful of groschen, a drunken smirk upon his face.

I looked around anxiously, feeling as if many eyes were upon me. Turning back towards the bar, I saw that at least one pair was. The woman was slender and fair, playing with her curly hair as she smiled at me. Though I blushed, I was tempted to go and talk to her. But by then Johann was on his way back from the bar. I was glad to see two pewter mugs in his hand.

'Here. For putting the old man in a foul mood.'

'Most kind, brother.' I took the mug and cradled it in both hands. We occasionally drank beer at home but it was weak stuff, designed mainly to quench the thirst. I saw that I had a dark beer, and knew even one mug would make me dizzy.

'Drink slowly,' advised Johann. 'Dunkel is quite fierce. Not to mention the fact that I can't afford to buy another round.'

I enjoyed my first swig: the dunkel was thick and malty.

'Kasebier?'

We turned to face the man who had spoken. Standing there was a fellow of around thirty I had not previously noticed. He was several inches shorter than me but very wide in the shoulders and chest. He possessed a round, plain face but there was something intriguing about his bearing and manner.

'Yes,' answered Johann.

'My name is Schmidt.' The pair shook hands and Johann introduced me. I did not often meet strangers and was flattered that he also shook my hand.

'You are in the cloth business, correct?' Schmidt had a low rumble of a voice and an accent I couldn't place.

'I am. My father is Johann Christophe Kasebier.'

Schmidt had his own mug of beer and took a long swig. 'I presume then, that you can obtain cloth of various types at a reasonable cost?'

'I can.'

'Would you be interested in making some money?'

I felt confused. Was this the contact Johann had spoken of?

'I might,' answered my brother.

'I know Brandenburg well,' declared Schmidt. 'Ravensburg too. And Bayreuth. I have many friends, many contacts.'

Johann nodded but he seemed bemused.

Schmidt continued: ‘You will be aware that cloth is not so cheap in Ravensburg and Bayreuth as it is here. Profits can be made.’

‘I’m sure they can.’

Schmidt took a step closer. ‘Especially if one can avoid needless bureaucracy.’

I wasn’t entirely sure what he meant. My brother, however, understood.

‘Needless bureaucracy – such as border taxes and tolls?’

Schmidt grinned then shrugged. ‘If a regular supply could be secured, I would expect to make an average of a thaler on every pound of cloth. And of course, I’d be willing to share that profit with my supplier.’

Johann smiled politely. ‘A pleasure to meet you, Herr Schmidt but that sounds rather like smuggling to me.’

Schmidt shook his head. ‘That’s a rich man’s word. An excuse for the king and his lackeys to rob working people to pay for his palaces.’

I chose not to point out that King Frederick was known to have reduced the huge personal staff retained by his father. This had included a personal chocolatier!

‘Unfortunately, I’m not sure everyone sees it that way,’ said Johann. Schmidt held up his free hand. ‘You are entitled to say no, Herr Kasebier. I shall not waste my breath trying to persuade you. I’m sure I will be able to find someone with a better eye for an opportunity.’

Schmidt moved on to the table of card players. He seemed to know them well and was invited to take the vacant seat.

Johann and I didn’t have any time to reflect on our encounter. He had spotted a familiar figure descending the steps. ‘Ah, there he is. No offense, Christian, but I'd prefer to handle this without my little brother in tow.'

'Of course.'

Despite my words, I again felt anxious once left alone. I observed Johann meet the man and the pair instantly began conversing in the shadows below the staircase. I had decided to occupy myself by watching the game of cards when I felt someone beside me. I turned to find the woman there. I suppose she must have been thirty or more but I was flattered by the attention.

'Good day to you,' she said.

'Good day, miss,'

'Do you play cards?'

'Only the simple games,' I replied. 'Not for money.'

'Oh, what a shame.' She was now twirling her hair with a finger. 'Very hot today, isn't it?'

'It is, miss.'

'An ale would be nice. Or perhaps some wine.'

Despite my innocence, I knew it wasn't wise to buy drinks for unaccompanied ladies. Not that I had any money anyway.

When I told her this, the woman swiftly departed, leaving me somewhat confused about the entire conversation. Telling myself to enjoy this rare sojourn and the taste of the dunkel, I approached the table of card players. But after a few sharp looks, I realized they might be wary of trickery, especially as I'd spoken to Herr Schmidt.

I moved towards Johann and took up a vacant stool, having asked the permission of the two older men sitting close by. Though appearing to concentrate on my beer, I listened in and discovered they were talking about the King and his eldest son. Apparently, the word from Berlin was that the heir to the Prussian throne wore his hair long and was a poor rider. It seemed to be common knowledge that the king openly criticized him.

The men left after a few minutes and I was surprised to see Johann's associate follow them up the stairs. My brother took a seat beside me, his expression glum.

'I assume it did not go well?'

'I'd been told he was keen on investing but some Dutch ship was wrecked off England last month. He claims there is too much risk.'

From all I knew, this seemed an entirely fair point. 'You'll get the money somehow.'

Johann sat there for some time, neglecting his beer, staring blankly at the floor.

'Spoke to one of the girls,' I said after a time. 'She seemed nice.'

'Is that right?' replied Johann. 'Well, I suggest you keep that to yourself, Christian. Mother and Father will be shocked if they hear you have been in a tavern, downing beer. I cannot imagine their reaction if you also disclose that you've been chatting up a prostitute.'

Even in his worried state, my startled reaction caused my brother to smile.

I did not see Johann again for a week. Fortunately, news of my trip to The White Hart didn't reach my father and I managed to stay out of trouble. On the Thursday of that week, a trio of officers visited the shop. All three were members of a Pomeranian regiment. They were passing through Halle and in need of some speedy repairs to various garments. Father generally preferred to be assisted by Johann, Mary, or Lucian but with the others absent or busy elsewhere, he had to make do with me.

The three officers planned to return the following day to collect their garments but one insisted on waiting for an urgent repair to a waistcoat. While Father withdrew to the workshop, I was left alone with them in the shop. They ignored me entirely but I was greatly struck by their conversation. They discussed several issues: the merits of a new artillery piece; a misbehaving infantryman who had troubled them all; varieties of Bohemian wine; and the wife of a major who apparently possessed 'the face of an angel'.

It wasn't just the speed and range of their exchange that impressed me but also the witty jibes and asides. I had no doubt that all three would also possess the arrogance and superior attitude dictated by class and rank but it seemed to me that they enjoyed their professions and their lives. A man of my class would not normally be permitted to become an officer but I knew exceptions did occur and that it was possible to move up from the lower ranks. Then there was the uniform, of course. Men seemed to enjoy wearing it, and women seemed to admire them.

There were at least two compelling reasons why I should not have even considered this alternative. Yet that did not stop me; and over the next few days, I began to seriously consider how I might achieve it. Even though Father's anger had diminished, with every passing day spent under his rule, I felt as if fresh weight was being piled on top of me. Something had to give.

On several occasions, I tried to persuade myself to take the path of least resistance; embrace my future as a tailor, and enjoy a quiet life. It did not work.

Upon Johann's return to the house, he and Father spoke at some length in private. While the rest of us waited for the outcome, I went to lie down in the bedroom I shared with Lucian. It was a warm evening and I opened the single window wide. Stretching out my aching limbs, I found my feet overhanging the end of the bed, as they had done for two years. The aptness of the metaphor was not lost on me.

Lucian entered the bedroom. 'I should have known you'd be skulking in here. Mother needs help with dinner.'

'Then help her.'

Lucian sat on his bed and pulled his good shoes out from under it. We were to attend church the following day and he set about polishing them. The sun was setting but we still had just enough light to see by. Ever since money had become tight, we were not permitted to keep candles or a lamp.

'Mary says no raised voices in the parlor. Perhaps Johann has seen sense.'

'Or perhaps Father has.'

Lucian snorted. 'I wonder if you ever will, Christian. This scheme of his is insane. If he and Maria go off on one of those ships, we'll likely never see them again.'

'God forbid anyone should actually want to do something with their life.'

'Do something? By throwing it away? If Johann's so desperate to travel and make his name, why not go to Berlin, even Holland, if he must? But across the ocean? The very thought of it gives me nightmares.'

'Everything gives you nightmares.'

Though less frequent in recent years, Lucian's dreams still tormented him. He could not help that.

It was his cautious, conventional character that I disliked.

'Why not offer to go with him then?' Lucian suggested.

The thought had occurred to me, and the idea of seeing the New World did appeal. But Johann was setting up his own tailoring business, and with him, I would end up in a similar position.

Lucian moved onto the second shoe, polishing with some vigor. 'I just hope they can settle all this. Then things can go back to normal. We need Johann here – earning for the family. He can help us turn things around.'

But it soon became evident that Johann was more determined to leave than ever. He had arranged a series of meetings with potential investors in Berlin and was departing the following day. He had come purely to make peace with Father and I believe we were all surprised to discover he'd been successful. When the pair emerged from the parlor, Father gathered us together.

'It is important in life to be honest. And the truth is that I hoped Johann would not continue with his plans. But he is determined, and I see now that he is doing this not only for himself and Maria but for the whole family. I …' Father was not given to emotion but he wavered here and placed a hand upon his oldest son's shoulder. 'I wish I could help him fund this venture but at the moment I cannot.'

I was surprised my mother had been able to contain herself this long. Seeing her clasped hands shaking, Father approached her and held them in his own.

'Margaretha, I know that you worry. I will worry for them too. But Johann has promised that he will write regularly, that'

Mother pulled free of him, an action that drew a gasp of shock from Mary. But this was no act of rebellion. Mother threw herself against Johann and put her arms around him. She could find no words but after a time turned to her husband and nodded. She had accepted it.

As Father gave her a handkerchief and sat her down, I believe I saw Johann wipe away a tear. Mary announced that she would take over the cooking of dinner and recruited Lucian and me to assist.

The rest of the evening passed pleasantly, with Father and Johann further discussing his plans. Mary and Lucian fired questions at him; Mother listened carefully but said little, occasionally offering an encouraging look for her eldest son. I was surprised by my father's accession and glad for my brother.

Yet I could not avoid the feeling that my own position was now even worse.

Chapter Four

The fruit market was a good place to meet and talk to girls. It was held on Tuesdays and Fridays and in July was almost overflowing with berries. Sellers large and small poured in from the countryside around Halle bearing sacks, boxes and barrels full of raspberries, strawberries, blackberries, blueberries and gooseberries. Apples were coming in now too; along with the rarer apricots, peaches and pears. Many farmers and traders were sly enough to place their prettiest daughter on the stand to attract passing men; and other girls were sent by their families to make a purchase.

I myself had empty pockets and was unlikely to see a single groschen from my Father any time soon. There had been yet another dispute but this time I had angered both my parents:

Though I knew there were numerous arguments against a military career, I'd been unable to shake my attraction to the notion. I even convinced myself that the sight of me in uniform – a young, dedicated patriot – might eventually be enough to win Mother and Father around. Though our family had belonged to the Brethren for several generations, Father had occasionally voiced the opinion that Prussia had to be defended. A devoted servant of God, he was also dedicated to his country and his king. As he was fond of saying, ours was not a land with great natural gifts; but one made great by the effort and unity of its people. Mother, however, abhorred violence in all its forms. She could not bear even to see we boys play fight. I had generally relied on my wits to avoid scraps at school and on the streets but even I fought on occasion. I was no battler and lost more than I won; but I enjoyed that odd combination of fear and excitement. Like a ride on a horse or a stolen kiss, it made one feel alive.

What caused this latest rift? I had been foolish enough to discuss my thoughts openly with Hugo. My friend approved entirely but unfortunately Lucian overheard the entire discussion. After Hugo left, Mother called me inside and sat me on a chair in the kitchen. She knelt at my feet and begged me to promise that I would never don the blue. It pained me greatly to see her crying but I didn't want to make a promise I couldn't keep. Even so, I was on the verge of conceding when Father stormed in to enquire what 'all the wailing was about'. Upon hearing the answer, he surprised us both by claiming, 'it might be for the best'. I suspect he didn't really mean it but I once again found myself desperate to leave the confines of the house. When Lucian and Mary also took their turn to berate me, I left, head buzzing with frustration and despair.

A walk in the sunshine improved my mood and for once fortune was on my side. As I strolled through the market, a passing cart deposited two apples right in my path. One I pocketed for later, the other I cleaned on my sleeve and set about eating. All around me, the folk of Halle were buying berries for cakes, tarts and pies. I have always possessed a sweet tooth and while the apple was pleasant, I wished I had enough to visit Hanna's, a famous bakery owned by a Silesian woman who made the most delicious strawberry tarts. Mother always bought me one for my birthday.

'Christian!'

Turning to my left, I saw a young woman waving at me from behind a stall. Initially bemused, I approached the table, which was packed with baskets of gooseberries. Once closer, I recognized the seller. She was the older sister of a former classmate but I couldn't recall her name. She was a plump, pretty girl, her dark brown hair identical in shade to my own.

'Good day,' said I. 'Er … how have you been?'

She was not alone at the stall. Beside me was well-dressed fellow with a pale complexion and a weak chin. He stood with one hand in his pocket, the other atop his cane.

'Very well, thank you,' replied the woman. 'Did you know that Elke is with child? Not long to go now.'

Elke – that was my classmate.

'Really? She married …'

'Gustav Draxler.'

'Yes, of course.' The name meant nothing to me.

With a pronounced sigh, the pale fellow strode away, shaking his head.

The young woman rolled her eyes. 'I was relieved to see you passing by. Herr Weber has been here for an age and he never buys a thing! Trying to impress me with talk of his travels as usual.'

'Ah, I see. I must ask your forgiveness. I have forgotten your name.' 'Oh. Frieda.'

'Sorry about that, Frieda.'

'Don't worry, it's been years since we spoke. Father puts me on the stall because I have such a memory for names and faces.'

'I'm sure that's not the only reason.' She flushed a little as I continued: 'I remember that you and Elke were very close. I presume she now lives with Herr Draxler?'

'They moved in with his parents over on Gerberstrasse.'

'So, you don't see so much of her now?'

'No but we all take a walk together every Sunday after church.'

'Please wish her well from me.'

'I shall.'

'How much for a basket?' asked a new arrival at the stall. I swiftly recognized the deep tones and broad frame of Wolfgang Schmidt. Without acknowledging me, he awaited Frieda's answer.

'Two groschen, sir.'

Schmidt ran a hand across his thinning, sandy hair. 'I can get twice the number for that at the stall by the well.'

'Not of this quality, sir.' Freida picked a gooseberry out of a basket. 'See the size and color.'

'I don't see much difference. One and a half groschen.'

'My father sets the prices, sir. It's two.'

'Your father isn't here, young lady. It's just gone eleven and you've hardly sold a thing. If you took a walk around, you'd see you're not doing very well.'

Freida now looked worried.

'You seem a nice girl,' added Wolfgang. 'I'll help you out. Three baskets for four groschen.'

'That's even less!' she exclaimed.

'Look around you – there's queues at most of these stalls. The other with the gooseberries was almost sold out. What will your father say if you return home with unsold baskets?'

At this point, I almost intervened, but I sensed this display was largely for my benefit.

'Very well, sir. Three baskets for four groschen. But please don't tell anyone.'

'Perhaps not now,' said Schmidt, 'but I'll give it some thought.' He turned to me, a smile upon his round face. 'Warm, isn't it? I think I shall buy myself a beer. Herr Franke over by the well always keeps his very cool. Good day.'

As he departed, Freida rolled her eyes again.

After I'd finished talking to her, I of course made my way over to the disused well at the center of the market. I had no doubt that Schmidt would try and use me to persuade Johann to take up his offer. Yet it occurred to me that I could also use him; and win myself a cold beer.

Herr Franke was well known; he and his sons could be relied upon to appear at most of Halle's markets. As ever, he was doing a fair trade and at least a dozen men had gathered at his stall, some leaning against the crumbling surround of the old well.

Schmidt was alone, a mug in his hand. 'I would have bought you one too but I thought you'd prefer it cool.'

I must say I felt a little tawdry while waiting for him to return with my beer but such treats were a rarity for me. I decided I would indulge the fellow with some talk and then go on my way. It was not dunkel this time but a Berlin wheat beer – very refreshing.

'Not bad, eh?'

'Very good.'

Though his face and frame were that of a farmer, I now noticed that Herr Schmidt was actually quite well attired. His boots were of fine red leather, his white shirt and brown waistcoat both of quality.

'You never had any intention of buying any gooseberries, did you?' 'What can I tell you? Pie-making is not my specialty.'

I couldn't help laughing at that.

He continued: 'As for the girl, I was only trying to illustrate a point. Opportunities are all around us – if one knows how to take them. If she'd sold to me at that price, I could have made a few pfennigs within a quarter-hour.'

'You were already here at the market?' I asked.

'No. You walked right past me on Bruderstrasse. I followed you.'

I was surprised by this brazen admission.

'Don't worry, lad. There's no great mystery to it. It's just that I'm not one to give up easily, especially when I can smell a profit. That brother of yours made a hasty judgment.'

'About smuggling?'

He wiped sweat from his brow. 'Once again - what I'm talking about is entirely legal. I have made a good deal of money simply by understanding supply and demand.'

'Why don't you go to a cloth supplier yourself?'

'I can and I have,' replied Schmidt. 'But the lowest cost yields the highest profit. Would you at least be able to tell me who sells cut cotton and brown linen at a good rate?'

I felt I could disclose this. It was usually Lucian and I who fetched cloth from my father's suppliers and I knew the rates well.

'Well there's Schulz, Richter and Konig – all very popular with tailors. My father also uses Zimmerman – cotton is six pfennigs per pound, brown linen is eight.'

Schmidt kept his expression neutral but I could tell that these numbers were of interest to him.

'Zimmerman is very reliable,' I added. 'Always good quality.' Schmidt nodded as he drank his beer. 'Since I last saw you, I've met a new associate who's planning a trip to Ravensburg. I know that he's had problems finding brown linen. I also know what he can get for it down there. Even a small amount – twenty pounds, let's say – would bring a decent profit.'

Now I drank my beer to give myself time to think. I noted that Schmidt hadn't mentioned a border crossing and the avoidance of tolls but the implication was clear. Then again, his associate took that risk. We would not be involved at all.

I knew that neither Johann nor my father would have anything to do with the scheme. I also knew that the thought of having my own money was very appealing.

'How much profit?'

Schmidt looked up at the bright blue sky while he made a few calculations. 'At least three thalers. I can give you one.'

'One and a half, surely. You don't even have to do any work.'

'But I have the connections.'

'Clearly not enough.'

'You're a sharp one, young Christian. Very well, if we go ahead – half each.'

One and a half thalers. For a young man at that time, it was quite a sum – enough to buy a new pair of shoes or a coat. It would have taken me a year to save that much of my allowance.

Schmidt added, 'Can you make a deal with this supplier?'

I had little doubt that I could. Zimmerman was well used to me turning up to collect Father's orders or make new ones. He would almost certainly have twenty pounds of cut brown linen available. All I would need was the money.

Of course, it wasn't entirely that simple. But a chance to strike out on my own and make a quick profit was hard to resist.

'Well?' asked Schmidt. 'Do we have a deal?'

'We have a deal, Herr Schmidt.'

He shook my hand. 'Call me Wolfgang.'

I almost didn't go through with it. Over the next few days, I mended a few bridges with Mother and Father by knuckling down and making no further mention of the army. I felt like giving Lucian a good slap for getting me into trouble but settled for simply ignoring him. Maria informed us that she had received a letter from Johann. His engagements in Berlin had gone well and he was expected home the following week.

I had agreed to meet with Schmidt on the Monday outside a church only a stone's throw from Zimmerman's warehouse. He would give me the money and I would return with the cloth. A day later I would receive my share of the profits.

My doubts struck me on Sunday night. I had spent most of the morning in church and the priest had spoken about choices and consequences. I was perhaps the least devout member of my family yet the sermon gave me pause for thought. I was to meet my cohort at the tenth hour of morning and had invented a favor for Hugo to excuse me from my chores. As I ate breakfast, I gave serious thought to not going and never seeing Wolfgang Schmidt again.

But then I was given cause to change my mind once more. Maria had brought an apple cake for us the previous evening and we had all eaten our share. There was some left and mother cut five slices: for her, Father, Mary, Lucian and myself. Unfortunately, I had been late to the parlor for morning prayers and Father clearly wished to punish me.

'None for the boy.'

Mother was holding the plate and had just offered it to me. 'But he so loves'

'He has to learn,' said Father, already eating his own piece of cake. 'He has to grow up.'

Boy I was called and as a boy I was treated.

'May I be excused?' I asked.

Father nodded.

It may seem a trifling matter but it was enough to dispel my doubts. I would make the deal and to hell with the consequences.

Having received the money from Herr Schmidt, I warily approached Zimmerman's warehouse. It was one of the largest in Halle and via one arched entrance cloth arrived from the city's numerous factories. Via the other, carts left for local tailors, markets, domestic customers and more distant destinations. Sweaty and anxious, I was pleased to see a friendly face; an elderly administrator named Hans. Herr Zimmerman himself was also present – shouting orders at his workers – but Hans showed me through to the little office in the corner of the warehouse. Here, two clerks worked busily, quills scratching.

Old Hans shifted some papers around his desk. 'I wasn't aware of any new order from your father. Don't you normally come at the beginning of the month?'

My mouth was suddenly dry. This was the moment in which I had to deceive the man in order to secure the cloth. Or did I?

'Er … this is a new order. Twenty pounds of brown linen.'

'Ah, business must be good.'

I simply smiled; continuing to avoid an actual lie.

Hans consulted one of the clerks and for a moment I almost hoped that they wouldn't have the linen. But both men seemed confident that there was sufficient.

'I shall have it wrapped and brought around,' said Hans. 'Daniel here will write out your receipt.' He made a few calculations then told the young clerk the price.

As Hans departed, Daniel took up two sheets of paper. I knew that he would actually write out two receipts: one for me as the customer, one for Zimmerman's records. I would be able to keep the customer receipt and theirs would be put with the others on my father's account. As I was about to make the payment, no demand would be made to him; and I hoped it would get lost among the many other transactions. With no outstanding debt, I thought the chances were good that he would never know. I could not recall the last occasion Father had visited Zimmerman's himself. His time was better spent with clients or with a needle in hand. I must admit I liked the idea of outfoxing him.

Even so, I grew nervous again as the voluble Herr Zimmerman appeared outside the office. For an aging, corpulent man, he seemed to possess a remarkable amount of energy. I subtly retreated so that he wouldn't see me. Three separate employees were berated while I waited and I was highly relieved when he moved away. By then Daniel had finished the receipts and I handed over the money. He counted the coins carefully then placed them in a strongbox under his desk. I felt almost ecstatic when Hans returned. With him was a tall lad holding a bundle of cloth so large that it reached higher than his head.

'Do you have your cart?'

'Not today,' I replied. 'I'll manage.'

'All done, Daniel?'

'All done, sir,' answered the clerk.

'All yours, young Christian,' said Hans. 'And do pass on our best regards to Herr Kasebier.'

With another forced smile, I took the great bundle of cloth and walked out of the warehouse. The weight was a strain, though not the only cause of my perspiration.

Wolfgang Schmidt was waiting around the corner. He seemed very pleased with himself and had a pony and a little two-wheeled cart waiting. A boy was standing by the pony and looked on as we placed the bundle on the back.

'Sent by my associate,' explained Schmidt. 'He is on the other side of the city.' He nodded at the nearby church where we had earlier met. 'What time tomorrow?'

I knew I had no chance of getting away again in the daytime. The evening was the only alternative.

'Eight o'clock?'

'Eight it is.'

While on my way home, I struck upon a fine idea: I would keep a little of the money for myself but donate the rest to Johann's venture. It would be unwise to disclose the source but I would surely be praised for my contribution.

Upon my return, I was called instantly into the shop. Not for the first time, Major-General Schroder of the Halle garrison had summoned Father. Many, including some of his subordinates, referred to Schroder as 'the peacock', such was his obsession with his uniform and appearance.

Fortunately, there were no clients so Mary and I busied ourselves by tidying up the displays. These included several wooden models bedecked with sample clothing and racks of coats, jackets, breeches, waistcoats and shirts. We also stocked a few canes, hats and shoes. These were not our specialty but chosen to compliment the designs of Father and Johann.

Although she was not an apprentice, Mary was as happy as everyone else in my family to give me orders. I generally went along with it, accepting that she knew far more about tailoring. I could never really understand why she didn't harbor resentments as I did, though I suppose the restrictions upon her were imposed more by society than our family. I did not dislike her as much as I did Lucian but I cannot say we were ever particularly close. Perhaps it was due to our similar age. I preferred the company of my older sisters.

Though doubts about the Schmidt affair continued to assail me, I was not glad of the interruption that came in the late afternoon. Father had still not returned and Mary and I found ourselves entertaining the esteemed Count Casimir, Johann's patron and quite possibly Kasebier's most important client.

As ever, the count was accompanied by two of his lackeys. Upon seeing his approach, Mary emitted a nervous noise and went to fetch Lucian. Left alone, I opened the door and bowed low, as custom dictated.

'Good afternoon, Count Casimir, and welcome.'

The count – who I believe was around thirty-five – appraised me with a frown. 'Which one are you?'

'Christian, sir.'

'Ah. I know your brother's away but what about your father?'

'I'm afraid he's currently with Major-General Schroder, sir.'

'Ah. I daresay the peacock needs a few more feathers.'

Casimir's manservants smiled obsequiously. Personally, I thought this was a bit rich; to me, Casimir had always appeared every bit as vain as Schroder.

'Count Casimir, good day to you!' Lucian hurried in, patting down his hair and almost stumbling as he bowed in front of the nobleman.

'Lucian, is it?' asked the count, passing his cane onto one of his men. 'Yes, sir. How may I be of service?'

'An urgent matter. I have a cousin arriving for a ball this evening and I'd like him to wear one of Johann's waistcoats.'

'I see, sir. Would you like to peruse our selection?'

'I shall but there is a slight obstacle. Sebastian is rather overweight. Not his fault – some medical condition, apparently. You will have to make considerable adjustments.'

'I see, sir,' replied Lucian. 'And when would you need this?'

'No later than seven o'clock. I suggest you summon your father right away.'

This was the height of arrogance. The Count was a member of the Landrat council of Halle but to expect our father to favor him over the Major General was ridiculous. Schroder's house was situated well outside Halle and Father had borrowed a horse to get there. We had no idea when he would return.

Lucian did quite well: 'I don't think that will be possible, Count Casimir, but rest assured that we can make the adjustment in good time. If you select a waistcoat, we will get to work right away.'

The count sniffed haughtily. 'Very well, young man – but I do hope you are not making promises you are unable to keep.'

'You know you can rely on Kasebier's, sir.'

I stood aside as Lucian ushered the count to the rack holding Johann's waistcoats. There were nine, all unique in design. Two were of a larger size and it was these that Lucian showed to our esteemed client.

Casimir was tall and very slender, with a narrow, oddly shaped nose. He moved in the deliberate, upright manner common among aristocrats.

'Mmm,' was his only reaction to the two waistcoats. 'I'm not sure these will flatter a fellow of Sebastian's shape. He is of average height but his stomach is very large. Show me those others.'

Lucian grimaced. 'Er … sir, the smaller waistcoats will be difficult to adjust. These two can be modified by inserting'

The count threw up his hands. 'I've no need for a lesson in tailoring. The adjustments are your concern, not mine. Show me those others.'

Glad that I was not in charge, I helped Lucian take several more waistcoats from the rack.

'A larger man needs more patterning to distract from his rotundity,' observed the count.

I generally avoided such encounters and struggled not to express the disdain I felt for the man. Like most, ours was a city where many labored all day long to make ends meet and deaths from starvation were not unheard of. Yet this man made the choice of a waistcoat seem like a decision of tremendous import. I lacked not only the interest in tailoring but the enthusiasm to serve such people.

Mary appeared. 'Good day, Count Casimir. Would you like some hot chocolate?'

'Yes,' said he without a glance at my sister.

It was a wise intervention. Though the chocolate was very expensive for my mother, Casimir loved the drink and it seemed likely the gesture might improve his mood.

'I think perhaps that one. Otto?'

Casimir called forward one of his manservants to examine a dark blue waistcoat decorated with red and gold flowers. It was quite obviously one of the smaller examples but this did not deter him. I knew just how long Johann spent on each garment and just how difficult it would be to unstitch one and add the required sections. I reckoned that even Lucian and Mary working together might struggle in the time they had.

Though he tried to hide it, I saw my brother's uncertainty; he wasn't sure whether to air his concern.

I decided I could help. 'Count Casimir, if I may. I'm afraid that may be an inadvisable choice.'

He stared at the waistcoat for a moment longer then turned to me, fixing me with unblinking eyes. 'Your brother assured me that they can be modified.'

'Yes, sir, but you did say that it was for a large man. I don't think we anticipated that you would choose one of the smallest garments.'

I had not intended to sound so blunt. My brother's face turned white and Otto cleared his throat in a contemptuous manner. Mary had by now also returned. Looking rather shocked, she offered the count his hot chocolate. It had been served in a china cup and saucer – one of only two we owned.

'In a moment,' said the count.

I feared a rebuke but it never came.

'Well, we wouldn't want it to lose its shape,' he added. 'I think the light blue then – that's not too small, is it?'

By now, Lucian had recovered himself. 'No, sir, I'm sure we can let that out without too much trouble.'

'Mmm. Otto?'

'A fine choice, sir.'

'Bloody difficult, purchasing for that bloater, eh!'

Otto and the other man chuckled along with the count. I laughed myself but Lucian and Mary still seemed too taken aback to join in.

The aristocrat soon found another cause for complaint. 'And all this walking has made my feet sore.'

'Please, sir,' said Mary, 'take a seat here and you can enjoy your hot chocolate.'

'I believe I shall do just that.'

Father returned home just after six o'clock. I was present in the workroom when he came in to find Lucian and Mary putting the final touches on the waistcoat. He held the garment up to the window to examine it.

'Just that last bit of stitching there.'

'We know, Father,' said Lucian.

'And the count's man is coming at seven?'

'Yes.'

Father handed the waistcoat back to Mary, who set about finishing. He looked exhausted from his ride and sat down upon a stool. 'Christian, take the horse back to Herr Hoffman. Tell him I'll pay him in the morning.'

I did not much care about being given another chore; I was just glad to hear Father use my proper name.

'Christian was rude to Count Casimir,' stated Lucian suddenly. Though used to my brother's sleights, I was shocked by this betrayal. As Father's face darkened, I was greatly relieved when Mary came to my rescue.

'Very unfair, and you know it, Lucian. Christian simply explained a difficulty. In fact, he helped us.'

Mary was generally regarded by all within the family as a fair, calm character. Her testimony was enough for Father, who let out a long breath before speaking.

'What matters is that the count will get his waistcoat. Well done.' He got up and walked through to the kitchen.

We three siblings said nothing. Such praise was unusual and I was so surprised that I couldn't summon a rebuke for Lucian.

I wished then that I had not made the deal with Schmidt. But the die was cast.

Chapter Five

I have always possessed a rather spontaneous, impetuous character and must admit that I vacillated yet again when I received my profits from Wolfgang Schmidt. I found him leaning against the church wall, cleaning out his pipe, oblivious to a priest dealing with some sobbing woman only yards away.

'You're early, Christian.'

'I can't stay long.'

'Oh?'

'I have to brush the courtyard.'

'A young man of your ingenuity and nerve is wasted as an apprentice.' I knew flattery when I heard it. 'The deal went through as expected?' 'It did. The brown linen is on its way to Ravensburg as we speak. Here.' Schmidt reached into his jacket pocket and produced a leather bag. He gave me the thaler first, then the twelve groschen. I looked down at one of the heavy silver discs: at the bewigged King Frederick and his name etched around the edge. I had never held so many coins. 'Plenty more where that came from,' said Schmidt. 'What about some cotton next time?'

I watched as the still-sobbing woman was ushered towards the church by the priest.

'I'm not sure there will be a next time.'

I had barely slept the previous night and this whole affair now seemed like a mistake. I even wondered if I should simply hand the money back. Schmidt seemed a little outraged. 'What the hell is wrong with a man trying to earn a few coins to make his way? Nobody got hurt.'

I wasn't entirely sure that was true.

Schmidt put a hand on my shoulder. 'We're a rare breed, you know – the ones who take risks. Most people are sheep. They just do as they're told – by the priest, the lord, the general. But that life's not for everyone. Some people don't want to live by the rules. You're one of them. I saw the look on your face when you came out of that warehouse.'

'I was worried.'

'Excited.'

Much of what he said appealed to me. I had known a few similar characters at school and had tended in that direction myself.

But for all their faults, I did love my family – even my father – and this was beginning to feel like a betrayal. At that moment, I just wanted to forget the whole thing.

'Sorry.' It was all I could find to say.

'Perhaps you're not one of the rare breed,' said Schmidt. 'But keep the money – you've earned it. And if you change your mind, ask for me at The White Hart.'

The rest of the day passed peacefully as I sorted a new delivery of thread, needles and other bits and pieces. Unfortunately, it was to be the calm before the storm.

With Mary and Lucian in charge of the shop, I was alone in the workroom when Father entered. Having been preoccupied with my chores, I had no idea he'd attended a meeting of Halle's tailoring guild. His expression cold, he picked up his yardstick and advanced towards me.

'Father?'

I stood up and he came to a stop right in front of me. We were exactly the same height: eye-to-eye. He had the yardstick up, ready to strike. He hadn't used it on any of us in years but I had seldom seen him so enraged. There could only be one cause.

'Admit it,' he said through clenched teeth. 'Admit what you did.' My reply was quiet. 'You mean the cloth?'

'I met Herr Zimmerman at the guild meeting. He asked me what I was intending to do with the brown linen. In my ignorance, I told him I knew nothing of it. And then I hear that you used my rate – a discount that only exists because of fourteen years of trade. Trade and trust. What did you do with it?'

There seemed little point in trying to deceive him at this point but I did not wish to mention Wolfgang Schmidt.

'I sold it to a trader bound for Ravensburg. I already have the profits. I was going to give them'

'To Ravensburg? There is a border toll. What profits could you make on'

He reached the inevitable conclusion without my help. 'Smugglers? You sold Zimmerman's cloth on to smugglers?'

Up to this moment, I had matched his gaze. But now I looked down; so I was not prepared for the attack that came. Father's yardstick was narrow but of solid birch and he struck with all his might.

The blow to the side of my head sent me reeling and a second impact caught me above the ear. I fell against the wall and could not prevent myself crying out.

'Damn you, boy! You are lazy. Ill-disciplined. Always the short cut. Always the easy way out. You have brought shame upon this household. Upon the Kasebier name.'

'Johann?' Mother came in, Mary just behind her. She saw me clutching my sore head, then spied the yardstick.

'What's going on here?'

Father simply looked at me, jaw set, eyes unblinking. I stood up straight, even though I feared he might strike me again.

'Johann? Christian?'

'You are no help to us, Christian,' Father said finally. 'You are a hindrance.'

He stared down at the yardstick for a moment then dropped it. Head bowed, he left.

Mother came to comfort me but persisted in asking what was the matter. I could not and would not tell her. Ignoring her pleas and cries, I once again fled my home.

Not daring to return, I wandered the streets until night fell. By now, I had two painful welts on my head that continued to throb. I considered walking to Hugo's home but that was a long way in the dark and robberies were not uncommon. I strayed close to The White Hart but did not enter. I also passed the church that my family attended with the other local Brethren. I could have sought out the kindly Father Roth but did not see how he could help me.

Though warm enough, I was now very hungry. My wandering path took me back to Fleishergasse and the alley opposite my home. I spent several hours there, occasionally spying a figure at the parlor window or within the shop. Not long after the city's bells rang for nine, two familiar figures approached the door; and I was greatly relieved to see them.

I reached Johann and Maria before they could knock. 'Evening.'

In the gloom we could barely see each other.

'Christian? What are you doing out here?'

'Long story.'

'Come in and tell it then. I've one of my own you might like to hear.' 'I can't. I had an argument with Father. I … it's difficult to explain.' 'By God, Christian, I've been traveling for three days.' He shook his head and sighed. 'Maria, you go in. We shall take a walk.'

We set off along the street and I recounted the story of recent events. Johann's reaction was more of disbelief and disappointment than anger. It might have been because of his weariness but he moved swiftly from past to future as we turned back towards the house. He suggested that I stay outside for the moment. He would talk to Father. I knew that if Johann could not help me, no one could.

I waited for a quarter-hour, alone in the darkness. Eventually my brother reappeared.

'Father will not even discuss the matter. Mother suggests that you come around the back and go straight to your room.'

I realized then that I didn't really want to enter the house; I simply had no other alternative. Once at the back door, I was bemused to find only Johann present. He escorted me to my room with such swiftness that I realized Father must still have been in a rage.

As he was about to shut the door, I asked him a question. 'Johann, the trip to Berlin? Were you successful?'

'I was. We are to leave in August.'

'That's good news. I was going to give you the money to help fund the trip. I didn't do it only for myself.'

I wasn't sure he believed me. Without a word, Johann shut the door and I sat there, alone in the darkness again. My thoughts turned eventually to a local neighbor named Franz Vogel. He had been a customer of Father's and often told us stories when we were younger. Vogel's father was a blacksmith and, as his only son, Franz had been expected to take on the family trade. But he was clumsy and imprecise and simply uninterested in the work. To his parents' dismay, Franz left aged just fifteen to seek his fortune elsewhere. After many adventures, he discovered that he had a gift for finding and evaluating old objects. He set up an antique shop in Stettin, where he eventually accumulated a small fortune. Moving back to Halle, he founded a second shop. By then he was past thirty but had mended the fractured relationship with his father. Old Vogel was able to give up the relentless labors of the smithy and helped his son run the shop. Though our situations were somewhat different, I felt inspired by Vogel's example and wondered why I hadn't considered it before.

Lucian entered. He said nothing and did not even look at me. He simply took his blanket and pillow and left. It was very late now and I could tell from the quiet that all were abed. I had expected Mother to look in on me but she did not. I believe that is when I made the decision.

I waited a while longer before escaping the room. A few glowing embers remained in the kitchen hearth, enough for me to light a candle. I returned to my room and placed it on the table beside my bed.

From my chest, I removed my knapsack. It was quite large: sufficient to accommodate underwear, socks, two shirts and a spare pair of breeches. I also took my woolen coat, heavy though it was. I owned four books: a Bible, two books of German grammatical exercises and another of mathematical formulas. Though I seldom studied the Bible outside church, I enjoyed reading certain passages and could not bear the thought of Mother discovering I had left it behind. The last items into the knapsack were my sewing kit and an old silver thaler that my grandfather had left me. It had been minted during the reign of Frederick the Elector and I knew it was worth more than its face value.

After snuffing the candle, I quietly left my room. My path to the rear door took me past my parents' bedroom. I listened for a time and thought perhaps I could hear Mother sobbing, though I was not sure. Wincing as I slid the heavy bolt that secured the rear door, I slipped out into the darkness. The bells of Halle were tolling midnight.

I could have spent some of my earnings on a room but I was determined to make the money last. It was summer and I knew a safe spot to sleep. Three sides of our church were occupied by graves but the other was a small grove of pear trees. There were two benches here and I was relieved to find that neither were occupied.

I settled down with my woolen coat for a blanket and my knapsack for a pillow. At first, it seemed impossible I would sleep. Among my numerous ruminations was the question of whether I should have left a note. Yet surely the fact that I had taken my knapsack and most of my belongings made my intentions clear. I resolved to at least write regularly to Mother, simply to reassure her that I was safe and well.

Considering its location in the center of Halle, the churchyard was remarkably quiet. Though woken several times by barking dogs and distant shouts, I did sleep for several hours.

Upon waking at dawn, I headed straight for Rathaustrasse, where there were several bakeries. One opened up shortly after I arrived and I ate a breakfast of bread rolls and apple tart on the bench outside. I could not say I felt happy but even these first moments of independence were somehow satisfying.

I had no second thoughts about then visiting The White Hart. Now free of my family, I was interested in making more money so that I could afford to travel; seek out adventures and opportunities to make a success of. I simply could not summon any guilt about avoiding tolls leveled by a king who hadn't the faintest idea what life was like for most of his people.

The beer-tavern did not open until midday. I didn't want to spend any more money so waited outside. Wolfgang Schmidt arrived just after noon and immediately noted the knapsack beside me.

'Good day, Christian.'

'Good day, Wolfgang. I want to make some more money. And I want to leave Halle as soon as I can.'

'Is that right? Why the change of heart?'

When I didn't answer, he added: 'None of my business, I suppose. Shall we get a beer?'

'Not now, if you don't mind. I've a suggestion. My father works with three other suppliers. We should order as much as we can before they catch wind of what happened with Zimmerman.'

For all his friendliness, I knew that a man like Schmidt was interested mainly in what I could offer. So, if I wanted to be around long enough to really learn from him, I had to make myself useful. My view was that I had already suffered the consequences; so why not repeat my crime?

'Well, well. You are keen. We must talk to my associate first, see what he needs. Then we can put you to work this afternoon.'

'Good. This time we'll need a bigger cart.'

Before the day was out, I'd made deals with Herr Richter and Herr Schulz. I decided against trying my luck with Herr Konig, who was a fiery fellow and would have beaten me had he suspected any deceit. We purchased fifteen pounds of best wool, twenty pounds of calico and forty pounds of cotton. The profits provided me with another two and half thalers: enough to get me through a few weeks on the road. That evening, Schmidt and I visited an inn on the eastern edge of Halle, where we dined on roast beef.

I found him good company. He was a rogue, of course, and very much liked a drink but my education had already begun. Schmidt told me about the products that currently made most profits: where to buy them, where to sell them. I learned that superior East Prussian corn could fetch a good price anywhere west of Danzig; that imported whiskey was beloved by South Prussians; that Russian vodka was the favored tipple of sailors in Hamburg; that coffee, salt and tobacco were amongst the easiest products to transport and sell.

There was so much to take in. And though he still never used the word smuggler, I gathered that this was the best description of his profession. He admitted that it was like a game; there were always risks and obstacles, peaks and troughs.

When he spied a real game – of cards – Schmidt couldn't resist. I found myself talking to his friend, a former reed-cutter who now traded in jewelry.

After three dunkels, I was more drunk than I had ever been in my life. I suppose I was trying not to face the consequences of my decision and another beer almost finished me off. I was therefore feeling very dizzy and weary when Schmidt returned from his game. He had won and showed me a great handful of thalers.

'Well, Christian. We have both enjoyed good fortune this week.'

He slumped beside me in a quiet corner of the inn. Though midnight was long past, there was still quite a crowd, some singing along to an accordion player.

'Perhaps it is time to quit Halle while we are ahead – seek some newer pastures. You see the man there I was playing with, the bald fellow?'

'Yes.'

'I've known him for many years. He tells me there is great demand for Bradenburg cotton down in Drezno. Even without using your contacts, a wagon load would make us a pretty sum. What do you say? Would you like to see the Elbe? It is a grand river.'

Even through the beer-induced haze, I was alarmed by how speedily events were progressing. Yet there could be no other answer than yes.

'Good,' said Wolfgang. 'Well, I don't know about you but I could do with some sleep. I'll go see about a room.'

'Very good.'

I sat there alone, sipping at my last beer. A large group of men had just entered the inn. There were several familiar faces and one of them approached. I could not recall his name but I knew him for a friendly fellow.

'Ah, young Kasebier – your brother is looking for you. I saw him in *The White Hart* and *The Bear's Teeth*. Seemed quite concerned. Anything wrong?'

'No,' said I. 'Nothing at all.'

Chapter Six

1729, Sagan

Though not yet twenty, I suppose I had become a man. Two years had passed since my departure from Halle but it seemed a lifetime away. The first few weeks and months had been the hardest. For all my determination to follow my own path, I had known no other home, no other life. Did I miss my father? My brother Lucian? My life as an apprentice tailor? Not particularly. But thoughts of Mother were seldom far away. I missed my sisters and friends too; and Johann, of course.

At least I knew how he was faring. That spring, I had exchanged letters with Mother, the fifth time I had done so since my departure. I always asked an intermediary to collect her replies from the post offices, fearful of some plot to drag me home. Johann and Maria had reached Pennsylvania. Mother disclosed that the ocean crossing had been awful, with many fatalities. Life in the New World sounded equally hard but Johann had established his business and was supporting himself and Maria. It encouraged me to know my brother had flourished as I had.

But we had taken very different paths. The unadorned truth is that I was now a criminal. This is not something that happens overnight. I was still with Wolfgang; and it had been several months before I became involved in an overtly illegal scheme. Up to that time, I had steered clear of such affairs and my friend and guide had offered no objection, on account of my age and inexperience. Among many things I'd learned was that Wolfgang's gambling habit prevented him holding onto coins for very long. Personally, I had accumulated quite a pile.

However, at the end of my first year away from home, our luck took a turn for the worse. Having invested most of our money in a purchase of Frisian leather, we had unwittingly done business with a vicious gang and were fortunate to escape with only a monetary loss. We were in desperate straits and I spent the second year at Wolfgang's side as he cheated, smuggled and double-crossed his way across Prussia. I suppose I could have left at any time but the truth is I enjoyed my continuing education; and my companion did have a moral code of sorts. He would only ever exploit the rich or a fellow criminal. I had seen him be a little rough with others at times but he always treated me fairly.

While in Drezno, we'd met up with a pair named Hans Muller and Stefan Beck. These two were ex-soldiers and, like us, did not favor the conventional life. We made a couple of decent deals but a better opportunity arose late that summer. Poor weather and the resulting poor harvest had afflicted Brandenburg and Pomerania, while the East had fared far better. Many products required high quality grain and the best place to find it was in neighboring Silesia. At that time, the province was still a possession of the Habsburgs but, like most borders, it was loosely guarded. If we could purchase our grain and return to Brandenburg without being seen by the troops that enforced the toll, there was a good profit to be made.

Upon arriving in the town of Sagan – which was situated just on the Prussian side of the border – we split into pairs. Stefan and Wolfgang toured the town to find a favorable buyer who would purchase our grain with no questions asked. Hans and I, meanwhile, were to arrange transportation and learn what we could about the local area.

We were staying at an inn and the proprietor recommended a reliable stable where we secured four wagons and horses. Although I could now ride a mount reasonably well, I was anxious about driving a vehicle, especially through perilous territory.

We then visited an old associate of Hans, who directed us to a local man named Lang. This fellow masqueraded as a traveling musician but was in fact a smuggler of rare metals and jewelry. He knew Silesia well and would tell us what he knew: for a fee, of course.

Sagan was a pleasant little town, rather quieter than Halle or Drezno. A summer shower had soaked the streets and given everyone relief from what had been a hot, stifling August. With the grey clouds moving off, townsfolk began to emerge, including a quartet of infantrymen, presumably from the local garrison. As we neared them, Hans subtly turned into a side-street. I had now spent enough time with him to realize he avoided soldiers when he could.

'How long since you left?'

'I didn't leave,' said he. 'I *deserted*. Eight years.'

'Surely you're safe now?'

I found it hard to believe Hans was scared of anything. Six-foot-tall and broad-shouldered, he also possessed a chiseled, rather grim face. When combined with the patch he wore to cover an eye lost to a bayonet, the overall effect was quite imposing. At first, I'd been reluctant to approach him but over the last few weeks, I'd discovered he was friendly enough, though he didn't like to talk more than necessary. 'I was in for twelve years,' he said. 'Met hundreds of soldiers from dozens of regiments. All it takes is for the wrong man to spot me and I'm in trouble.'

'How bad?'

'They'd hang me. They hang all deserters. Doesn't matter if you've given your best or killed for your king or lost an eye.'

I wondered what had prompted Hans to leave after so many years but did not feel it was something I could ask. I'd found that a great deal went unsaid between those in our trade. Only Wolfgang knew my story.

Following the directions given to us by Hans' contact, we eventually located a row of small red brick houses. This was the Prinzenstrasse and my companion knocked on the door of number twelve. After a worryingly long delay, the door opened and a middle-aged man appeared. He was a short fellow with fine, sandy hair and deep-set eyes. He appraised us suspiciously.

'Yes?'

'Herr Lang?' inquired Hans.

'Who's asking?'

'Michael Ziegler gave me your name. My friend and I are planning a trip to Silesia. He said you know it well.'

'Ziegler has a big mouth. I'm busy.' Lang tried to close the door but found it blocked by Hans' boot.

Lang frowned. 'I don't take kindly to bullying.'

I placed a hand on my companion's shoulder. It was plain to me that he did not always take into account the effect of his appearance.

'Hans, we would not want Herr Lang to think ill of us. If he wishes to close his door and be rid of us, so be it.'

As Hans didn't seem to want to move, I removed my hand. Ziegler whispered a curse.

I spoke quickly. 'But I can assure you, Herr Lang, that we need only a quarter-hour of your valuable time. Would that not be worth a few groschen?'

'A *few*? What do you take me for? A beggar?'

'Not at all. We know you are a respected and successful man. We may be happy to part with a considerable amount. But, as you will appreciate, that must depend on the value of what we learn.'

Hans at last retracted his foot.

'A quarter-hour,' said I. 'Not a minute more.'

We were admitted to a dingy parlor and saw Herr Lang's wife briefly as the two conducted a short but sharp argument. He shook his head wearily as she withdrew. Mounted upon the parlor wall were several stringed instruments. Lang gestured for us to sit upon a bench and took a chair for himself.

I thought it best to speak before Hans set us back again. 'Herr Lang, we understand that you have good reason to be suspicious of strangers at your door. For all you know, we could be spies in the employ of the garrison or the court.'

Lang scoffed at the suggestion. 'Not likely, young man. I know every single spy and informer on this side of the border and the other. What I'm waiting for is payment. six groschen or I say no more.'

Hans was in possession of half our group's limited funds. He placed the coins in Lang's hand and was sensible enough to leave the discussion to me.

'What are you moving?'

'Grain,' said I. 'Four wagons.'

'Taking advantage of the bad harvest, eh? A decent idea but I must tell you you're not the only ones. Under instruction from the court, the guards have doubled their patrols. Where will you buy?'

'We were told that there are sellers in the villages of Gablenz and Trebendorf.'

'And where will you sell?'

'Here in Sagan.'

'Where will you cross?'

Hans sighed. 'Aren't we supposed to be asking the questions?'

Lang leaned back in his chair nonchalantly. 'I can give you the answers. But I will first warn you that you are taking quite a risk; and that if caught, you will be shown no mercy. The local magistrate spares no one.'

Lang turned his gaze on me. 'Regardless of age. If, however, you wish to proceed, I can tell you what you need to know. For another eighteen groschen.'

Hans snorted. 'A *thaler*?'

Hiring the four wagons for a week had not cost us that much.

Lang shrugged. 'If you know someone else who can provide the necessary information, you are free to leave now and question them.'

I did not wish to argue the point in front of our calculating host. 'May we have a moment?'

'Please.' Herr Lang stood and left us alone in the parlor.

'It's lot of money, Christian,' said Hans. 'Do we really want to spend all that without asking the others?'

'I don't see that we have much choice. We might spend another week here and not find anyone who knows what this fellow does. Your friend Ziegler vouched for him. You trust his judgment?'

'I do.'

'Then as long as he is specific, I believe the trade is worthwhile. Let us pay him his thaler in the name of goodwill and see what we get.'

'And if we don't get what we need?'

I grinned. 'Then we can just take our thaler back, can't we? Unless you're scared of his wife? She does sound quite fierce.'

Two days later, we put Herr Lang's information to the test. He'd suggested that we buy the grain from somewhere close to the village of Krepa. Apparently, there were sufficient farms here to supply what we needed and it was some distance from any sizable settlement. Lang felt it unlikely that any other smugglers had used this area so we would hopefully avoid any entanglements. We knew that two companies of garrison troops covered the sixty-mile border. This meant a total of over two hundred men but that was not many for the distances involved. Soldiers also manned the six toll-stops on the main roads that crossed the border. Lang concurred that our own troops were far more likely to cause us a problem than the Silesians. There were few sites of strategic value to the Austrian empire in the region and only a small force of local militia.

Even more important than this information, Lang was able to plot a precise route in and out of Silesia. The six main roads were of course out of the question, even for the outgoing trip – four empty wagons would raise too many questions. But there were only so many other routes that could accommodate the heavy vehicles. Two paths popular with smugglers were known to have been blockaded by the army earlier in the year. Lang had a solution:

A nobleman named Count Sommer possessed a large tract of land that edged the Silesian border. A member of the Landrat, he refused to allow the border guards on his territory but had pledged to monitor it with his own staff. According to Lang, the count was experiencing financial difficulties and had let go of many of the men supposed to carry out the patrols. The southern sector of his land could be approached via some quiet lanes and the only physical barrier was an ancient Roman wall with as many holes as intact sections. Once inside the count's territory, we faced only four miles of meadow before crossing the border. And once in Silesia, we had only another ten miles or so to reach Krepa. When questioned about the ease of crossing these meadows, Lang explained that he'd used the route in June. The ground was even and dry and there'd been only the occasional cloudburst since.

And so, it was with some confidence that we set off from Sagan at dawn, first heading north to put off any interested parties. Upon turning east and striking the old Roman wall we didn't have to travel far to locate a gap. Though it took us half an hour to clear a wide enough space, we soon found ourselves moving quickly across the lush meadow. Negotiating a rise, we spied Count Summer's mansion some two or three miles to the north. Hoping that we hadn't attracted any attention from that direction, we pressed on through the afternoon.

I cannot say that I enjoyed it. Each in charge of a vehicle, we had little opportunity to speak or rest. My compatriots had generously assigned me the most biddable horse but driving a wagon was very different to being on horseback. More vocal commands were necessary and this horse didn't seem to understand me. On several occasions I inadvertently took the path of most resistance and the other three had to wait. I could not blame them for cursing me; I was slowing them down. Worse still, I belatedly realized that I now found myself embroiled in a highly hazardous mission.

I worried about the army patrols. Personally, I had no desire to fight and carried no weapon. But Wolfgang had a cosh and Hans and Stefan both possessed swords. I had no doubt that they would strike if they had to. Hans lived in perpetual fear of the hangman's noose while the others had previously endured spells of imprisonment.

To me, our scheme was barely an offense; certainly not in comparison to crimes like robbery and rape and murder. But I also knew the reality of my situation, the risks I was taking. If faced with armed men, would I give in or fight for my freedom? I simply did not know.

With great relief we cleared Count Sommer's land and came eventually to a narrow track. It was bumpy but led directly south-east, towards Krepa. As dusk neared, we spotted a useful copse of trees where we hid our wagons and ourselves. Needing no fire for warmth due to the season, we ate then settled down for the night. It had already been decided that we would post a guard. Due to my poor performance on the wagon, I went first.

Our good luck continued during the morning of the next day. After a couple of wrong turns, we consulted a passing goatherd and found our way to Krepa. The villagers – like most Silesians – spoke German and believed our story that we hailed from their own province. One of those we encountered was a farmer's son who claimed his father had sufficient grain and would offer a competitive price. When this turned out to be true, a deal was swiftly made and we began emptying his barn. Some of the grain had already been placed in sacks and these we loaded up first. The rest had to be moved from barrels into the sacks we'd brought with us. Though the assistance of the farmer and his three sons was part of the deal, our labors took us deep into the afternoon.

Though exhausted, we rallied when the farmer's wife provided us with bowls of a tasty lamb stew. A celebratory flask of wine was then handed around and we set off northwest towards Count Sommer's estate. We were in good spirits; our plan was to rest up overnight just short of his territory then cross in early morning.

With the sun setting ahead of us, we entered a flat, even area of grassland. Wolfgang guided his wagon up alongside mine.

'Better today, Christian. I do believe that beast is at last doing your bidding.'

'On occasion.'

'I'm starting to wish we'd hired some men and brought four more wagons. That Lang fellow clearly knows what he's talking about.'

I nodded, glad that at least this part of my contribution had proved telling. I was trying not let myself get excited; about the prospect our success; about what I might spend my earnings on.

We plodded on across the meadow, insects buzzing around us as the darkness closed in.

'You all right?' asked Wolfgang after a while. 'Not your usual talkative self.'

'Tired.'

'Me too. Poor sods like our farmer friend spend the whole days breaking their backs. It's no kind of life.'

I agreed with him about that. Our new business partner was clearly comparatively well off – especially after our purchase – but I knew that, for most, living off the land was a relentless, thankless struggle. There were some with their own holdings but most rented land from local aristocrats and had to pay taxes and pledge two or three days a week to work their masters' fields.

I wondered about Count Sommer, about the change in his fortunes that had provided us with this opportunity. So much in life was connected by cause and effect. As I drifted off into rumination, Hans called a halt. I narrowly avoided riding into his wagon.

'Off your horses!' ordered the ex-soldier. 'We need cover.'

I was about to ask what was going on when I spied a bloom of color in the twilight. Directly ahead of us, someone had lit a fire.

***

We were stuck on open ground, plain for any watcher to see; and if not for the evening gloom we would have undoubtedly been spotted. We followed Hans' order immediately and led the horses and wagons onto the lowest piece of ground nearby. The fire was no more than a half-mile distant.

'Who the hell is camping out here just before nightfall?' spat Wolfgang.

'Could be gypsies,' said Stefan. 'Hunters maybe?'

'With an open fire on the count's land?' replied Wolfgang. 'I doubt it.'

I said: 'Maybe we're not the only ones who know he's low on manpower.'

My tired horse jerked its head, almost pulling the reins from my grip. Stefan's horse was also unsettled.

'Let's get them unyoked,' said Wolfgang. 'We need to keep them calm.'

This was no easy job but once we'd tethered the horses, they were happy enough to chew on the thick, high grass that had been tempting them all day. By placing the wagons in front of them, we at least shielded their movements from any observers.

After refreshing ourselves with water from our flasks, we gathered together. I could not take my eyes off the spark of firelight.

'Sommer's men?' suggested Stefan. 'Maybe they got wind of us. Perhaps some peasant saw us come through yesterday.'

'Could be,' said Wolfgang. 'Whoever it is, they'll see us as soon as the sun's up. We can set off at first light but if we head south we're off the count's land and bloody close to that toll road. If we go north, we'll be too close to the manor.'

'Maybe they'll move off before that,' said I.

'Why light a fire then?' countered Hans. 'They mean to stay the night.'

'Could be army,' said Wolfgang. 'They might have got word of us too. That bloody goatherd, I swear I saw a crafty look in his eye. Probably made himself a couple of'

'No point guessing,' interjected Hans. 'I'll go and see what we're dealing with.'

We others waited in the darkness, none of us able to rest until we knew more. I remained silent while my companions exchanged theories and plans. I did not like what I heard from Stefan about using his blade 'if necessary'. I knew that he'd escaped the army for attacking a compatriot and he clearly had a short temper. While Hans had been an elite grenadier, Stefan had been recruited only to a provincial battalion.

After what seemed at least an hour, Hans finally returned. 'Soldiers. Three of them on foot. Muskets and lances.'

'Only three, eh?' said Stefan.

'Young lads,' added Hans. 'Not much older than Christian.'

'What do you think?' asked Wolfgang.

'I think there's no easy way around them. There's not much moonlight, we could slip past on foot without a problem.'

'Abandon the haul?' said Wolfgang. 'Not a chance.'

'Then what do you suggest?'

'Wait for them to fall asleep then creep up and stick 'em.'

I can't say I was entirely surprised by this comment from Stefan but t shocked me nonetheless. He spoke about it so casually.

'It wouldn't be difficult,' said Hans evenly. 'But I can't say I'm one for cold-blooded murder.'

'We don't need that kind of attention,' said Wolfgang.

'Who would ever know?' said Stefan. 'By the time the bodies were found, we'd be a hundred miles away.'

I felt I had to say something. 'I … can't do that.'

'You wouldn't have to, lad,' said Stefan. 'Leave it to me and Hans.' At this point, silence ensued. I feared that with no other alternative, Stefan's solution might win out. Though heartened by Hans' words, it was perhaps now that I realized how ruthless Wolfgang could be. Profit was everything to him and any soldier was the enemy. It didn't seem to matter that each was a man: with a mother and father somewhere.

Desperation forced me to move quickly. 'There is another way. Please hear me out.'

At dawn I found myself alone. The meadows were still cloaked in a damp gloom but I was heading directly north, away from my compatriots. On the wagon behind me, half a dozen sacks full of grass, hopefully enough to attract the attention of the soldiers. Grateful that my horse was continuing to behave, I saw the distant angular outline of Count Sommer's manor. I hoped the three border guards were the only enemies who would see me. The success of my diversionary rouse depended on them doing so.

As the sun rose higher, I turned the wagon westward and continued along a low ridge, hoping to be noticed. Gazing to the south, I saw no trace of the fire but after a few minutes I caught sight of figures on the move. They were at least a mile away but the red and white of their uniforms was unmistakable. I gave no sign that I had noticed them and continued steadily on my way.

Now I had a judgment to make: I needed to draw the soldiers close enough to distract them from Wolfgang and the others, who were to veer south then press west with maximum haste (their wagons were now also weighed down with my share). Yet I also had to give myself time to ensure I could escape. Hans had reassured me that the troops would be hampered by their packs and weaponry. I had nothing to slow me, and a pair of well worn-in boots. Then again, I could not outpace a musket ball, nor did I wish to try my luck.

I was glad to see that all three soldiers were advancing, now trotting across the meadow on an interception course. I suppose they were about a quarter-mile away when I stopped the wagon beside a dried-out ditch. Abandoning the vehicle would eat into our profits and I felt rather sorry for the horse but needs must when the devil drives.

Still giving no sign that I'd seen them, I dropped into the ditch, crouched over and sprinted westward. After a hundred yards or so, I encountered thick vegetation and was forced to abandon the ditch. Crawling upward, I saw the soldiers now closing in on the wagon. They were spread out, muskets at the ready.

Now on my hands and knees, I continued to a stand of trees. Using them to obstruct my foes' view, I was again able to bolt away unsighted. I was too far north to see any sign of Wolfgang and the others and didn't even try. My only goal was to reach that Roman wall and escape the count's estate.

Those hours were not pleasant. I have always been a good runner and did not stop until sure the soldiers were far behind me. That didn't mean there might not be others in the area. I expected the mist to disappear as the day progressed but it in fact got worse. Thankfully, I could still see the sun and was able to find my way west. It was around midday when the mist finally cleared. I was within sight of the wall when an awful noise reached me.

It was the sound of barking dogs. Hiding myself within a clump of bushes, I saw a great flurry of movement. Five or six hounds were running south, noses to the ground. Close on their heels were a similar number of riders. They were quite far away but I could see they were not soldiers. Then I realized: this was a hunt, perhaps one of the horsemen was Count Sommer himself. My initial relief faded when I reflected that the hunters might easily encounter the soldiers. In that case, they might turn their attention to human prey.

Despite my weariness, I sprang away, desperate to get over the Roman wall. Once past it, I began to relax a little. In mid-afternoon I happened upon a cluster of blackberry bushes and gorged myself. Newly invigorated, I pressed on. I sighted a pair of men dressed in green clothing, both armed with muskets. Glad that they did not have a dog, I gave the hunters a wide berth.

Eventually I picked up a country road and met a vagrant who directed me towards Sagan. It was almost midnight when I finally reached the inn where we'd agreed to reconvene. I found Wolfgang and Hans in the parlor and was greeted most warmly. They had concluded the journey with not a single sight of a soldier, arrived in early evening and hidden the wagons just outside Sagan, where Stefan now watched over them. Wolfgang would relieve him during the night and the sale would take place in early morning, to avoid any prying eyes. While Wolfgang went to order me some much needed food, Hans clapped me on the shoulder.

'Very good effort, lad. Very good indeed.'

I reached down and loosened my boots. 'By God, my feet are sore.' 'I'm not surprised,' said Hans. 'By my reckoning, you've covered more than twenty miles.'

Chapter Seven

The sale went ahead as planned and we left Sagan in a hired carriage, each having made six thalers from the deal. For me, the satisfaction was two-fold: firstly, I had made a crucial contribution to our success; secondly, I had avoided any bloodshed. Though concerned that some future clash with the authorities seemed almost inevitable, I was thrilled by the excitement of the whole affair. True, I had been afraid much of the time but for a young man with my zeal and ambition, this was just the type of adventure I was crying out for. Though I tried to appear humble, I indeed felt proud of myself for extricating our party from peril.

We were now bound for the city of Cottbus, a center of wool production, where we hoped to execute our next scheme. None of us had any contacts there but Stefan seemed convinced that there would be money to be made in such a busy, thriving place. The roads were dry and I suppose we would have arrived in good time if not for what occurred in late afternoon.

I may have mentioned that Wolfgang Schmidt had an eye for the ladies. He had a particularly keen eye for what he called 'dusky beauties', that is womenfolk from the eastern and southern parts of the continent: provinces of the Habsburg empire such as Wallachia, Bulgaria and Transylvania. Some from those parts were what we Brandenburgers called gypsies. I cannot say that they were treated well in Halle but my Mother and our church had always insisted that all folk were equal in God's eyes. I knew that gypsies traveled widely and were often viewed suspiciously by locals.

When we passed a group by the side of the road that included three 'dusky beauties', Wolfgang ordered our driver to halt. He had a ready-made excuse: the travelers' wagon had lost a wheel and there was only one man to attempt the repair. Hans complained at the delay but Stefan also wanted to play hero. Both were practical men while I knew nothing about such things. Our driver was happy to lend a hand though, and was soon retrieving some tools from the rear of his carriage.

Though their German was heavily accented, we soon realized we were dealing with a family: husband, wife, and two daughters. While Wolfgang and Stefan assisted the father, I found myself conversing with the elder daughter, who was around my age. I discovered that the wagon was old and in need of replacement parts. She and her mother had warned her father but he was desperate to attend the funeral of his uncle in the town of Wiesengrund. To Wolfgang's credit, when he and the others heard this, they redoubled their efforts.

I spent a pleasant half hour talking to the girl, who was named Boyka. The practical men seemed to be making progress and Boyka's father seemed greatly relieved and grateful. Unfortunately, this cheerful scene was rudely interrupted:

From behind us came a plush, gleaming carriage escorted by four armed men and trailed by a wagon. The men were equipped with swords, breast-plates and helmets, undoubtedly bodyguards of some sort. A shout from within the carriage halted the driver. There was only a single occupant and he emerged with a curious look on his face. He was clearly an official and wore a grey wig and a black frock coat. I noted that my three compatriots suddenly appeared nervous.

'By god, more of them,' he uttered in a refined tone. 'If we're not careful, Brandenburg shall be inundated.'

By now, two of the soldiers had dismounted.

Their superior pointed at Boyka's father. 'You there, where have you come from?'

The man hurried over and bowed his head politely. When he gave the name of some obscure town, the official frowned. 'What? Never heard of it? Which state?'

'Bulgaria, sir.'

'Then what are you doing here?'

Even when he heard of the funeral, the official's hostile expression did not change.

'Well we must have something for the coffers. The Landrat has had enough of providing for itinerants who seem to think they own the whole of Europe. We shall say five groschen and you had better hope you don't see me again.'

I'll confess I was surprised when Wolfgang spoke up; and I could see from their faces that Stefan and Hans wished he hadn't.

'Might I ask, sir, what the Landrat has provided for this man and his family?'

The official sneered at him. 'What makes you think I have to explain myself to you?'

'It's just that we Brandenburgers see no benefit, so I can't imagine how a Bulgarian would.'

'Such ignorance. Tell them, Winkler.'

'Roads, walls, sewers, hospitals, schools.'

The second soldier continued. 'Army, navy, government, administration.'

'Precisely, Pfieffer,' said the official. 'All essential. Humble servants such as ourselves ensure that all can live safely and securely within the realm of King Frederick.'

Wolfgang shook his head but knew better than to push his luck. This official seemed like the type who would happily have anyone he didn't like thrown in jail. Such occurrences were common. A man with the force of the Landrat behind him could act with impunity.

'Five groschen,' said he.

Boyka bravely approached the man. She clasped her hands together and spoke with great articulacy, asking the official to spare her father. His response: 'Quite charming for a gypsy. Pretty too. But neither charming nor pretty enough. Five groschen. Hurry now.'

The rest of us looked on as Boyka's father handed over the coins. With a smug grin, the official returned to his carriage and went on his way.

***

All four of us were angered by the incident. We agreed to compensate our new friend for his loss and, once the wagon was roadworthy, accompanied the family to Wiesengrund. I would have liked to see Boyka again but they had to attend the funeral and we pressed on to Cottbus. Here we accommodated ourselves in the city's largest and most famous inn, which was located beside the Muhlgraben River. On the opposite side was a series of water mills, some several hundred years old. I was fascinated to see the wheels powered by the fast-flowing water and longed to see the inside of one of the buildings.

Before we had much of a chance to investigate the local scene, another matter came to my attention. After eating breakfast on our first morning in Cottbus, we spied none other than our tax collector friend exiting the inn. His hulking enforcer, Winkler, who now had a blackjack hanging from his belt, again accompanied him. My companions cursed him but swiftly returned to their coffee and pastries. I noted that two other fellow guests were discussing the official.

Shifting my seat so that I could better listen in, I learned that he was a tax collector named Walter Wolff. He was indeed a senior official of the Landrat and distantly related to Margrave Scholz, who apparently owned 'half of Cottbus'. One of the men stated that he'd heard many people – of varying rank – complain about Wolff's ruthless methods and personal avarice.

As we left the parlor, the others discussed our duties for the day. Finding the right places to get the right information was still not something I did well. Due to my youthful appearance and lack of experience, I was never quite sure who to ask and how to do so. Wolfgang had a real knack for spying fellow rogues and always knew the best moment to buy a man a beer, hand over or coin or – as importantly – walk away. It was decided that I would stay with him while Hans and Stefan embarked on their own fact-finding mission. I knew this would inevitably involve markets, taverns, taverns, post offices, coach stations and numerous other places where 'opportunists' dwelt. This was the term that Wolfgang often used for us. Stefan considered himself a smuggler, while the plain-speaking Hans referred to himself unashamedly as a criminal.

When Wolfgang and I reached the room we were sharing, I asked him if I could have the day to myself, assuring him that he would approve of how I spent the time. I was apparently still in his good books following the Silesian success for he readily agreed.

I didn't have a specific plan in mind but the presence of the enforcer led me to believe that Herr Wolff was still carrying out his official duties. The inn contained no less than thirty-six rooms, arranged across three floors. Ours was on the first floor and I made some adjustments to my appearance before leaving.

I still had my trusty knapsack but also another, larger pack.

As well as buying clothes for everyday use, I'd purchased some others that came in useful. Wolfgang had occasionally asked me to scout out a building or area and there were obvious methods of blending in. I had a dusty smock that would help me mix with farmers at a market or a village. Then there was the plain black coat that suggested a personal attendant or a junior member of a household staff. I also owned an impressive dark green jacket which I had embellished with buttons and patterning. In combination with my best breeches and shoes, I could therefore pass for a wealthy young gentleman.

On this occasion, I chose the black jacket and ensured that my breeches and shoes were spotless. When Herr Wolff and his associates had previously seen me, I'd been on the road and would have appeared unkempt. I had shaved that morning and now brushed my wavy, brown hair into a tidy but modest style.

Satisfied by my transformation, I made sure there was no one outside our room, then left. I first toured the ground floor, my manner efficient and deferential, imagining myself as an attendant carrying out some duty for his master. It wasn't until I reached the second floor that I saw something of interest. That something was a man: none other than the second enforcer, Pfieffer. He had found himself a stool and was sitting outside the room, clearly keeping guard though presently picking his nose. I pretended to be studying a painting then reversed my course so he didn't get a good look at me.

Returning to our room, I removed the jacket and stood by the window. Entranced once more by the nearest water wheel, I began to plan.

Not long afterward, I positioned myself on a bench outside the inn. It was interesting to observe the watercraft passing and the comings and goings at the mills but the object of my surveillance did not return until midday. Once I saw Herr Wolff head up to his room, I strode swiftly to my own. Donning my fine jacket, I reminded myself of the details I had established for my new identity and proceeded directly to room twenty-one.

'Good day,' said I to Pfieffer. 'I'm led to believe that Herr Wolff is currently staying here?'

Pfieffer looked me up and down. He was an intimidating character: his nose had clearly been broken more than once and upon his cheek was a long, pink scar.

'Who's asking, sir?'

'My name is Pohl. Christian Pohl.'

I did not pitch my tone at the refined heights of someone like Count Casimir but ensured that I sounded like an educated gentleman.

'If Herr Wolff has time, I would like to ask his advice.'

'Wait here, please.'

A moment later, Wolff appeared. Now without his wig, I saw that he had only a few patches of dark hair upon his head.

'Good day to you.' His manner was indeed different when he believed he was conversing with a man of his own station.

'Good day, Herr Wolff. Forgive my presumptuousness, but I am told you are an official of the Landrat?'

'Indeed.'

'Then I believe you may able to help me. If I might explain?' Wolff acceded with a nod.

'I am from Leipzig. My family own several clothing concerns and often send and receive deliveries via Cottbus. Unfortunately, several of our wagons have been robbed recently. My father hired a man to investigate and we learned that the gang are based here in the city. We have approached local officials but they seem to have made no progress so Father sent me down to see what could be done. Last night, I overheard someone mention that you are staying here, that you are a very efficient and well-respected official. I am a stranger in Cottbus and know not even who to approach. Would you be able to assist me?'

I felt sure that an unprincipled and ambitious man like Wolff would ensure he gained personally from every operation. The pursuit and arrest of this fictitious gang might bring him a cut of any penalty; or a valuable bribe.

Wolff's eyes narrowed and I feared that he might have recognized me. Had I been naïve? Exposed myself for no reason? Surely, such a man would have an excellent memory for faces and a nose for trickery.

'What was the name?'

'Christian Pohl.' I bowed my head once more. 'At your service.'

'Herr Pohl, I am sorry to say that these greedy swine are everywhere. It is only right that your family should recover these lost earnings. Do you have any details?'

This had been part of my preparation. 'Indeed, I do.'

'I believe I can spare you a few moments. Please, come in.'

'Sounds like your day's been more productive than mine,' said Wolfgang as he slumped down on his bed.

'Possibly. What about the others?'

'I believe Stefan has a couple of leads. Anyway, tell me what you saw in that cheating bastard's room. Any sign of his strongbox?'

I had in fact not seen the strongbox, nor had I looked for it. My aim was not to commit such a crime for the risks were grave and the complications numerous. My wish was only to exact some form of revenge on behalf of Boyka's family. I simply couldn't stand the thought of Herr Wolff crisscrossing his domain, fleecing innocents as he pleased.

'No but it's clear to me what he spends his earnings on. He has a snuff box fit for a prince – emerald and ivory.'

'Is that right?'

Wolfgang now set about removing his boots. In fear of the inevitable odor, I crossed the room to the window and opened it wide.

'That would fetch, what …'

'Forty thalers,' said I. 'Possibly more.'

'Any other trinkets in there?'

'Some. Nothing else of such value.' I had been granted a good look at the snuffbox when Herr Wolff sniffed its contents. He kept it in his pocket and had offered me some but I'd refused, largely because I didn't like the stuff.

'I must say the emeralds took my eye. The box would go so well with my jacket.' I looked at the dark green garment, now hanging on the back of the door.

Wolfgang grinned. 'How you have changed, Christian. I thought I was supposed to be the rogue and you the innocent. And yet here you are, intent on pure thievery.'

'When one steals from a thief, one is simply righting a wrong.' My companion seemed impressed by this articulate statement. I wondered if I believed it.

'Herr Wolff is attending a musical recital at the home of the mayor this evening. I would like to relieve him of his snuffbox upon his return. I'll need your help – all of you.'

***

I don't imagine it was the most innovative operation of its kind but my three compatriots were happy to take part and even offered a few suggestions. As it would be unwise to remain in the same inn, we relocated in mid-afternoon, then returned to the riverside as evening approached. Taking turns with our pursuit, we followed Herr Wolff and his two bodyguards the short distance to the mayor's townhouse. Wolff now sported an ostentatious outfit complete with cloak, cane and hat. Stefan remained outside to await his reappearance while we other three retraced our steps.

We spent the next two hours skulking around near the bridge that connected the inn to central Cottbus. I was now once again dressed as 'Christian Pohl' and, as time passed, I began to grow increasingly anxious. Defeating Herr Wolff was a prize indeed but after the Silesian success, was this a risk too far?

'Don't be nervous,' said Wolfgang as we waited in the shadows of a park.

'I'm not,'

'Nonsense. You always pace around when you're nervous. You have it ready?'

I checked the pocket of my jacket. 'I do.'

'Everyone knows their part. Just make sure you do yours.'

About half an hour later, Stefan came sprinting up to us. Wolff was on his way. We all moved to the edge of the park, just a stone's throw from the bridge. Much of my role was about timing. There were four sets of lanterns alight on the bridge and I could not be too close to them when I encountered Herr Wolff. Ten minutes elapsed before he appeared. There were some couples taking a romantic walk but no one – such as a watchman – who might interfere with our scheme.

With everything already agreed, no one spoke as I emerged from the shadows, and then ran towards the trio as they passed the first of the lanterns.

'Herr Wolff, is that you?' I yelled, already slowing down.

The official and his enforcers spun around surprised.

'Help me, please!' I darted behind his party towards the side of the bridge.

'By god!' spluttered Wolff as three more figures reached us.

As instructed, Stefan and Wolfgang made an attempt to grab me but were put off by Hans, who was wielding his own blackjack. Pfieffer and Winkler drew their weapons but by then Stefan and Wolfgang had abandoned their 'attack'. As they sprinted across the bridge and away, Hans pursued.

'Werner, no!' I cried. 'You've done enough. Werner!'

As the sounds of their footfalls faded, I leaned back against the side of the bridge, panting hard. 'What a brave fellow.'

'What the hell happened?' asked Wolff as Pfieffer handed him his hat – it had fallen off during the commotion.

'Werner is an old friend of my father's,' said I. 'Without him, those two ruffians would have done me in. They fought and knocked him to the ground then pursued me. But he gave chase.'

I forced myself to breathe harder and harder, gasping and coughing as if having a fit.

'Calm yourself,' said Wolff, striking me on the back with no little force.

'They're gone, sir,' said Pfieffer wearily.

I slowed my breathing but stammered and made my hands shake. 'I'm s-s-sorry but I have always been of a s-s-somewhat nervous disposition. I seem to have lost control of'

'Here,' said Wolff. 'This will calm you down.' He offered me the snuffbox and opened the lid.

Perturbed that he hadn't actually handed me the box, I grabbed it nonetheless, acting as if still deranged.

Wolff sighed as I plucked some snuff and snorted it wildly.

Hans timed his return perfectly, jogging back onto the bridge.

'Sons of bitches got away from me. Where are the bloody watchmen when you need them?'

'Th-th-thank you,' said I to Herr Wolff. 'I do believe that helped.' In fact, the snuff had made me feel very light-headed.

He took the box offered to him and replaced it in his jacket.

'Not at all. You should make a report to the watchman in the morning. We can't have this sort of thing going on in Cottbuss. You might also consider hiring a professional for your personal protection, Herr Pohl.'

'Yes. Yes, indeed.'

'You were not hurt?'

'No, sir, thank you.'

'Then I suggest that you return to Leipzig and inform your father that you are not really cut out for fighting crime. Goodnight.'

We reconvened at our new inn. Wolfgang ordered a bottle of fine Bohemian wine in celebration and we toasted Herr Wolff while taking our turns to examine the exquisite snuff box. I could not help smiling when I thought of him turning out his pockets to find the pewter box of equal size but minimal value that I'd purchased that afternoon. With no light to see by and so much going on, he hadn't even suspected the deceit.

Did I feel guilt at this, my first robbery? I would like to say yes but if there were any such feelings they were subsumed by the glory of success. I had graduated from trading to smuggling to theft. The first real scheme of my own had gone very well. It was not to be my last.

Chapter Eight

Danzig, 1734

Taking a seat upon a mooring post, I gazed out at my favorite part of the city. The docks on both sides were hemmed in by tall white houses, black bars across their windows and red tiles upon their roofs. Of the ships themselves, some were a hundred feet long, with three great masts covered with nets for the sailors to clamber upon. I watched in amazement as two youths scrambled upwards, bags over their shoulders. Halting a good forty feet from the base of the central mast, they listened as an older man bellowed instructions before beginning some repair. Two rowing boats towed another ship along the Weichsel River. I waved to a ruddy-faced mariner and wondered where he and his fellow sailors had come from. The flag at the rear of their vessel meant nothing to me but I knew that brave men sailed here from as far away as Russia and Ireland, even Portugal and Spain. A trio of fishermen had just returned with their morning's haul. They seemed to be in a jovial mood and I understood why when I saw half a dozen baskets full of slithering, grey fish.

'Good catch!' I exclaimed.

'Very good, sir,' came the reply from a man now wrestling with a net.

I suppose I was used to being called 'sir'. Now in my twenty-fifth year, I had accumulated enough wealth to buy any clothes I desired. It was inadvisable to draw too much attention to oneself but I possessed three fine pairs of shoes, four excellent jackets and two waistcoats of which Johann would have been proud. My companions often mocked me for my vanity but they knew that my appearance was useful to us all. When meeting strangers, I now described myself as a merchant, which was not so very far from the truth. We sold and we bought; and on this – my third visit to Danzig – we were awaiting a shipment of Dutch gin from Rotterdam. As is often the case with seagoing transport, there was a delay. We had already been in Danzig for a week and while I had my own reasons to enjoy the longer stay, I was concerned about the others, who tended towards drink and gambling when unoccupied.

There were six of us now. Stefan had been lost during another grain run three years previously. While the rest of us elected to flee a fearsome cavalry patrol, he and another man had stupidly chosen to fight. We had not seen either of them since. Wolfgang was still with me; Hans too. Hans I never worried about. He was as steady a man as I have ever met. Still taciturn and given to dark moods, he had become a valued friend. He was not far from his fiftieth birthday and I suppose there was something of the father and son in our relationship.

In the years since Sagan and Cottbus, I had increasingly become the plotter within our band, though it was often Wolfgang's endless search for the next 'opportunity' that drove us on. Wolfgang did concern me. He was now forty-one yet in many ways seemed to be going backwards. He drank more; he gambled more; and he used any spare money on prostitutes. I was also no longer sure about his feelings towards me. True, there were moments when I detected pride about how his apprentice had turned out. But at other times, I sensed resentment. Nobody could dispute the fact that my influence had mitigated risk and improved our earnings.

As midday was near, I supposed Wolfgang and the others would have found some tavern to spend the day drinking in. Our wagons were ready and we had secured several buyers in quiet locations south of Danzig. Our profit would be made by avoiding the import tax levied at the port. I had established a relationship with one of the deputy harbormasters, who would ensure that the local customs officials were otherwise occupied while we unloaded the ship. Herr Engel charged a considerable amount for his services, which was only fair considering the risk to his reputation and livelihood.

We had come to know of him – and his 'pragmatic' tendencies – in an unusual manner. During our first trip to Danzig, Wolfgang and I worked hard to find a local official who might cooperate with us but to no avail. As I've mentioned, I initially found such tasks difficult but over time – and with Wolfgang's help – my skills improved. Yet it was never easy. Approach the wrong man; offer too low a bribe; push a contact farther then he wished to go; and danger could come quickly. In fact, one of our previous compatriots was now behind bars in Hanover due to one such misjudgment: he had tried to recruit a clerk at a tax office only to find a squad of soldiers at his door the following morning.

I learned of Herr Engel through his daughter. I had met Clare while visiting the tall clock tower in The Basilica of Saint Mary. Here was housed Gdansk's famous clock, which possessed many dials and unique features. Clare was a little younger than me and there with a friend. Seeing my interest in the clock, she told me a grisly legend that the maker had put out his own eyes for he knew he'd never make a clock to better it. From there, the conversation took on a lighter tone and I enjoyed a long walk with the girls.

For our next meeting, I took Clare for coffee. She was very talkative and I soon learned that she was rather bored by life in Danzig; and trying to resist her parent's intent to marry her off to some rich boat captain. She knew the worries and travails of such a life and proudly told me she'd rejected a dozen such suitors. Strange as it may sound, I retained an interest in clothing and we exchanged opinions on some of the current fashions.

It was during a later meeting that I learned of her mother's concerns about her father. Nothing specific was said but I learned enough to gather that Herr Engel might not be averse to a moneymaking scheme. I recruited Wolfgang to approach him and we soon had the deputy harbormaster on side.

He helped us make a good profit on that first occasion and was now doing so for the third time. I did feel guilty at this method of approach; especially as I had exchanged letters with Clare ever since and was about to meet her again. Herr Engel did not know, of course, and Clare did not tell him. She had grown exhausted by her parents' matchmaking and I suspected she enjoyed sneaking around behind their backs.

We had arranged to meet at a coffeehouse far from the harbor. Knowing that Clare always came late to make an entrance, I did not arrive until some time after our eleven o'clock appointment. Despite the occasional correspondence, we had not seen each other in months and I was quite apprehensive. Yet as I waited there, another matter took my attention. Sitting opposite me within the coffeehouse was a mother and her son, who was about the age I had been when I left home. The young man was a handsome, well-presented fellow and I could see the pride in his mother's eyes as he offered her a plate of cakes.

Seven years. Seven years since I had seen her. When I thought of the young Christian who had packed his knapsack and left that night, he seemed like another person. Hans sometimes asked me why I never went home. My mother had asked me to do so on several occasions in her letters. After dispatching the last refusal, I'd received no reply.

Two concerns stopped me returning to Halle. First, I had maintained the 'merchant' pretense in my letters and I worried that upon hearing the truth, she would want nothing to do with me. Second, I wondered why the correspondence had ended. Perhaps she had simply given up. Or had something happened? To her? To the family?

Just forget it. Forget them. Keep looking forward.

This was Wolfgang's repeated advice to me. Sometimes it seemed wise, sometimes the height of foolishness.

'Good day, Christian.'

Suddenly Clare was there beside me; and what a sight she was. Slender yet shapely, she had a fine head of auburn hair and pale blue eyes. Attired in a dress of cornflower blue and a white shawl, she was quite a picture. I stood and bowed.

'Good day, Clare.' I took her hand and kissed it.

'I can't get this thing to close,' she said, gesturing to her parasol.

'Allow me,' said I as she sat down.

Flushing as I realized one of the foldable struts was stuck, I nonetheless persisted. As the battle between myself and the parasol continued, the other customers began to look at me. Clare shrugged, her face also reddening. At last, the strut folded and I was able to hang the parasol from a nearby coat stand.

'Victorious at last,' said I.

A waiter appeared and we ordered coffee. I had never lost my sweet tooth but did not order cake because I knew Clare wouldn't. She was very proud of her figure.

'How nice to see you again,' she said. 'I do enjoy your letters but there's nothing quite like meeting face to face.'

'Indeed,' said I, reflecting that hers was a very beautiful face. On one hand, I was proud that such a young woman would want to spend time with the likes of me. On the other, I felt a vague sense of shame; presuming that if she knew the truth, she would reject me. Clare did not even know my real name. We exchanged letters via the postal service and she knew me as Christian Frank, one of my many pseudonyms.

'That is a superb dress.'

'Thank you, Christian.' Clare leaned forward. 'A birthday gift from Father. Mother told me not to ask where the money came from but I suppose I should just be grateful.'

'Are they well?'

'A touch of gout for Mother, but otherwise, yes.'

'And Hette is to be married?'

Clare simply nodded. I'd gathered from the tone of her letters that she was not too pleased about her younger sister's engagement. I suppose it made her position even more difficult.

Again, the guilt. I had made no formal commitment to Clare but even by maintaining relations was I leading her on? After all, what could a man like me offer her?

'How is business, Christian? You said something about calico?' Another lie.

'Yes. I need to secure a supplier. I have several meetings arranged.' I was spared further elaboration by the arrival of our coffee. Over the years I had acquired a taste for it; one of many luxuries I could now afford. As we drank, Clare continued to question me. I tried to turn our conversation to general matters but she was persistent. Some answers were honest but many were by necessity false. I'd told her I'd been born in Drezno, so fearful was I of the emotions brought about by recollections of Halle. It was not difficult for me to lie; it was the ease by which I did it that disturbed me.

Finally, I was able to turn the conversation back to her. Clare spoke with enthusiasm about Danzig's cloth market and some of the new French and Dutch patterns. She was very well educated and her interest in France was not limited to fashion. She spoke of the intellectual Voltaire. I knew the name but required Clare to explain to me that the man was very critical of his own government and had been forced to flee Paris, not for the first time. Apparently, he argued that religions should tolerate each other and that people should not be subject to the whims of monarchs. In Prussia, where the followers of Calvin and Luther clashed endlessly, I thought this sounded very sensible.

The questioning continued. Clare asked me if I thought I would ever settle down in one place and argued in favor of Danzig. The pressure of her interrogation eventually forced me to request that we take a walk to get some air. Fortunately, she agreed.

***

After we'd gone our separate ways, a feeling and a thought struck me. The feeling: she was a lovely girl and I looked forward greatly to our next meeting. The thought: that I was being highly unfair to her and that continuing to see her was unlikely to do either of us any good. I had not previously considered it a courtship, though I now knew that was precisely how she saw it. And therein lay the problem.

Upon returning to the inn, I was greeted by Axel Bettmann. He was the only member of the gang younger than me, a small but energetic fellow and an orphan since his tenth year. Axel came from a rural area and still wore the baggy trousers and leather waistcoat of a farmer.

'At last. I thought, you'd never return,' he said, intercepting me outside the inn. 'Hans sent me to fetch you. The Middelburg is in.'

'About time,' said I. This was the Dutch ship we had been waiting for.

'Hans is speaking to the first mate now. He's hopeful we can get the gin off tonight.'

This was good news but it meant I had to seek out Herr Engel urgently. We had to ensure that he could keep the customs officials busy while we transferred the gin from ship to wagon.

'Where are they docked?' I asked.

'The south harbor.'

I gave an approving nod. Though still surrounded by houses, the south harbor was the least busy area of Danzig. We had considered meeting the Middelburg further down the river but concluded that this would actually attract more attention. Unloading ships at late hours was not uncommon in the busy port; doing so without paying the considerable Brandenburg import tax was. This was especially high on alcohol, which meant there was no shortage of merchants happy to buy from us.

It was generally Wolfgang and I that made these arrangements and we knew the Middelburg's captain and first mate from a previous operation. I expected Axel to tell me that Wolfgang was ensconced in some tavern, but that was not the case.

'He ran into an old friend on the street. Apparently, the fellow's down on his luck and Wolfgang took him to buy some new clothes.'

'Is that right? Well, let's go and see how Hans is getting on.'

As it turned out, my presence was required. The first mate did not speak much German and Hans was struggling. The sailor and I both had passable English and French but used English on this occasion. The Dutchman apologized for the delay – some problem with their rudder – but said the captain was happy for the unloading to commence at ten o'clock. We discovered that a couple of kegs had been damaged during rough weather and adjusted the fee accordingly. We were to take sixty-four kegs of gin in total, to be sold to three separate purchasers, all within forty miles of Danzig. With this arranged, I left Hans to gather the men.

Taking Axel with me, I sought out Herr Engel. Not wanting to risk a meeting with Clare, I sent Axel to the harbormaster's headquarters and we later met Herr Engel on a towpath under a bridge, well away from any prying eyes. He was generally calm but, on this occasion, seemed anxious.

'Is tonight not possible?' I asked. Axel had sensibly moved away so that Engel could speak freely.

'As good as any other night. Or as bad.'

'What's going on?'

'Bloody Voigt. The man is an imbecile. He doesn't have the wit for this type of thing.'

'I don't know the name.'

Engel let out a long sigh before continuing. 'An assistant harbormaster.'

I knew this meant Voigt was ranked below Engel. Danzig was such a busy port that dozens worked for the chief harbor master.

'Fancies himself as some master criminal. He's started taking money from the Danish skippers – small fry but somehow it's got back to the mayor. He doesn't know who's involved but I've seen a lot of watchmen around this week.'

'Ah. So we might see some tonight.'

'If you're unlucky. South harbor's still the best place to be.'

'And the customs men?'

'On that count, you're in luck. Allenbach and Busch are off with illness. That leaves only two and I can keep them busy elsewhere.

Now that the wind's picked up, we'll have plenty of ships on the move.'

'Much appreciated. We shall post two guards.'

'Very wise. And if anything happens'

'We don't know you.'

Herr Engel seemed to have calmed down a little. 'Now then, to the subject of payment.'

I cannot say that I was particularly happy to meet Wolfgang Schmidt's old friend. This man was named Horst Bohm: a stout, balding individual with a wine-colored birthmark across the left side of his neck and face. As youths, the pair had begun their smuggling careers in the city of Luckenwalde. Bohm had spent eight years in prison for various offenses and struggled to make ends meet ever since. I could not reasonably deny Wolfgang's request that he join our group but I did not much like the timing. We faced a delicate operation that night but when Wolfgang promised to keep Bohm at his side at all times, I acceded. We often involved Hans in such decisions but the ex-soldier was not an imaginative man and it was generally Wolfgang and I who led the way, occasionally using the veteran for a casting vote if we did not agree.

Our plan was to leave Danzig in the morning, once the gin was safely transferred onto our wagons. Having collected the two vehicles, we made our way through the darkened streets towards the south harbor. With so much spare time, we'd been able to study the patrol patterns of the city watchmen and successfully avoided them. We had a convincing cover story ready but I was glad when we reached the harbor without incident. Along with Wolfgang and Bohm, Hans, Axel, and myself, were the two other members of our gang. Gunter and Emil had both joined us in Wittenburg the previous year. As usual, we gave them a few testing tasks before granting them permanent membership. Both had repeatedly proven themselves.

We found the Dutch sailors keen to complete our risky transaction. They had already moved the kegs off the Middelburg and onto the high stone quay. Wolfgang and I spoke briefly to the first mate, who then set off into town to join captain and crew: this way they could creditably claim their innocence if we were caught.

Posting Emil and Axel as sentries, we set to work. Though small, the kegs were very heavy and it took two men to safely load them onto the wagons. Horst Bohm seemed determined to impress and before long we were moving on to the second wagon. I estimated that we'd been there only a quarter-hour and seen only a man walking his dog. Directly behind us was a row of houses but at this time of night there were no lights on. We were working quietly and under a combination of moonlight and two half-shuttered lanterns. We had carried out such operations dozens of times. While most others were sleeping, men like us were creeping through the fields or the streets: shifting products, making money. Night was our ally.

The second wagon was almost fully loaded when Axel came sprinting along the dock from the direction of town. At the time, I was steadying one of the horses.

'Two watchmen coming this way,' said Axel between panting breaths.

'How far?'

'Hundred yards. Less.'

I could actually see their lantern. Both men would also be equipped with heavy clubs and a bell to summon others if necessary. We were exactly what they were looking for. Without documentation to show we had paid the import tax, every one of us faced imprisonment. Worse, I knew that the likes of Hans and Wolfgang would fight any watchmen brave enough to take us on.

Wolfgang jumped off the wagon and landed beside me. 'That looks like trouble.'

'Do we have time?' I asked.

'Not unless we can stall them. Any ideas?'

I always had several up my sleeve for just such an eventuality.

However, these often depended on me taking a personal risk and I was rather tired of doing so. I decided that I could give our newest member another chance to prove himself.

'Mind if I put Bohm to work?'

'Go ahead. He'll do as he's bid.'

Wolfgang summoned his friend and recruited Axel to help with the last of the kegs. By now the watchmen's lantern was no more than fifty yards distant.

'What do you need?' asked Horst.

'See the houses to the right? Go around the back and put in a window or two. Make plenty of noise. Head towards town and do the same to two or three more. Give it half an hour then come join us at the warehouse. Go now.'

With a nod of reply, Bohm ran towards the houses.

From the wagon, I took a hat and a cane. 'Wolfgang, they're close.' 'Everyone quiet,' he said. 'Lanterns out.'

He and Hans stood by the horses; keeping them quiet with pats and whispers.

Imagining myself a gentleman out for a late stroll, I set off along the quay, only stopping when I was well away from the wagons. I saw the lantern up ahead and could now spy the two watchmen caught within its glow.

'Hurry up,' I murmured, hoping to avoid an encounter with the pair. If Bohm failed to lure them away, I had a plan for turning them around. If that did not work, there was always the silver thalers I kept on me for emergency bribes.

The watchmen were no more than thirty feet away. I could see the thick beard on one of them; hear the other whistling.

Twenty feet. I reckoned they could probably see me. I was about to hail them when

A smash. A scream. Moments later came several shouts. The watchmen responded instantly, retracing their steps, then bolting towards the noise.

I ran back to the wagons, dropping my cane and hat into one as the others loaded the last kegs. The noise had brought Emil running and we were soon all aboard the vehicles. I had still made little progress with driving so it was Hans and Gunter who guided us away from the harbor. The warehouse was less than a quarter-mile away. When we reached it, we could still hear the watchmen's bells far behind us.

Since the arrival of the Middelburg, events had marched on quickly, giving me little time to consider what to do about Clare Engel. We had to depart the next morning. I could have left a note for her at the post office but time was short and I had no idea what to write. I suppose I took refuge in the strategy that had served me well since my youth: I would leave; keep moving; avoid anything too difficult. I didn't know when I would return to Danzig but it seemed for the best if I did not see Clare again. After this abrupt departure and no more letters, surely she would soon forget about me.

With our kegs covered, we set off from the warehouse. Hans and I now both owned a horse and followed along behind the wagons. There were dozens such vehicles on the move and no reason for us to be concerned. We had planned a route to avoid toll stops as we headed for our first buyer in the town of Zuckau.

We'd not gone far when the traffic slowed to a halt. Word came back that a cart had turned over and we soon heard the pained shrieks of an injured horse. My horse became skittish and I nervous because of pedestrians close by. Once it was under control, I became aware that I was being watched.

Sitting on a bench outside a store no more than twenty feet away were three young women. Two were talking to each other. The third, Clare, was staring at me. I can still remember the expression on that lovely face. She seemed confused and hurt; trying but failing not to show it.

I have seldom felt so ashamed of myself. How pathetic – to pretend there was nothing between us. How cowardly – to flee without another word.

I never saw her again.

Chapter Nine

By the following afternoon, I realized I needed to tell someone of my woes. I have always liked to communicate and I generally feel better about a troublesome issue when I have discussed it. Poor old Hans usually ended up playing priest to my confessor and so it was in this case. We had sold a third of our load in Zuckau and were now continuing south. All around us, spring flowers were in bloom yet the natural beauty did little to improve my mood. I had been tarrying at the back but now urged my mount forward so I could ride alongside Hans.

'Seems a decent fellow,' I said, nodding forward.

Horst Bohm was sitting beside Wolfgang on the second wagon, pipe smoke drifting up from both of them.

Hans offered only a neutral nod. He was not one to make swift judgments. Like me, he respected Wolfgang's numerous abilities but wearied of him at times.

'You remember Engel's daughter?'

'Yes. Did you see her?'

'Just once. Well, twice. I … I didn't know how to say goodbye to her.'

We rode on past a field where a father and his sons were scattering seed. The younger lad stopped to wave and I returned the gesture.

'I just wonder sometimes. What's the point of even buying a girl flowers or taking a walk? With the life we lead, what can I possibly offer?'

'A big pile of coins, Christian. When it's big enough, perhaps you can buy a house and find some fair maid to share it with you.'

I knew Hans had experienced this for a time. He'd married just before joining the army and returned from a campaign two years later to find his wife dead. She'd been thrown from a horse and died instantly from a broken neck. Hans had missed the letter sent to summon him and arrived a day after the funeral.

When I heard this tragic tale, it made me view the man in a different light.

'I don't know,' said I. 'What would I do for work?'

'You've pretended to be a merchant for so long – why not actually be one?'

'It's not the worst idea in the world.'

'There's nothing wrong with our life. This life,' said Hans. 'But there's a lot to be said for coming home to a kiss and a good meal and a warm bed. Especially if you find the right woman.'

In my earlier years with the gang, I would have seen no merit in such a proposition. And I still had little desire to settle down. But I could now see some appeal in what Hans described.

The veteran was not given to long conversations, so I was surprised when he spoke up again. 'We'll be heading towards Halle. You could call in on your mother. Just to say good day.'

Karthaus was in many ways a typical West Prussian town. However, it had grown up amidst several small lakes, giving the place a unique appearance and atmosphere. I had only visited once before and was glad to return. There were more spring flowers on show here and a brilliant May sun to illuminate them.

We completed our second deal swiftly, leaving us with one to go. Wolfgang and I had decided to wait until all the gin was sold before distributing the profits. Hans was always happy to leave such matters to us. In general, no one in the gang questioned we three as the most experienced members. If there were complaints or new ideas, we usually gave them a fair hearing. But the world of smuggling was a small one and we had built a strong reputation as a crafty, hard-working, well-connected group. Any man with any sense who joined us knew better than to upset the apple cart. We had got rid of several troublesome individuals over the years. The combined force of Hans and Wolfgang was generally sufficient to dissuade any from violence. Though Wolfgang was given to shouting and insults when riled, I knew he could also take care of himself. Hans did not lash out unless he felt there was no choice. So far, I'd only seen him do so with his fists. I had no doubt he'd be equally dangerous with his sword.

There seemed to be no soldiers in the area at all, leaving myself and my compatriots in a relaxed frame of mind. We decided on an overnight stay and were accommodated at a pleasant inn. We were all tired from traveling and most settled down for an afternoon nap. We had hired one large dormitory room and, though also weary, I had an urgent task to attend to: my horse had lost a shoe just short of Karthaus and a replacement was urgently needed. Consulting the innkeeper, I learned that there was a blacksmith close by. Just as I left, young Axel appeared and asked to accompany me.

Our path to the smithy took us past the monastery at the center of the town. It was the biggest building in Karthaus: constructed of red brick with a long sloping roof of black tiles. I knew that the monastic order had founded the town many centuries before; and the monks themselves were a common sight in their voluminous white robes and peaked hoods. The innkeeper had reminded us not to attempt communication. Silence and solitude were tenets of the Carthusian order.

Axel seemed to be following their example and I wondered if he was preoccupied by something. Once we'd delivered my horse to the blacksmith, we found a bench on the town's main street and sat down. The young man was keen to know more about our next operation but our plan was a loose one: we had heard of some potential opportunities in Berlin. In truth, I'd spent most of my time thinking of Halle and my family.

I knew that Axel was saving up for a horse of his own and was pleased to hear he'd accumulated a few thalers. Knowing my mount wouldn't be ready for several hours, I suggested we head back to the inn. Only then did Axel express what had obviously been concerning him.

'I'm not sure if I should even mention it.'

'Come, Axel, you can tell me.'

'It's the new man –Horst.'

'What about him?'

'I saw him unpacking back in the room,' continued Axel. 'He has some money – a few thalers. No harm in that but'

'He's supposed to be destitute.'

'Yes.'

'It's possible that Wolfgang lent him something. You're sure they were thalers?'

'Five at least. They slipped out of a wallet onto his bed. He collected them quickly; didn't realize I'd seen him.'

'Well, I wouldn't worry too much, Axel. Wolfgang has vouched for him. Come on.'

I didn't want the young man to concern himself with this matter but I now was. Wolfgang might have lent Bohm a few groschen but five thalers was no small amount.

As events transpired, myself and the rest of the gang would have considerable cause to be thankful for Axel's watchfulness.

Back in the dormitory, the others all appeared to be sleeping and Axel soon joined them. As usual, Wolfgang was snoring and a noxious combination of smells now filled the room. Such were the 'pleasures' of traveling with a band of men. Having opened a window, I settled down upon a blanket, hoping to get some rest myself. I had little doubt that with a night to spare and no sign of any troops, Wolfgang would be determined to enjoy the evening. The problems that often arose from such occasions – drunkenness, gambling, brawling – could generally be avoided if Hans and I kept a lid on things.

But I could not rest. I was thinking of Berlin, how easy it would be to leave the gang for a week, continue southwest to Halle. In my mind, it would all look the same, but after seven years I could not know what might have changed.

I closed my eyes and thought of a cartwheel turning. This was Hans' trick for falling asleep and it sometimes worked for me. Not today.

I believe I was the only one awake when Horst Bohm got up. He did so quietly; carefully. I knew this might just be consideration for we others, and if not for what Axel had told me I might not have watched him at all. I was at the opposite end of the dormitory and kept my eyes narrowed in order to obscure my surveillance. I watched Bohm tap his waistcoat pocket, as if checking something was there then leave on tiptoes.

I waited a minute then put on my shoes and followed him. Once outside the inn, I caught sight of him turning down a side street. I hurried up to the corner and watched him striding away. This did not look like an idle stroll; he clearly knew where he was going. To my knowledge, Bohm had not been to Karthaus before.

Following him was tricky but I had a little experience in the practice and was careful not to get too close. Fortunately, he was not going far, only to the town's post office. There was one to be found in almost every place at that time and they performed a crucial service that I used regularly. Though the movement of correspondence was slow, it was rare for a letter to go missing.

I didn't dare go inside but crossed the road and hid myself behind a cart. Bohm exited the post office after only a minute or so. I was expecting him to be holding a note or an envelope but all I saw was a pencil, which he replaced in his waistcoat pocket before departing in the direction of the inn.

'Can I help you?' The inquiry had come from a large man wearing a bloodstained apron. He placed a possessive hand on the cart and glared at me from beneath bushy eyebrows.

I gathered he had exited a nearby doorway and looked up to see a butcher's sign.

'Er …'

I glanced again at the post office. If Bohm had left a note, I wanted to know who picked it up. There was no sense even attempting to bribe a postmaster: they were a loyal, fastidious breed and post-tampering was a serious offense. This was a busy street and there were no other obvious locales from which I could monitor the building.

I smiled at the butcher. 'Perhaps you can.'

He was a forceful negotiator and I was charged three groschen for the privilege of sitting on a stool at the back of his store. Customers occasionally obscured my view but my host didn't seem to care what I was up to. There weren't that many customers so I guessed he was satisfied with his earnings.

I was there for over an hour, looking for a very specific type of man. If Bohm was working against us, either the courts or the army would have recruited him. It was possible that someone had tipped off the authorities in Danzig. If they were using Bohm, they would want to keep in close touch. Spies were generally recruited from the ranks of the army. Some were more skillful than others but I knew what to look for.

Just after four o'clock, I saw him. The man was around thirty, dressed unremarkably but very upright and martial in his bearing; and then there was the mustache – thick and oiled like any good infantry officer. The timing interested me. The last hour of the working day had begun; a busy time at the post office as locals came in to check for correspondence before the place closed.

It was guesswork, of course, but educated guesswork.

Thanking the butcher, I set off down the street, following my mustachioed friend. When he entered a small inn, my suspicions grew. I knew of one reasonably reliable way to establish his identity. Sneaking around to the rear of the inn, I saw that it was equipped with a small stable. Outside the three occupied stalls, saddles and tack hung from hooks: a typical arrangement. I waited for a few minutes to see if the courtyard was busy. It seemed quiet so I nipped over the gate and inspected the central stall. The horse inside was a fine beast. This fact was instructive but proved nothing.

I then examined the saddle, which was easily the most impressive of the three. Officers of the Prussian Army were equipped with the best riding gear money could buy. I knew where to look and soon spied the maker's mark. Better still was the stamp of the Ninth West Prussian regiment. I knew they were based in Marienburg, which was not far from Danzig.

Escaping the courtyard without detection, I hurried back to the inn. The evidence was not conclusive. It was perfectly possible that I had misread the signs: put two and two together to make five.

My head and my gut told me otherwise.

By the time I showed my face at the inn, Wolfgang was itching to visit the town's most popular tavern, which – fortunately for the monks – was situated on the far side of a lake, some distance from the main town. Claiming weariness, I let the others leave. Left in possession of the dormitory key, I locked the door then searched Bohm's belongings. I emptied his rucksack, examined the meager contents but found nothing incriminating. He owned a coat but it was a warm night and they had all left them behind. I checked this too but again found nothing. I would have to employ another method of investigating Herr Bohm.

I found the gang sitting at a large table outside the inn, only yards from the lake. Despite the heat, there was a pleasant breeze that moved the rushes bordering the water. Upon it, a few ducks and geese idled. There were a dozen other patrons, none of whom seemed very interested in our group.

Every man had a mug in front of him and, given the pleasantness of the scene, I wished I was without the burden of my suspicions. Only when I bought my own dunkel and joined them did I notice something else out of place.

We all owned headgear of various kinds: wide-brimmed sun hats, common cloth caps and I myself possessed a gentleman's three-pointed hat. But because of the clement weather, only two of the gang had brought them. One was Emil, who had taken his off and placed it on the table. Bohm's cap was on his knees and he had one arm resting protectively across it. Unlike the rest of his clothes, it appeared new. This gave me a ready-made excuse.

'May I see your cap?' said I.

Upon seeing Bohm's reaction, I knew instantly that something was wrong.

'My cap?'

'Yes. May I see it? I'm thinking of buying one.'

'Too cheap for you, Christian,' said Wolfgang. 'No offense, Horst.' Bohm was still looking at me. 'It's just a cloth cap.'

'I know good workmanship when I see it.'

'Once a tailor, always a tailor,' said Emil.

'Quite so,' I replied.

Bohm handed the cap across the table to me. Axel was watching closely and I believe he also noted the anxiety in the newcomer's face. The exterior of the cap was typical. But within the interior, I felt an unusual feature along the back edge. Peering closer, I saw that a flap of material obscured a row of tiny buttons. A hidden compartment.

By now the others were more interested in a returning serving girl. Keeping the cap below the level of the table, I opened the buttons. I was already reaching inside when Bohm leaned across and spoke.

'All right. The game's up. But let's not do it here.'

The seven of us stood on a sandy beach, a remote spot further around the edge of the lake. Wolfgang squatted by the water, now silent after a vicious tirade against his old friend. Emil, Axel, and Gunther looked on as Hans examined the three pieces of paper I'd just handed to him. One was a map of the region, one a list: the addresses of post offices in no less than twenty-nine towns in the Danzig area. On their own, not exactly incriminating. The third document left no doubt: it was a brief statement signed by a magistrate granting Bohm immunity from prosecution as an agent of the crown. I understood fully why he would carry it. While with us, he might find himself under arrest or attack at any time. The document he had carried to protect himself now threatened his life.

The traitor stood alone.

I continued my questioning. 'How long were you to stay with us?' 'Until the gin was delivered. Longer if I could learn more.'

'When will they arrest the buyers?'

'Once the last load is sold and we clear the area.'

'The man you left the message for – is it just him?'

'I believe so. He is to travel a day or so behind us. I was to leave messages whenever I could.'

'Why?' yelled Wolfgang Schmidt as he got to his feet. 'You know I would have given you money. By god, I bought the very clothes you're wearing.'

'I had no choice,' said Bohm quietly, clearly hoping that a reasonable tone might help him. 'What I said about trying to survive after prison was true. I had nothing. When I was caught selling knocked-off ironware, the magistrate said I could work for the court or go back inside. I just couldn't face it. I'm sorry. All of you, I'm very sorry.'

Hans spoke up. 'Your handler is here in Karthaus. What about other soldiers – close by?'

'I don't know.'

I thought the worst of Wolfgang's rage had passed. How wrong I was.

He caught the traitor unawares with a powerful punch. Bone cracked and Bohm staggered backward. Wolfgang grabbed his former friend by the collar and dragged him into the water, then tripped him and forced him under.

'Wolfgang!'

He gave no sign of having heard me.

'Hans?'

My friend wouldn't meet my gaze. It seemed he didn't disapprove of Wolfgang playing judge, jury, and executioner.

Bohm was struggling fiercely but Wolfgang was the stronger man. I approached him. 'Let him go. Please. Hans, will you not help me?' 'It has to be like this, Christian. That bastard would have been happy to see us all hang.'

I couldn't believe what I was hearing. I looked at the others. Emil and Gunther turned and walked away. Young Axel was weeping but now followed the others.

I hesitated for a moment. Could it be that I was wrong and they were right?

No.

I walked into the water. Bohm's hands flailed but Wolfgang kept his head under. Eyes unblinking, jaw set, he seemed a man possessed.

I gripped his shoulder. 'Please. You're no murderer.'

He ignored me.

In desperation, I grabbed one of his arms and pulled it free. This gave Bohm a chance and his head broke the surface. I believe it was the sight of the animal terror in his eyes that changed Wolfgang's mind.

He let go.

'You're no murderer,' I said again.

'You have no idea what I am.'

Still on his knees, Bohm wheezed and spluttered. I helped him up and back to the sand where he fell again.

Wolfgang lurched out of the water then walked away.

'He'll go back to them,' said Hans as he gazed down at Bohm. 'We leave him alive and he'll tell them all he knows. They won't give him any choice.'

I understood what he meant. Bohm had heard of our plan to visit Berlin and that was not all that would change. We would have to abandon the rest of the gin and get out of West Prussia immediately. We would have to leave that night.

'We are not murderers.'

Hans walked away.

I was the last to leave. Behind me, the traitor coughed, retched and sobbed.

Chapter Ten

Drezno, 1740

My appointment upon the bridge was at midday. As was my habit, I arrived early to ensure that I was not walking into a trap. Such worries were now a daily concern but I had known no other life for more than a decade; and I doubt my burdens weighed more heavily upon me than any other man.

I can say, without exaggeration or excess pride, that I was by this point an infamous figure. My name – or rather my various aliases – appeared on numerous 'rogue lists' of the type kept by the authorities in cities and states across central Europe. Though the gang's operations occasionally failed, we had achieved a remarkable run of successes. We combined daring smuggling missions with audacious thefts, and I must confess that I was the driving force behind the latter. There was no better or better-known criminal enterprise within or without Brandenburg but this was not the sole reason why we'd achieved a degree of fame.

We had also begun to share out some of our ill-gotten gains. It all started when we snatched a tax collector's haul after distracting his guards with hired dancing girls. Fleeing the scene with bags stuffed with coins, my compatriots and I doled out handfuls to homeless men and families. We had so enjoyed the looks upon their faces and the knowledge that they could put the money to such good use. It was now common for us to donate a portion of our booty to whomever we deemed fit. In return, we often received help from common folk who allowed us the use of their barns or cellars to hide our goods. We had become known as The Lucky Thieves; and, yes, I myself was termed the King of Thieves.

Some said I was an aristocrat, who had turned against my own, others that I was a disillusioned army officer. I don't imagine anyone believed me to be a humble tailor's son. Some thought me a Brandenburger, others were sure I was a Saxon or a Pomeranian; and one rumor contended that I was a descendant of none other than Robin Hood! I was glad no one knew my real identity, partly because I did not want word to reach my family. And I was glad of my mysterious moniker; no one knew my true name.

Reaching the central arch of the great sandstone bridge that had been constructed across the Elbe only a decade earlier, I stopped and examined my surroundings. A few carriages were rattling past and a few men were peddling tobacco, candles and cheap trinkets. Several young couples of a superior rank were also enjoying the spring day; the ladies wielding parasols, the men canes. Nobody paid me much attention – I was clad in the dowdy attire of an artisan. I had come to enjoy my disguises; and carrying out our daring schemes while tedious everyday life went on about me.

Mine was a life of adventure and risk; and I admit I loved it. We were criminals – I had long adopted Hans' definition regarding this matter – but we played by a set of rules. We only robbed the crown and the rich; and we always avoided violence if we could. It's true there had been the odd scrap but no blades or guns had been used in anger.

This was one reason why Wolfgang Schmidt had left us the previous year. Looking back, I realize the Horst Bohm episode had been the beginning of the end. My judgment had proved more accurate than his; and over time there could be little doubt that I'd become leader. Wolfgang resented this; and no longer shared my reservations about who we preyed upon and how we conducted ourselves. In some ways I missed my old mentor; I owed him a lot and we had been through so much. But Wolfgang had always remained a slave to his vices and life was simply easier without him around.

I always listened to Hans' advice – and indeed the others – but I was now the one who selected our targets and ran our operations. I kept us on the move, always at least one step ahead of the authorities, always seeking the next adventure.

Was I happy? Happier, I think, than I had been in previous years. I'd accepted that this was to be my life and I was fully aware that it was far better and more exciting than most. This acceptance had helped me deal with thoughts of family and home.

In the year 1737, I had actually returned to Halle and stood alone, disguised, in my old observation point on the Fleisherstrasse. Seeing my father and my mother returning from church, I confess I wept at the sight of them. There had been no more letters and in part it was simply relief that both were alive and appeared well. I was halfway across the street and about to hail them when I turned and fled. The thought of all the difficulties and complications and explanations overwhelmed me. I felt like a vessel that had traveled so far from shore that there was simply no way back.

On most occasions, I was glad I had not crossed the street that day. On a few, I regretted it.

In the year 1739, a fortunate encounter led me to hear news of my family. I was in a tavern – rather the worse for wear – when I was approached by a man of about my age. He recognized me and shook my hand warmly. Seeing my confusion and blaming his lost hair for my failure to recognize him, he identified himself as none other than Willem Bassler. This was the friend of Hugo and I whose soldier brother had so inspired us as young lads. Willem had recently returned to Halle after several years in distant Ravensberg. When he mentioned my family, I claimed that a long-running dispute with my father prevented my return, which was not entirely untrue. Upon realizing that Bassler could bring me up to date, I put my beer aside and ushered him to a quiet corner of the tavern.

I was greatly relieved to hear only good news. Bassler was not entirely sure about which of my sisters had just given birth but when I listed their names, he reckoned it was Mary. My mother and father were apparently in good health and the Kasebiers were doing well. Lucian was now a married man and, for all our differences, I smiled at the thought of my annoying brother somehow finding a woman who would tolerate him. A foolish reaction perhaps: Lucian could have changed beyond all recognition. God knows I had.

Unfortunately, Bassler knew nothing specific about Johann's progress but we agreed that if there was bad news from Pennsylvania, he probably would have heard it. When we went our separate ways, I asked him to make no mention of our meeting to my family or anyone else in Halle.

I was glad of the encounter; and though I felt pangs of emotion at what I'd heard; I realized that thirteen years alone had hardened me. I never felt that I had made the wrong decision for myself in leaving. My aim had been to carve out my own path, break free of expectation and convention; and no one could deny that I had done so.

The scuffing of feet snapped me out of this reverie. I looked up to see that my associate had arrived.

I'd first heard of the Udaipur Emerald while in Berlin. After a run of jewelry thefts, I had become acquainted with several gem dealers. The fellows who purchased from the likes of me were not the most respectable in their trade but they were experts nonetheless. One jewelry in emeralds and had previously regaled me with the tale of this particular gem. It was in fact the largest of several emeralds mined near Udaipur, India earlier in the century. It had passed through half a dozen owners and was currently mounted in a silver ring and in possession of a notable lady. She was Swedish – the Countess Zulich –and her husband, the count, was now ambassador to Prussia.

A month earlier, I had checked one of my many postal accounts – this one in Rossbach – and heard from the dealer. The man was exceptionally well connected and informed me that the Zulichs were to attend a grand ball at the royal palace in Drezno on the fourteenth of April. He also advised me that 'if the emerald were to come into my possession', he could remove the gem and sell it on to a Russian buyer. We would share the profits. Once I'd advised him that I would expect two-thirds (as I was taking most of the risk), we agreed to cooperate. As usual, the gang would assist me and receive their share but I also needed some local guidance. After some lengthy, awkward inquiries, I had identified the man now before me.

He too wore anonymous, drab clothing; and like me resembled many of the passing pedestrians.

'Cold for this time of year.'

'Warm enough for me.'

The simple code had been arranged via letter. My new associate nodded and introduced himself. 'Jean-Pierre.'

'Christian. That doesn't sound like a Saxon name.'

He led the way to the side of the bridge. We both rested our arms on the thick stone wall and looked outward.

'Indeed not. My father is French, my mother Bohemian. They settled here. How can I help you, Christian? I do not have much time and my wife is ill.'

'I'm sorry to hear that. Rest assured that I will pay well if you are of use to me. I'm told you know a considerable amount about the great buildings of this fair city?'

'I do have some knowledge of architecture,' answered Jean-Pierre coyly. He was a small, unassuming fellow but there was an astute, piercing quality to his eyes.

'The royal palace, for example?'

There were several other issues I would need to address but accessing the famous structure and home of the Saxon electors would be essential.

'You're not serious?'

'I'm afraid I am.'

'It is the most heavily guarded building in Saxony. The exterior wall alone is fifteen feet high and there is a permanent garrison of over two hundred guards.'

'My dear fellow, I will not be approaching the place in a hooded cloak with an empty sack over my shoulder. I shall be in disguise. But I would like to know as much as possible about the layout of the place, the dispositions of the guards and so on. Can you help?'

Jean-Pierre looked down at the swirling river below. 'Augustus II had the place rebuilt after a fire about forty years ago. I believe there are plans, diagrams available. For the right price.'

'And current security arrangements? Routines, shift patterns and so on?'

'There are hundreds of staff employed there. I'm sure some are open to persuasion. For'

'-the right price. Money is not a problem. Here.' Ensuring that the transaction was not seen, I handed Jean-Pierre five thalers. 'There'll be plenty more if you can provide what I need. Shall we say Friday?

Same place, same time?'

Jean-Pierre secreted his coins with a practiced hand. 'See you then.' I was about to turn away but his keen eyes were still upon me.

He kept his voice low. 'You're going for the Jewel Room, aren't you?' I knew that this section of the palace contained the priceless collection of crowns, jewels and other valuables accrued over many centuries by the House of Wettin.

I laughed. 'Some consider me daring, Jean-Pierre but even I am not that daring.'

As well as good old Hans, Axel and Gunther were still with me. Emil had left the previous year, having met a lovely young woman who we all agreed he should marry. I could tell that Axel and Gunther were rather jealous of our friend, though they all enjoyed our adventures as much as Hans and I. As for myself, while I always hoped that a great romantic love would enter my life, a quiet existence was not something I coveted. I enjoyed women's company as much as ever and there had been a few brief affairs but not one had yet been able to tame me.

One would not wish to sound boastful but I did receive quite a bit of attention from the fairer sex. Much of my earnings went into clothes and I suppose my unusual career had given me a certain confidence. Another factor was my skill with languages, which had now become something of an obsession. I was fluent in Polish, Russian and French, with passable English and some skill in several other tongues. I took every opportunity to practice and had amassed a sizable collection of instructional texts. If I was not busy of an evening, I would commit two solid hours to my study. I'll concede that I had a natural aptitude but it was my constant practice that set me apart. Now approaching thirty years of age, I realized that I was in my own way a very dedicated and hard-working individual. There was still some Kasebier in me.

My approach to our schemes had become highly methodical as I grew older; and later that day I sat down with my three compatriots. These days we had enough money to hire a room each and were currently ensconced at a pleasant inn not far from the bridge. A window was open and outside we could hear the hubbub from a nearby market. Hans had bought some cider and poured us all a mug as I began.

'We will know by Friday if Jean-Pierre can get what we need. In the meantime, our other preparations must continue. Axel?'

'There are two carriage companies taking bookings for the ball. No one would talk to me at the first place – I'll have another try tomorrow – but I got to a groom at the other. With a few more thalers, I reckon I can get a good list together.'

Axel had become a valued member of the group. No longer a youth, his sunny disposition enabled him to chat to working men of his own type. I knew I could rely on him to make progress without exposing himself to unnecessary risk.

'Keep at it,' said I, keen to amass information on the guests attending the ball. 'Gunther?'

He sipped his cider then grimaced. 'Not a lot of good news, chief. Most of the aristocrats will stay with family or friends at their mansions scattered around the countryside. Difficult for us to get to. I've been around the better inns, got a couple of servants to spill the beans. Sounds like there will be about two dozen or so staying in the city.'

'Two dozen, eh?' said I. 'Seems likely our mark will have to be one of them. We have to focus our efforts there. Hans, can you go with Gunther tomorrow?'

This was not the ex-soldier's area of expertise but he agreed.

'How did you get on today?'

I had asked Hans to carry out a preliminary scouting mission. Though I'd never harbored any serious intention of breaking into the palace, I would need a swift method of escaping the area.

Hans sighed. 'Assuming you come out via the main gate, there are no good alternatives. The whole area is teeming with guards, day and night.'

'Any *acceptable* alternatives?'

'There are not only guards but many city watchmen. Their uniform is easily copied. They always work in pairs, one with lantern, and one with lance. I could accompany you.'

'I like it.'

'Not sure Hans does,' observed Axel.

I already knew that the veteran was not wildly enthusiastic about this scheme. Then again, I had never known Hans to be particularly enthusiastic about anything; though there was a buxom milkmaid in Potsdam he was very fond of.

'Well?' said I to my old friend.

'Why does it have to be the palace?'

'We've been over this. The man is a state ambassador. He does not freely advertise his movements and is well protected wherever he goes. But at an occasion like this, he and his wife will be off their guard.'

'You can't even be sure she'll be wearing it.'

'Men who buy their wives big emeralds want everyone to know they buy their wives big emeralds.'

Hans frowned. 'But the palace? Just for a gem? I don't see the sense in it.'

'Because we can,' said Gunther with a grin.

'We still have eight days,' said I. 'Let's see how we get on. If it's too risky, we walk away.'

Seven days later, I felt sure we had made sufficient progress to go ahead. Jean-Pierre had furnished me with an up to date plan of the palace and some information about the guards' dispositions and routines. Better still, Axel had identified a likely candidate for me to pose as. The Duke of Bartenstein was distantly related to the Wettin family but his seat was hundreds of miles away and he had not attended a function in Drezno for more than a decade. Now newly married, and perhaps eager to show off his wife, he was accommodated at a luxurious inn where we had cultivated an informer.

Crucially, the duke was around my age and, having observed him twice, I would try to appear as similar as possible. We could not mitigate against someone at the ball knowing him personally but I did not intend to remain within the palace very long. The key was getting in.

I had spent most of the morning working on the outfit I'd purchased and adapted to resemble the one he was planning to wear. Having considered several methods of stopping the duke himself from attending, I believed we'd found a good one. We didn't anticipate needing to delay he and his wife for more than an hour.

Another servant (who had demanded an astronomical fee) had allowed us to see one of the invitations sent out by the palace. Gunther – who'd developed some useful forgery skills – had created a passable facsimile.

But although we knew something of the Swedish ambassador, we'd been able to discover little about our target, the countess. With such limited knowledge, I had little guidance for planning my approach. I was confident in my ability to improvise but this left a great deal to chance when perhaps enough was being left already. I could tell that Hans was still uneasy.

As I continued to work on a jacket, the veteran came to my room. 'You have the uniforms?' I asked.

'I do.'

'And they fit?'

'Well enough.'

It would be Gunther's job to masquerade as an officer from the palace garrison. We knew that Russian insurgents had made an attempt on the Duke of Bartenstein's life and felt confident that by raising the specter of another threat here in Drezno, we could delay him long enough for me to do my work. Gunther was to hold the pair and their bodyguards until he knew I was out. Emil would then arrive, posing as another officer, and report that the threat had been removed.

I was currently stitching in some golden patterning and needed some assistance. 'Hans, hold this steady.'

With a weary shake of his head, he did so. 'Bloody seamstress's assistant, now am I?'

'In our line of work, one must be many things.'

'Too many, if you ask me.'

Smelling tobacco on Hans' breath made me crave one of the cigars of which I'd become fond.

'Why are we really doing this?' he added.

I shrugged. 'As Wolfgang would have said, an opportunity came our way.'

'But the royal palace, Christian?'

'You don't think we can pull it off?'

'Actually, after the way the week's gone, I think we have a decent chance.'

I took my eyes off my tailoring for a minute to look at my friend. This close, I saw how the lines beneath his eyes had become more pronounced in recent times.

'What is it then?'

'What if you do succeed? This theft will only bring more attention upon us.'

I couldn't help smiling at the thought of how this might add to our fame.

'It is not amusing!' snapped Hans, who was not given to such outbursts. 'This will be an affront not only to the ambassador and the Swedes but to his host the elector and all of Saxony.'

'Well, we should certainly make ourselves scarce afterward. I was thinking perhaps Ansbach? Bayreuth?'

Hans rolled his eyes. 'It's not just this job, Christian. I worry that you don't know where to stop. Always a bigger prize. Always a bigger risk. It can only end one way.'

Chapter Eleven

Even though I had visited the city before, the center of Drezno was a compelling sight. Most of the repairs to the palace were now complete and it was one of several immense, white-painted buildings adorned by countless arched windows that added elegance to the imposing bulk. The palace was of course the most impressive of all, centered around a rebuilt tower visible from every corner of the city.

I could see it now, as my carriage rumbled its way towards the main gate. Had Hans' words of warning given me pause for thought? They had, but the pause did not last long. I understood his concerns but most of the risk was mine and I simply could not resist the lure of this challenge. Stealing the Udaipur emerald would be a success. Taking it from the royal palace of Drezno? Nothing less than a triumph.

My driver and I had been waiting two streets away while Gunther intercepted the real Duke of Bartenstein and spun his tale about the Russian assassins on the loose. Gunther was not an actor of my caliber but the duke and his bodyguards followed his advice to hide in a nearby courtyard until further notice. Hans had been observing this and sprinted to my location to inform me all was going well. I instructed my driver – who was entirely ignorant of our scheme – to proceed to the palace with all haste. The ball was to formally begin at eight o'clock, with guests welcome from six. It was approaching seven when we reached the gate.

With my driver dismissed, I joined the short line of aristocrats and notables now gathered outside. Behind the gate lay a wide courtyard where several cavalry patrols could be seen; beyond them the palace itself. Despite the darkness, the area around the gate was well illuminated by countless lanterns and I saw some wonderful gowns on show, many of them silk and decorated with colorful stripes. I also glimpsed some of the high heels and square toes that were currently fashionable. Many of the male guests were in military attire, and most – including myself – wore three-cornered hats.

I was relieved to see that my dark blue outfit, complete with a wide sleeved jacket and waistcoat, would enable me to blend in with the other guests. I'd also had my hair cut short and darkened my skin with powder to match the duke's tone. It would not be enough to convince anyone who knew him well but every little bit helped. I reflected that my job would have been considerably easier had this been a masquerade ball but the occasion was apparently to celebrate the completion of the palace repairs.

Upon reaching the gate, I passed my invitation to a military man who bowed low.

'Good evening, sir.'

I nodded haughtily, as if impatient with the queue, and gave him my invitation. As I waited, I glanced at the twenty or so guards lurking nearby. They seemed to have been selected for their great height and everyone was armed with a thick-shafted lance. As the glittering tip of one glittered in the lamplight, I tried to ignore the butterflies in my stomach.

'Is your wife not with you, sir?'

'The Duchess is not well.'

The officer nodded. 'I hope she recovers swiftly, sir. Please, an attendant will guide you to the palace.'

Determined not to show my relief, I passed the officer and strode under the ornate arch of the main gate.

I will confess that my nerves did not improve upon entering the palace. Along with several other new arrivals, I was guided along two long corridors to a grand chamber where perhaps a hundred were already present. Thanks to Jean-Pierre's work, I knew my location and the surrounding rooms.

The chamber was a beautiful space with a high, decorated ceiling and dozens of portraits upon the walls. In each corner was a banner bearing the Saxon coat of arms: a halved shield with two red swords on one side and a green crown upon the other. A selection of more unusual objects was also on display, including a spectacular statue of what looked like a Moorish king clad in sparkling silver; and a coffee set made entirely of gold. I could have spent hours inspecting these pieces but quickly continued my survey of the room. Though there were chairs and instruments in one corner, no music was currently playing. I imagined that our host, Augustus III, Elector of Saxony, would make a speech before the festivities commenced.

After handing my hat to an attendant, I proceeded through the chamber, hands clasped behind my back, endeavoring to appear utterly at home. A faint smile fixed upon my face, I glanced this way and that, desperate for a glimpse of the Zulichs. We'd been unable to establish where they'd been staying and knew only that the couple were in their forties: he a stout fellow, she an elegant woman.

I had not gone far when I felt a hand upon my arm. Fearing the worst, I turned to find myself confronted by a tall, mustachioed man clad in a pristine uniform. He smiled.

'Your grace, I am Colonel Petersen of the royal household. Pleased to make your acquaintance.'

I shook Petersen's hand, unsure why he had accosted me. I feared that he knew the real Bartenstein yet he did not seem suspicious.

'Please forgive my intrusion. His Highness the king asked officers such as myself to welcome those attendees not well known here in Drezno. It would be my privilege to make some introductions. I understand that the duchess will not be joining us?'

'Indeed,' said I. 'One of her headaches. They can be quite severe. I must thank you for your kind invitation, colonel.'

'His Highness is greatly looking forward to meeting you later.'

I forced a smile. I could see no obvious way of ridding myself of Petersen and knew I had considerably less than an hour to work with. Regardless of whether I had the emerald or not, I did not want to still be here when the king appeared and gave his speech. Then I would be trapped, and any attempt to leave would attract attention.

'Excellent.'

'How was your trip?' inquired the colonel.

'Fair. I suppose we were fortunate with the weather though there was rather a lot of rain in Posen.'

'It is such a long way. I believe that's another reason why his Highness is so keen to see you.'

'How kind of him. We are distantly related, of course, and it's a great regret that I've been unable to visit of late.'

'I believe the last visit was eleven years ago? I'm told that you enjoyed a hunting trip with his Highness?'

'That's correct. As I recall, his Highness is quite the marksman.'

Petersen's hesitant smile seemed as unnatural as mine felt. For all I knew, Augustus III was an appalling shot.

I was on dangerous territory here. I knew a military man of the royal household was likely to be a sharp fellow and it seemed Petersen had been briefed on the Duke of Bartenstein. I would have to tread carefully.

The colonel caught the eye of a passing gentleman and introduced him as the French ambassador. Putting my linguistic skills to good use, I exchanged chatter while planning my next move. The ambassador insisted that Petersen and I join him in a glass of champagne; apparently, he'd had several cases sent from Paris for the occasion. While he collared two passing ladies to join us, I turned to my companion.

'Colonel, I wonder if you could help me. I am very much interested in meeting the Swedish ambassador to Prussia, a count …'

'Count Zulich.'

'That's him. I was led to believe he might be attending tonight? There is a diplomatic matter that my staff asked me to raise with him.' 'Indeed, he is. The count is a great friend of his Highness' son, Frederick Augustus.'

'Ah.'

Petersen nodded towards the French ambassador. 'As our friend seems to be occupied, perhaps now?'

'Excellent.'

As the colonel led me across the chamber, I was already looking ahead for the countess. My heart sank when I soon found myself amidst a cluster of five middle-aged men, though one was Count Zulich. Petersen politely waited for a halt in an energetic discussion about the intentions of the new Prussian king, Frederick II. I was alarmed to hear it was thought possible that the monarch might attack Silesia.

My eyes moved quickly across the nearby women. Their fingers were of particular interest but I did not spy an opulent emerald. Then came a moment of fortune. I was too far to hear the conversation, but I spied a middle-aged woman holding up her hand for others to admire. She was a good twenty feet away, but there could be no mistaking the glittering green jewel of quite remarkable size. Surely this was the Udaipur Emerald.

Before I could be embroiled in more introductions, I spoke quietly to Petersen. 'Colonel, I'm not entirely sure the champagne agrees with me. I need a tonic – something to settle my stomach.'

'Of course, I'll fetch a servant right away.'

'Colonel, could I impose on you to fetch it yourself? As you'll no doubt be aware, my grandfather was poisoned by an assassin during such an occasion.'

I doubted that Petersen's briefing regarding the Duke of Bartenstein extended to the fate of his grandfather, fictitious or otherwise. Outlandish though the story and the request were, the erstwhile colonel did as people generally do when a request is made by one of their betters.

'Of course. I won't be a moment.'

Hoping that he'd take a good deal longer than that, I hurried over to a very elegant but quite aged lady who I'd noticed earlier. To be precise, I had noticed her diamond brooch. She was talking to a younger woman but I had no time for social niceties.

'Excuse me ladies, but I must talk to you regarding an urgent matter. I am Hermann, Duke of Bartenstein; and my guards suspect there is a jewel thief at large here tonight. Your names?'

To her credit, the elder of the pair responded to this alarming introduction quite calmly. 'Your grace, I am Dowager Jansen but I must assure you that what you suggest is impossible. His Highness would not allow'

'-Dowager, I must inform you that one theft has already been reported.'

Hearing this, the lady put her hand to her mouth in shock.

'Please control yourself. We must not alert the thief, for he is well disguised. But we can prevent any further crimes while the king's men hunt him down. Young lady, you are …?'

'This is my niece,' interjected the dowager. 'Miss Cristyne Jansen Holstein.'

I nodded and pointed across the room at Countess Zulich. 'Miss, do you see the lady there, close to the statue?'

'I do.'

'She too is at risk. Please escort her immediately to the anteroom just over there. We will be safely out of the way until the thief is unmasked. Quickly now!'

Miss Jansen-Holstein simply stared at me, then at the dowager.

I gripped her arm. 'Young lady, the thief is among us. We must act now. Speak only to the duchess in case our enemy is close.'

'Do as he says, Cristyne,' instructed the dowager, now placing a protective hand over her diamond brooch.

'May I?' Offering my hand to the lady, I escorted her from the grand chamber into the anteroom. It was comparatively plain, containing more couches than paintings. A servant was on duty where it met the chamber, and on the opposite side of the anteroom were two doors.

'You,' I said to the servant. 'The second door leads to the library, correct?'

'Yes sir.'

'Very good. That will do.'

The dowager was looking warily towards the chamber, where new guests were still arriving. 'Can we not alert the guards?'

'Dowager, the thief's identity is not yet known. We must'

Just then Miss Jansen-Holstein arrived, the Countess Zulich behind her.

'Your name, my lady?' asked I in an urgent tone.

'Countess Zulich.'

She was indeed elegant but upon her face was an indignant frown.

What's all this about a thief?'

Before I could answer, Miss Jansen-Holstein addressed me.

'Your grace, there is a man looking for you – one of the king's officers.'

'He must know I'm onto him,' I replied, improvising as best I could. 'By God, he's disguised himself as one of the king's men. They told me this bastard was crafty. They call him the King of Thieves.'

'I've heard of him,' said Miss Jansen-Holstein, eyes wide. 'Quite handsome, so they say.'

'Really?' I told myself to concentrate on the issue at hand. 'Ladies, we must keep you and your valuables safe with this rogue on the loose. Come – to the library. I'm sure the king's men will have him in a matter of minutes.'

There is little doubt that if I'd appeared anything other than a nobleman, all three would have ignored me. But dukes are seldom ignored even by duchesses and dowagers and the ladies dutifully followed me to the library. Once there, I opened the door and ushered the panicked trio inside. I then joined them and pulled the door to, as if watching for a threat.

'This is a disgrace,' uttered Countess Zulich.

'The king will have the thief's head off,' added the dowager. 'Of that, we can be certain.'

Shutting the door abruptly as if alarmed, I spun around. 'The officer! Looking for us, no doubt. My guards told me that the villain is always armed. Please, ladies, with me.'

With a whimper of anguish, Miss Jansen-Holstein took the hand of the dowager and escorted her across the library. It was a voluminous room with a single door at the far end.

I reached for the hand of Countess Zulich but the forthright woman batted it away.

'I am quite capable of conducting myself, thank you very much.'

As the other fleeing pair were now some way ahead, I tried a second attempt to get at the ring. Those experienced in the finer arts of theft will know that distraction is key. Wolfgang was a decent practitioner; I had taken what he'd taught me and improved upon it.

'Countess Zulich.'

When I stopped, she did the same and turned towards me.

'What is it?'

'I'm sorry but I must do this.' I took her hand – the one with the ring on it – leaned forward and kissed her on the lips. Entirely as expected, Countess Zulich used her free hand to slap me with considerable force.

I was ready for it and – at the moment of impact – slipped the ring from her finger. Her face was a picture of outrage and confusion; emotions that create a fog to confound the senses. While she launched a litany of surprisingly colorful insults at me, I slipped the weighty ring into my waistcoat pocket. My only aim now was to escape.

The other two ladies had stopped and turned around.

'What's going on? demanded the dowager.

Countess Zulich's face was getting redder by the moment. 'This pig had the temerity to'

'-Please forgive me,' I said. 'I simply don't know what came over me. I should take my leave.' I turned and hurried back to the door, fearing that the countess would discover the theft at any moment.

'How dare you!' she shrieked as I slipped through the door and shut it behind me.

I knew I didn't have long. Without a single glance at the mass of guests, I hurried across the chamber past the new arrivals. Fearing interference from Colonel Petersen, I marched along the two corridors, encountering only servants.

Within a minute, I was approaching the main door – two great slabs of mahogany only slightly ajar. It seemed that all the guests were now present and the men stationed there were surprised to see me. Apart from four guards armed with the nasty-looking lances, there were several other members of the palace staff.

'Sir?' said one.

'It's no good,' said I, clutching my stomach. 'Whatever ailment my wife is in bed with has now struck me. If I stay a moment longer, I fear the worst. Please pass on my sincere apologies'

'Your grace! Your grace!'

Colonel Petersen. Now my stomach really did pain me as I turned to find the accursed man running along the corridor. I was considering making a dash for it when he stopped and held up a small glass vial.

‘The tonic, sir.’

‘What an excellent fellow you are, colonel. But I’m afraid nothing can help me now. I feel quite appalling. Good night to you.’

‘Your carriage’

‘I will find it, fear not,’ said I, already on my way out.

Willing myself not to walk too quickly, I passed through the great doors and down the broad stone steps. Only when I had entered the gloom within the middle of the courtyard did I increase my speed. I don’t suppose it was more than a hundred paces but it felt like a thousand. I heard a shout from somewhere and feared instantly that soldiers would appear from the shadows to arrest me. But then came another shout and I realized it was nothing more than sentries announcing that all was well.

The men on duty at the main gate didn’t seem concerned about my reappearance but asked if they could fetch my carriage. Dozens of vehicles were lined up on the broad avenue outside the palace. I declined the offer, claiming that I needed some fresh air.

Once clear of their view, I ran around a corner to the agreed meeting place with Hans: an overhanging willow tree that gave us adequate cover. Without a word, I removed my luxurious jacket and waistcoat and stuffed them into the knapsack he was carrying. I put on the dark watchman’s coat he offered me and took the lantern. He was carrying a lance and the pair of us set off at once. We passed two quartets of patrolling soldiers before we felt safe enough to speak.

‘Don’t tell me you actually have it?’ said my old friend.

'Oh, ye of little faith.'

'By God, Christian. I don't know how you do it.'

I smiled to myself and, as so many times before, the Lucky Thieves disappeared into the night.

Chapter Twelve

Altenburg, 1745

Our king, who would come to be known as Frederick the Great, had ruled for five years. The rumors of invasion I'd heard in Drezno had proved accurate and, only a few months after replacing his father, he launched an assault on Silesia. One might ask why? I must admit that the nuances of international affairs were beyond me but I was aware of the varying explanations.

For many, the answer was political. Prussia was a rising power, a state forged from dozens of territories over centuries under the Hohenzollerns. Most of the other European powers were weak or preoccupied by their own concerns; and the death of Charles VI, Holy Roman Emperor, had added to the chaos. Frederick clearly considered the Habsburgs our chief enemy and believed we must strike first.

Others maintained that our king's motivations were personal. It was common knowledge that his father, Frederick William, had considered his son effeminate and an unsuitable heir. He regularly struck him and shamed him in front of the court. I knew from my occasional encounters with well-informed individuals that these tensions had come to a head in the year 1730, when the young man made a doomed attempt to flee to France. Discovering the plot,

Frederick William ordered that his son be imprisoned and interrogated. The youth's accomplice was a lieutenant named Katte and this man was to suffer a far worse fate: the king had him beheaded in front of his wayward son. There were rumors that the two had been romantically involved; and that Frederick William had intended on killing them both, only to be dissuaded at the last moment by his advisors. In any event, after many months the young man returned to the court and further scandal was avoided.

And ten years later, when Frederick William died, it seemed that the son wished to eclipse his father and carve out his own place in history.

Frederick ordered his army across the Oder in December, 1740 and had claimed most of Silesia by January, including Breslau. Aged just twenty-eight, he'd proved himself an excellent general, winning a hard-fought battle at Mollwitz. By all accounts, Frederick dedicated himself to continually improving his army and after a second victory at Chotusitz, all Silesia was his.

In 1744, after learning of a new Austrian alliance with Britain, he again decided to strike first. This time Frederick fared badly, and his decisions led Prussia to the brink of failure. But during 1745 he rallied his forces and defeated the advancing Austrians several times, including a victory against Charles of Lorraine in September of that year. Like all Prussians, we followed the twists and turns of his campaigns, knowing that all our fates were tied to his.

As autumn turned to winter, the Lucky Thieves found ourselves just north of the city of Altenburg. The hostilities had brought us both opportunities and dangers. On one hand, there were few patrolling soldiers for us to worry about and plenty else to occupy the authorities. On the other, everyone was concerned about spies and many of our previous wealthy targets now hid in remote mansions and castles. I'd had few chances to repeat the audacious success of the Udaipur Emerald. It had been our biggest win to date and we'd lived off the proceeds for many months. But times were a lot harder now, and not only for us. During our travels, we often came across deserters, casualties, and families affected by war.

Of our king's campaigns, I daresay our disparate views reflected those held across Prussia. Hans kept abreast of developments and maintained a great sympathy for his former brothers in arms. Axel regarded the king with disdain, contending that thousands had suffered because of his thirst for conquest. My view? It may sound strange considering how I'd conducted my life, but I was in some ways a proud Prussian and a loyal subject. Such feelings run deep and perhaps in this way I was still my father's son. For all the contempt I felt towards the dissolute, uncaring aristocrats, I could not help admire a man who had cast off the shackles of his upbringing and followed his own path with such single-minded determination.

Yet I hoped peace would return. It seemed that the king had done enough to force the Habsburgs to negotiate but the conflict was now so lengthy and bitter that anything was possible.

'Glad I'm not out there,' said Hans. The former grenadier nodded towards a window and the snow-covered ground beyond. 'No time to be a fighting man.'

'Is there ever?' said I before tucking into a bowl of pea soup. Around us, dozens of other travelers and locals sheltered from the weather. The gang had been staying at the inn for three days while we decided on our next move.

Giving no reply, Hans reclaimed his spoon and ate his soup. Once finished, I looked up and caught the eye of Heike, the oldest – and most attractive – of the innkeeper's daughters. I'd gone to check on our horses in the stable that morning and enjoyed quite a long discussion with her. She was only twenty-three but had already suffered a terrible loss – her husband had been one of the many thousands who perished at Mollwitz. Heike seemed to have recovered well and freely admitted to me that she was seeking a new husband. I'd tried to discourage her interest but – judging by the way she kept glancing at our table – I had not been successful.

Gunther was still with us and we had added two more to our number earlier in the year. Dieter Becker was another deserter like Hans and the two got on very well, so much so that at times I felt almost jealous at their closeness. Dieter's brother Roland had been excused military service on account of his poor eyesight. Roland was not particularly bright but very strong, hardworking, and loyal. Axel was really a third in command by this point and currently in Altenburg with the others, selling off the last of some silk we'd acquired in Potsdam. Hans and I often excused ourselves from onerous duties; we felt we deserved some benefits for being the oldest hands.

'What are we down to?' asked Hans, leaning back in his chair and adjusting his eye patch.

'That depends,' said I.

'On what?'

'On whether you mean what we have here or what we have in total.' Over the years, I had stashed quite a considerable amount with several different bankers (using false identities, of course). Unfortunately, I'd had to draw even on these reserves in recent times.

'Here,' said Hans.

'Eight thalers.'

The veteran rolled his single eye. 'By God, perhaps we should move to a cheaper inn. This winter is going to be a struggle.'

'Don't worry. I'll think of something.'

The truth is that opportunities were thin on the ground. It wasn't only the current circumstances that had led me to forgo my more daring operations. There had been several close calls and with every passing year, I felt I had more to lose. The arrogance and sense of invulnerability that I'd possessed as a young man had dissipated. I was still a confident fellow but over the years many of our associates had ended up at the end of a noose or left to rot in a hellish prison. I suppose I was more fearful and realistic now and had no desire to meet such an awful end.

Now thirty-five, I planned on a few more years of the adventurous life, during which I would try to save for a property. I even toyed with the idea of returning to Halle, perhaps inventing some story about where I'd been. Not since my chance encounter with Willem Bassler had I heard anything of my family. Times of inactivity were difficult for me; I wondered about them all.

Heike came over to take our empty bowls. She was a pretty, statuesque woman. It was my habit to study people and I'd quickly gathered that she was greatly respected by the patrons of the inn. Like my sister Mary, she was perhaps one of those women who longed for more than the role she'd been given.

'How was the soup?'

'Not bad,' said Hans, which from him was effusive praise.

'Very nice, thank you,' said I.

'Can I get you something else? Mother's just taken some apple pies out of the oven.'

As ever my sweet tooth tempted me but we needed to keep our bill down.

'Perhaps later.'

With a smile, Heike took our bowls and headed for the kitchen.

A moment later, the door opened and our four compatriots lurched in. The innkeeper's young son came forward with a brush and helped them get the worst of the snow off their hats, coats, and boots. This was quite a job, and their pink, pinched faces further testified to the cold. We were four miles from Altenburg and they had each carried a pack full of silk.

Hans snorted with disdain as the frozen quartet approached our table. Gunther simply shook his head before following the Becker brothers to the nearby fire. The three of them settled down on a bench, stretching out their arms towards the heat. Dieter called out to the innkeeper for some hot wine.

Axel slumped down on a chair opposite us. 'By God, I can barely feel my fingers.'

'Only eight miles,' remarked Hans. 'A mere stroll.'

'How did you get on?' I asked.

'That depends. Do you want the good news or the bad news?'

***

The bad news was the price they'd negotiated for the silk. The buyer claimed that the local courts were very aggressive and that without a bill of purchase, he would struggle to move the product on. Even so, I was glad to see the coins Axel had returned with. The good news was an opportunity that had come to them quite by chance.

While waiting for the buyer at Altenburg coach station, they had seen a column of grenadiers passing through. This had provoked some interest among the townsfolk and one fellow announced that troops were arriving from several directions. Apparently, Frederick had summoned reinforcements and a large force was gathering at an encampment between Altenburg and nearby Meuselwitz.

Where there are a large number of soldiers, there are generally large amounts of supplies; and it was this that interested us. So, on the following morning, when the latest snowfall had ended, Hans, Axel, and I rode out to the camp. Because cash was short, it was only Hans and me who had sufficient savings to maintain a mount; Axel had to borrow an aged nag from the innkeeper.

We knew that the camp was on a local estate, centered around some farm buildings. Such arrangements were common and the king's officers were not slow to commandeer any site, structure, provision, or equipment they were in need of.

As we approached, Hans reminded us to keep a sharp eye out for patrols. As I've mentioned, commanders were always on the lookout for spies; enemy agents and informers were often hanged as an example to others. We first circled the area and Hans identified a hill that would give us a good view of the camp but was distant enough to avoid arousing suspicion. At his order, we urged our steeds into a gallop. Clouds were gathering once again and we knew that visibility could fade in an instant.

Once upon the hill, we tethered our horses to a tree and used the vegetation to obscure us from any observer. We were perhaps a half mile away but Hans had his trusty telescope. He'd also chosen our location so that there was no risk of the sun striking the glass and betraying our position – such were the benefits of working alongside a military man. After he'd taken a long look at the encampment, Hans passed me the telescope.

There were half a dozen buildings, including two very large barns, and here numerous soldiers were at work. We could see a line of wagons coming in from the Naumburg road to the northwest and unloading their cargo. Closer to our location were three lines of white tents, where many more soldiers could be seen.

'Lot of men,' said Axel uneasily.

'And there's going to be plenty more,' said Hans, now pointing at the Naumburg road. There were not only wagons on the move. We could see towed artillery pieces and beyond them, another column of infantry, easily identified by their colorful uniforms and gleaming equipment.

'The next few days will be the busiest,' said Hans.

'Indeed,' I replied. 'And the most chaotic.'

'Lots of different units,' he continued.

'Which means there might be an opportunity.'

'But how can we even get in there?' asked Axel.

'Maybe we can't,' said I. 'We need to know more. Firstly, if there's any chance of doing so; secondly, if there's anything worth stealing.'

'And how do we do that?'

'Gather intelligence,' said I. 'Which means we're going to need to be closer, preferably on the Naumburg road. What's that village there? We'd be able to see everything coming past.'

'Kreibitsch,' said Axel. 'I believe there's an inn or two.'

'Might be officers billeted there,' added Hans.

'Even better,' I replied, 'providing I can get a room. One man won't attract much attention. I'll go and inquire.'

'Well you better be quick,' said Hans.

I had been so intent on our plans that I had failed to notice the falling snow.

Over the next two days, I developed not only some useful intelligence but a nasty cold. There were in fact two inns in Kreibitsch but only one adjacent to the road. It was a tatty, dirty place with three rooms and a malodorous proprietor who communicated largely through grunts. The man was, however, open to persuasion; and with a few groschen, he displaced one of his guests for my benefit.

Taking over the ground floor room, I was in a perfect position to observe the traffic approaching the encampment on the Naumburg road. Though the snow had lessened, the temperatures remained freezing. The fireplace in my room was too small to do much good so I sat in a chair, wrapped in blankets, with several handkerchiefs on hand. By leaving the shutters just open, I could study those passing without fear of giving myself away. I kept paper and pen beside me as well as one of my instructional texts: this one on French verbs. In the quiet periods, I studied.

My intelligence gathering was not limited solely to observation. I suspect my inn was not of sufficient quality for the recently arrived officers but several were accommodated in Kreibitsch's second hostelry. Only in one regard was my establishment superior: the innkeeper was an enthusiastic drinker and had amassed an exotic collection of liquor. During the first night of my stay, a major and two lieutenants visited to sample his Russian honey vodka, American whiskey, and something called Arrak which apparently came all the way from India. While the officers drank, I planted myself in a corner with my book of verbs and listened in to the conversation. Much was of no use to me – talk of King Frederick's intentions; an upcoming marriage; the lack of decent blacksmiths in the area – but there were also some snippets of interest.

While manning my observation post, I also had the displeasure of seeing the army at its worst. None of the behavior surprised me but on at least two occasions I was sorely tempted to intervene. First, I saw a goatherd forced to hand over half his meager flock – apparently with no compensation. Then a passing family with a young daughter had to endure a tirade of insults and crude remarks from a party of injured soldiers in a wagon. Worst of all was what happened to the elderly woman who set up a little stall selling socks. No soldier made a purchase but one wretch simply stole a pair and marched on, ignoring the woman's cries. I was sure there were many noblemen serving the king but it was often the lowliest of people that suffered at the hands of his army.

On the first afternoon, Hans had delivered my bags. On the second, he came to exchange information and discuss our plan of action. As I sat there blowing my nose, he described what he'd learned.

'I came via our observation point. I could hear the camp before I saw it – trumpeters and drummers practicing. Christian, it is three times the size it was two days ago. Plenty of guns – six and twelve-pounders, by the looks of it. I counted more than a hundred tents, probably fifty wagons. And they're still coming.'

I nodded. 'There are several companies of musketeers, several of garrison troops, and a unit of dragoons. They've come from all over the place.'

'Anything interesting on the wagons?'

'Oh yes,' I replied. 'And I must say I do appreciate the army's habit of labeling every box, barrel, and container. Ammunition, timber, guns, fodder, grain; what looked like an entire field bakery. Plenty of coffee and sugar too.'

'Your thoughts?'

'Today some sutlers arrived. That changes things.'

Civilian merchants could be found wherever there were large concentrations of troops. While the army generally maintained its own stocks, these vendors filled in the gaps. Like many traders, sutlers often employed female sellers to lure the soldiers and secure a good price. I'd seen none on this occasion but the presence of other civilians would make our task considerably easier.

I continued: 'Remember when Gunther knocked up that camp pass? Something similar would suffice this time.'

'We would need the name and signature of the senior officer.'

'The commander is a Colonel Von Munchow.'

'Or a commissariat officer if we're to be sutlers.'

'I know. I shall find a way.'

Hans sat down on the bed. 'You don't mean to steal from the sutlers?' Given what I'd seen in the last few days, I took a little offense at this. Hardly, Hans. No – but as sutlers with a pass we stand a good chance of getting into the camp.'

'And then?'

'I wouldn't risk more than one wagon. It needs to be something light and easy to move.'

Hans leaned forward. 'You've already made up your mind. Tell me.' 'It came through this morning. Conveniently labeled as usual. Tobacco.'

Once Hans had gone to brief the others, I set about addressing the issue of the signature. These were often little more than a scrawl but whoever was on guard duty would likely know that scrawl. A convincing pass and the signature of another officer might suffice but it was not a chance I wished to take. I needed the mark of a commissariat man.

Robbing an army camp was risky in itself but the prize was a very lucrative one: a wagon could hold several hundred pounds of tobacco, which would be worth hundreds of thalers. Despite my advancing years, I did enjoy a challenge.

In the corner of my dank, dusty room were four saddlebags and my knapsack. I'd had to rationalize my various disguises over the years but kept a small supply of useful clothing, not to mention three wigs and some cosmetic items. In amongst a bag stuffed with bits and bobs, I found a panel of black cloth embroidered with the insignia of the Prussian postal service. After a moment's thought, I hurried to one of the saddlebags and retrieved my sewing kit.

Not long afterward, I put on my boots, coat, and hat and ventured outside. The tide of traffic had slowed and I could see only a single unit of troops some distance towards Naumburg. There had been no snow since the night and while it still lay upon the roofs, the road was largely clear, the verges covered in a dirty slush.

It seemed that my enthusiasm had somehow dispelled the worst of my cold for I was feeling considerably better. I made my way to the second inn and hurried into the parlor, hoping that at least one of the officers would be present. Those I had overheard the previous night were not there but two others sat in front of the hearth. Also present behind the counter was a woman who did not have a chance to welcome me.

'Excuse me, is there a Major Jager here?'

The two officers were deep in conversation and did not respond. I took a step closer.

'Excuse me, sirs, do you know where I might find Lieutenant Jager? One man shrugged.

The other said, 'Never heard of him.'

'The senior commissariat officer at the camp? I've a message for him.'

'There's no Jager that I know of. It's Captain Bauer.'

'Ah. I seem to have been misinformed. Is he staying here?'

'Not likely,' said the man, drawing a grin from his friend.

The pair looked like cavalrymen and I don't suppose they held supply officers in great esteem.

'Apologies for the inconvenience,' said I.

Now armed with the name I needed, I fetched my horse from the inn stable and set off for the encampment. Though I had seen most of the men, horses, and wagons pass my window, I was still not prepared for the scale of the place. What had previously been no more than a farm and a few fields now resembled a small town. Trotting my horse off the Naumburg road, I passed the side of the camp. I saw a company performing drill; a mass of men sorting through supplies; and a huge queue awaiting food. Other than those training, most wore gloves and hats with their coats of Prussian blue.

The camp had spilled far beyond the farm but the center was within the walled compound that contained the buildings. A young lieutenant and a trio of guards manned the gate that led to it. Reining in, I dismounted and approached the officer.

'Good day to you, sir.' I had already unbuttoned my coat and now pulled it back to show the insignia of the Reichspost upon my jacket.

'Postal courier. I have a note for a Captain Bauer.'

The officer seemed a little taken aback. 'You can only enter with a pass.'

'I don't need to enter, sir, thank you. As long as you can give the message to the captain.'

I knew how the postal service arranged such things and had placed the letter in a good envelope and sealed it with wax. The contents were entirely an invention of mine – a letter of greeting from a mysterious woman. When he opened it, Captain Bauer would simply assume there had been a mistake.

The young officer ushered one of his men forward; a spotty youth who looked no more than sixteen.

Before handing him the letter, I added a small slip of paper.

'I will just need the lieutenant to sign for it.' I shrugged. 'Rules are rules.'

The youth waited for a nod from his superior before taking the delivery and running through the gate. The officer was clearly not in the mood for discussion so, while waiting, I surveyed the camp. The area around the two huge barns was exceptionally busy and I was relieved to see sutlers already selling to the soldiers.

Ten minutes later, the youth returned with the receipt containing the full signature of Captain Wilhem Ernst Bauer. With a heartfelt thank you, I mounted up and rode away.

Chapter Thirteen

When we returned the following day, a bitter northerly was blasting the camp. Many soldiers could be seen adjusting their tents to resist the wind and horses gathered for warmth within the corrals. I felt that the gale was to our advantage because preoccupied people are less likely to notice something unusual. A serious snowfall, however, would be a problem; we had only one wagon and I did not want our escape to be impeded. With me were Axel, Gunther, and Roland. Dieter and Hans awaited us in Kreibitsch with our mounts and gear. Hans had wanted to come along but it seemed an unnecessary risk. Though he'd been out of the army for many years, he was a memorable character, especially with his eye patch.

As we approached, I was glad to see a different officer guarding the main entrance. Even so, I left it to Axel to get down off the wagon and present our fake pass, complete with the forged signature. The officer examined it briefly then waved us through. Our covered wagon contained a dozen barrels of turnips, which we hoped to swap for a far more valuable crop. Typically, sutlers provided more luxurious products but also delivered basics such as bread and fodder.

Having examined the layout the previous day, I instructed Gunther to head for the area in front of the two big barns. I felt nervous whenever an officer came close but no one questioned us and we halted alongside the first of the buildings. Despite the vicious wind, the sutlers were doing a reasonable trade. There seemed to be at least a dozen different outfits, each with its own stall. I could smell roasting meat from one and another seemed to deal solely in bottles of wine.

Looking around, I spied some smaller tents and a row of wagons. Leaving the others, I took my knapsack and strode through the camp, endeavoring to look as purposeful as everyone else. Not all the officers were accommodated in Kreibitsch. I knew there would be dozens within the camp and they were of course allocated the small, individual tents. Officers were also permitted to travel with heavy chests for their belongings; some senior men even kept a retainer and brought along luxuries such as silverware or musical instruments. It was evident here that some of the officers had only recently arrived and were still settling in. Pretending to tie a bootlace, I stopped and perused the area. It didn't take me long to spy a likely target. Beside one wagon, several chests had been opened and junior officers were moving their belongings into the tents.

I approached them, pass in hand, again asking for the fictional Lieutenant Jager, as it at least gave me a reason to be there. The officers and rankers helping them either shrugged or ignored me. I passed an empty tent and eventually came upon an untended wagon and four chests. Two of the chests were locked. One contained a jacket that was far too small for me. In the other was one that would do. Discreetly folding it up and placing it in my knapsack, I continued my search and was able to pilfer the hat of an unsuspecting lieutenant very much occupied with his tent pegs. With these two crucial items secured, I sneaked into an empty tent to transform myself. The jacket belonged to a captain and within my knapsack were breeches and boots Hans had purchased for me in Altenburg. Once my three-corned hat was on, I waited for an opportune moment, then marched confidently back to the barn.

Despite our perilous situation, Axel and the others smirked as they watched me approach. I had seen enough military men to affect the confident bearing and did not break character for my cohorts.

'You men there, bring your wagon. Follow me.'

I continued around the corner and found two infantrymen guarding the entrance to the barn. They both had muskets upon their shoulders and straightened up as soon as they saw me.

'You two, is there space left in here?'

The older of the pair answered. 'Yes, sir. How much do you need?' 'Oh, not too much. Just a wagon full of fodder. Is Captain Bauer around?'

'He's with the colonel, sir.'

'Ah, well, I'm sure he won't mind. It's all got to go somewhere.'

'Everything that goes in and out has to be signed for, sir.'

'Of course.'

'The list is just inside the door there, sir.'

As the wagon approached, I gave more orders. 'Start unloading. I shall find a space.'

I hurried past the guards and into the barn, which was at least a hundred feet long and perhaps half as wide. There were several windows but, with the overcast weather, much of the building was shrouded in shadow. The only other occupants were two youthful soldiers stacking kegs close to the far wall. Despite the cold, they had stripped down to their shirts. The barn was about half full, the supplies arranged around the edges and in two neat lines along the middle. I passed countless ammunition boxes; barrels of cider, beer, oil and vinegar; casks of flour and dried biscuit; bundles of blankets, clothing and spare cloth. Reaching the end of one line, I was dismayed to find no trace of tobacco. There was an obvious place for our fodder but there was no point unloading if we couldn't locate our prize. I checked the second line but my eyes and nose were again disappointed.

Once back outside, I instructed the trio to cease unloading.

'What's wrong, sir?' asked one of the sentries.

'Too much dry stuff close together,' said I. 'Fire risk.'

The men exchanged a confused glance.

'We shall use the other barn,' I added.

'Wouldn't worry, sir,' said the older guard.

'Well, unfortunately, we officers are paid to worry about such things.'

I added an admonishing glare.

'Yes, sir. Of course.'

***

'Shall we unload, sir?' asked Axel.

'In a moment.'

I waited for the major to depart then addressed the guards. 'You two will have to move so we can put the wagon right beside the entrance. These barrels are very heavy.' This was quite true but not the reason for my order. I needed a way to obscure the theft.

'Very well, sir,' said one of the men, a tall, imposing fellow.

'Fodder,' I explained. 'But these sutlers need to keep their barrels. Captain Bauer is aware. Shall I sign?'

As I did so, Axel and the others guided the horses forward and positioned the wagon as I'd described. It took the three of them to lower each barrel and roll it inside. I then guided them to an appropriate space and pointed out the tobacco. I knew they would work swiftly and was particularly grateful to have the brawny Roland along.

Once back outside, I fulfilled my main task – distracting the guards. This I first did by pointing out a couple of deficiencies in their uniforms. Both were imaginary but it had the desired effect of reinforcing my authority. I then questioned them about their unit, in case I might later need such information. The sight of several infantrymen chasing an errant tent across a nearby field all temporarily distracted us. The wind had not abated and I had to keep a hand on my hat to hold it in place.

I suppose the men took fifteen or twenty minutes to unload the turnips and seize the tobacco. I was running out of ways to keep the guards looking away from the wagon by the time they secured the covers.

'All this for a pile of turnips,' I remarked. 'Well, I suppose the cavalry need their horses fit and strong.' With a cordial nod, I sauntered away beside the departing wagon.

Reclaiming my knapsack, I used the vehicle for cover as I nipped into the narrow space between the two barns. Here I discarded my uniform (feeling somewhat guilty for leaving the immaculate jacket and hat in the mud) and emerged from the other end of the space, now clad again in the smock and loose trousers of a peasant. Altering my hair and keeping my head down to ensure the friendly artillery officer saw nothing amiss, I circled around and met my compatriots at the gate.

The Lucky Thieves departed the Altenburg encampment unmolested and in possession of several hundredweight of tobacco. In many ways, the scheme was one of our very best.

Unfortunately, we would never profit from the raid and would soon find far more than our earnings at risk.

At first, all went reasonably well. Hans and I hunched upon our mounts as they trudged along the Naumburg road and behind us on the wagon were Gunther, Axel, and the Becker brothers. On several occasions, we had to make way for military traffic but soon reached Meuselwitz and put a few miles between the encampment and ourselves. Light snow and cloud now obscured the sun but we knew we had at least five hours of light left. All agreed that Meuselwitz was simply too close and that we should push on to the town of Zeitz, though it was another eight miles away. For all we knew, the theft of the tobacco might not be discovered for days; but it might only take hours. Depending on the attitude and other concerns of the commanding officer, we might face the wrath of the Prussian army.

We were still in sight of Meuselwitz when one of the horses hurt itself. The first I heard of it was a shout from Gunther. Hans and I reined in and turned to see the horse fall to its knees and shriek with pain. Throwing my reins to Hans, I dismounted and hurried back. By then, Axel was also on the ground and pointing at a hole in the road.

'Damage from all the wagons probably.'

We next turned our attention to the poor horse. No bone had broken the skin but the creature was evidently in great pain. The men set about unyoking it while Hans and I looked warily back along the road. It was immediately evident that the horse could no longer work. They are such strong creatures but often do not recover from even minor injuries. We had just passed a small house and Hans swiftly led the limping creature there. We knew the inhabitants would be grateful and could at least use it for meat.

Neither of the other mounts was a wagon horse so the one remaining animal had to continue. It was clearly disturbed by the fate of the other and had to be whipped hard. We'd lost valuable time but plowed on through the worsening weather. We saw no more houses; in fact, we saw little of anything other than the road in front of us. Though all of us had gloves and hats and the best coats money could buy, that biting wind chilled us to the bones.

Around five o clock, we called a halt, if only to give the horses a break. Hans watered his then leaped back into the saddle, announcing that he wanted to check the road behind us. As was usually the case, he endured difficult circumstances far better than the younger men and myself. It did not take much imagination to appreciate that the trials of a soldier had prepared him well for the worst in life. I was very grateful for the flask of rum that Gunther produced and shared with the rest of us.

'By God,' said he as I took a sip. 'I did not expect this.'

'Can't be far to Zeitz now,' said Axel, ever the optimist.

'Maybe the Almighty's punishing us,' suggested Dieter.

'This weather's bad for everyone,' I countered. 'Not just us.'

'Cavalry will move quicker though,' said Gunther gloomily.

I'd barely had a chance to reflect on this statement when we heard the sound of galloping hooves. Hans was first a blur, then a dark shape, and only his recognizable self when he reined in just a few yards away.

'They're coming after us.'

'Cavalry?' I asked.

'Who else?'

'You saw them?' asked Roland Becker.

'I didn't need to!' snapped Hans. 'I heard them. We have to get off the road.'

The others stood there looking at each other and I confess I did not understand the gravity of the situation as Hans did.

Gunther said, 'With the one horse, I don't think we'll get the wagon.' 'Forget the wagon!' bellowed Hans, now as angry as I'd seen him. He dismounted, pulled our packs off the wagon, and threw them at the younger men. 'We have to go. Now.'

'And leave it?' said Gunther. 'Leave it all?'

'Gods' blood!' bawled Hans. 'Christian, talk some sense into them.' I believe a combination of tiredness and the cold had lulled me into a moment of paralysis but I, at last, saw the light. We would have to forget our haul and flee the road. As only Hans and I had mounts, we could not all ride away.

'Let's go,' said I, dismounting.

'To the left,' instructed Hans. 'If we're lucky, we'll strike Kuhndorf forest.'

I led my horse over a shallow ditch then watched as the others pulled on their packs. Axel stared at the wagon but was soon grabbed by Hans and pushed after the others.

'I can hear them!' yelled the veteran. I broke into a run, bowing my head against the wind and sheeting snow.

'Stay close together!' I shouted, knowing how easily we might lose each other in such conditions.

The snow was landing in thick, heavy flakes and before long it was up to our knees. More than once I stumbled, using my hold on the reins to stay upright. I looked back over my shoulder but could see nothing more than I could ahead; an impenetrable grey-white fog.

Some time later – I don't know how long – Hans called a halt. I dropped the reins, knowing my horse was too exhausted to go anywhere. We met in a circle; gazing at each other with pale, snow encrusted faces.

'Are they behind us?' asked Dieter.

'They were,' answered Hans.

'They've got their bloody tobacco,' moaned Axel. 'Why would they chase us in this?'

'Depends on their orders,' said I.

Though the snow had worsened over the last half hour, the wind had become weaker.

Hans raised a hand to quiet us. Nobody said anything because we'd all heard what he had.

Shouts. Moving horses. Not far away.

My mount began to whinny, which in turn unsettled Hans' horse. He ran up to me, gripped me by the shoulders. 'We have to set them loose. They might even distract the cavalry.'

I knew instantly that he was right and was grateful that the others helped us unstrap our saddlebags. Hans used his belt to whip both mounts, sending them galloping away. The six of us crouched down, trying to make ourselves as small as possible.

More shouts, closer this time.

I imagined the cavalry bearing down on us, slashing us to pieces with their murderous blades. Even if they didn't kill us there and then, we would face some awful punishment. As I crouched there in the snow, freezing and afraid, I had never felt so disheartened. Was this how my life would end? Is this what I had taken all those risks for? Why had I followed this path? Why did I constantly endanger my friends and myself?

I saw something flash through the snow, no more than twenty feet away. I heard a man call out for Colonel Von Munchow. It seemed the camp commander led the hunters himself.

Suddenly Hans' sword was in his hand. Then Gunther and Dieter drew daggers. They were all ready for a fight. Was I?

I'll confess that I uttered a prayer then and perhaps it was answered for we saw and heard nothing more of the cavalry. Once we had recovered ourselves, Hans led us away. Axel helped me with my saddlebags and we struggled on through the storm. To this day, I cannot grasp how Hans found his way in such a situation but no more than an hour later, we reached the edge of Kuhndorf forest. At last, we had a little respite and with the dying light of the day, we constructed a rudimentary shelter.

Any observer of our little band would have been surprised to see us soon joking and laughing, a result no doubt of profound relief. We had lost our prize and a good deal more besides.

But we were alive.

Chapter Fourteen

Goslar, 1747

In hindsight, it was an obvious mistake, yet at the time it seemed like the right thing to do. Wolfgang Schmidt was once again a Lucky Thief, a development I would not have predicted.

While passing through Regensburg, a mutual associate informed us that Wolfgang was also in the city. None of us had seen him in five years but when I learned that he was homeless and without a pfennig to his name, I felt duty-bound to help my old mentor. Hans and I eventually found him living with some other vagrants in an abandoned mill. Wolfgang was utterly bereft, all his money lost to gambling and his meager possessions contained in an old sack. The only advantage to his parlous condition was that he could not afford alcohol and professed himself free of his addiction.

Hans and I had discussed our strategy and we told him he was free to join us once more on two conditions. The first was that he never gambled or drank to excess again. The second was that he accepted that we were in charge. He would have no more say in matters than the junior members of the gang. Given his circumstances, Wolfgang readily accepted our terms. We gave him enough money for a shave, a bath, and some new clothes and he was a Lucky Thief once more.

Looking back, I think I was partly influenced by the wider situation at the time. The war with the Habsburgs was long finished, though their refusal to accept the loss of Silesia ensured a febrile situation, which meant that the Prussian courts and army could once again direct their energies toward domestic threats, which we were certainly one. Worse still, our previous victim, Colonel Von Munchow, was now a lieutenant general and had been tasked by the king with bringing the criminal fraternity to justice. Like Hans, Axel, and myself, Wolfgang was a name that appeared on the rogue lists kept by the authorities. In recent years, several well-known criminals had been captured, put on trial, and publicly executed. Such a fate awaited us all unless we were careful and cunning. Wolfgang had reached a dangerous, desperate situation, with little defense against the powers of the state. For all his faults, I did not want to see him hang.

In recent times, we had once again concentrated on smuggling operations. It was now almost expected that the Lucky Thieves would make donations to the poor and we still took great pride and enjoyment from doing so. Other than the audacity of some of our schemes, I believe this is what set us apart and ensured our infamy. We doled out silver coins to urchins in Potsdam only a stone's throw from the royal palace. We gave a bottle of stolen gin to every household in the village of Oberhof, and on one famous occasion hijacked two wagons of luxurious food meant for a baron and gave the entire contents to a camp of destitute veterans. This last gesture had been Hans' idea and we departed the scene with the grateful soldiers singing our name.

For the first few months, Wolfgang toed the line. He did seem to have his drinking under control but once back on his feet, old enmities returned. Nothing was said openly but it became obvious that he resented his lowly position. He suggested various operations but, to my mind, all were far too risky. As ever, he favored what Hans called 'get rich quick' schemes, failing to realize that it was only our careful planning that had enabled us to evade the authorities for nigh on twenty years.

Though I said nothing even to Hans, I was running out of patience with the life. In the years since the near-disastrous theft from the army camp, I had concentrated on building up my earnings and stashing it in three separate bank accounts. I had enough to leave crime behind and plans to establish a new identity — perhaps buy myself a nice inn somewhere and settle down. I was not about to let Wolfgang Schmidt ruin it.

And so, as we neared the end of a delicate operation in the town of Goslar, I was forced to explain to him that he would not be taking part in the final stages. I simply did not trust him to carry out my orders.

The gang was gathered in a small warehouse we had rented for the week and I broke the news to him in a dusty corner. It was April and a brisk spring wind rattled the timber walls.

'That's how it is. I'm not going to change my mind, Wolfgang. You can remain here with the Beckers.'

He ran a hand across his head, where there was now little hair. 'And Axel and Hans will assist you, of course.'

'They will.'

'At least let me occupy myself, Christian. I can be in and out of Zimmermann's in no time. I'll be back before you are.'

Not for the first time, I found myself exasperated by his misplaced enthusiasm and poor judgment. 'By God, will you stop this nonsense. You are not to go anywhere near the place.'

Josef Zimmermann was one of the foremost jewelers in Prussia. He and his sons were exceptionally skilled and they specialized in adapting rings and bracelets. Wolfgang had apparently harbored ambitions to rob the place for many years and saw our presence in

Goslar as his chance. What he seemed unable to appreciate was that Zimmermann's shop was on the same street as the local army garrison. Even assuming he could get out of the place with something, if the alarm went up, he would be surrounded in minutes.

Wolfgang was not easily deterred. 'Some noble was there earlier in the week – dropped off several items. Zimmermann has only one guard. He's practically asking for trouble!'

'We are here for the chocolate, and only for the chocolate.'

Sixty pounds of the stuff had been seized during a raid on a nearby manor house. The thieves lacked the connections to move it on so we were taking it off their hands. Chocolate was increasingly popular across the continent, and we knew most would be used for drinking. We had dealt with this gang once before but their leader was a fiery character named Fuchs. The presence of another hothead like Wolfgang during the negotiations was not an appealing prospect. Hans, Axel, Gunther, and I were to meet Fuchs and three of his men at an abandoned mine later that day.

'Chocolate? This is petty stuff, Christian. What happened to your ambition?'

'As I've explained already, it will be a good, solid earner. In any case, are you really going to lecture me on how to make a living?'

My words were perhaps ill-advised because this seemed another bone of contention. Though he'd accepted our assistance willingly, Wolfgang clearly felt ashamed that he'd had no choice.

I tried another tack. 'Haven't I asked you for help at other times?' 'For donkey work. Don't forget who taught you this business.'

'That was a long time ago. Things change.'

'People too.'

His comment hung in the air for a moment before he waved a hand at me. 'Ah, go ahead. I'll just sit here and twiddle my thumbs.'

'Next time.'

He gave a reluctant nod. Trying not to show my annoyance, I crossed the warehouse where the others were waiting with our wagon. Though we were only buying sixty pounds worth, this was still the easiest mode of transportation. At the rear of the warehouse was a small stable where our two hired horses were kept. They had already been brought through and yoked to the wagon.

Gunther was seated with reins in hand while Hans and Axel sat in the rear. All three were armed. I was slightly concerned about the possibility of Fuchs deciding he would keep the chocolate and take our money. He had been straight in our previous dealings but his reputation for recklessness was long-established and times were hard.

Dieter and Roland opened the double doors and Axel drove us out into warm afternoon sunlight. With my last glance at Wolfgang, I saw he was still lurking in the shadowy corner.

Goslar is an ancient town on the northwestern slopes of the Harz mountains. I believe that iron ore was extracted from the area by the Romans and mining has continued in various forms ever since. There were several active operations extracting silver and zinc but we were bound for a long-disused site south of the town and it took us an hour to get there.

The route meandered around several low hills covered mostly by dense forest. We saw a number of people on the outskirts of Goslar but only a few farmers as we ventured further into the countryside. The track was bumpy and poorly maintained but our horses were resilient and Gunther an excellent driver. We passed roughly made signs directing the way to various mines, all clearly no longer in use. We came eventually to the Kohler Mine, which sounded grand but turned out to be little more than a clearing in which several small shafts had been dug. The afternoon had become evening and I was anxious to get back to Goslar before nightfall.

Herr Fuchs and his men were already present. Their horses were all tethered to a tree and as we approached, they assembled in a line. Like me, Fuchs himself was not armed. But two of his men had muskets and the third wore what looked like a cavalry officer's sword. They were a grim, tough-looking bunch all with heavy beards and heavier brows. Though attired in dark breeches and jacket like the others, Fuchs set himself apart from his henchmen with a grey three-cornered hat. On the ground behind the gang were several wooden trays holding glass jars and the valuable powdered chocolate.

Fuchs watched from beneath his hat as we halted. Leaving Gunther with the horses, Hans, Axel, and I strode across the brown earth of the clearing. Though nothing was said, I could tell the sight of the rifles disturbed Hans. He had his sword and Gunther and Axel their knives but blades were no match for muskets.

'Good afternoon, Herr Fuchs, a pleasure doing business with you again.'

'Haven't done any yet, have we?'

'Fair point. You have the goods?'

'I do. You have the money?'

'Of course.' Hans and I had split the thalers between us – we carried a bag each inside our jackets. 'May I try a sample?'

Fuchs nodded to one of the men, who fetched a glass jar. When I approached, he removed the stopper. I had brought a spoon for the occasion and now lifted out some powder to taste. As we'd been informed it was good quality and already mixed with vanilla.

'That will do nicely. I believe the amount is sixty pounds - so I assume you have twelve jars?'

'That we do. Let's talk money.'

'Of course. I'll give you three thalers a pound. That's one hundred and eighty in total.'

'Not enough.'

It was an entirely reasonable offer. I had expected Fuchs to drive a hard bargain but I didn't have much room to maneuver if we were to make a profit.

'Feel free to counter,' said I.

'Four thalers a pound. I'll take nothing less.'

'Two hundred and forty? We'll make nothing on that.'

'Feel free to counter,' said he with a smirk.

'I can't go higher than two hundred and ten.'

'I can't go lower than one ninety.'

'Herr Fuchs, let us both remember that you've had trouble offloading this. Otherwise, we wouldn't be having this conversation.'

Fuchs smirked again. 'But you're the Lucky Thieves. This is a small deal for you.'

'Shouldn't believe everything you hear.'

'Let's call it a round two hundred.'

'Very well.'

We both stepped forward. As we were about to shake hands, a twig snapped. All eight of us turned to where the sound had come from – a stand of trees thirty feet to my right. If there was someone there, they were well hidden.

Hans put a hand upon the pommel of his sword and eyed the other gang. 'Bring some help, Fuchs?'

Wishing he hadn't opened his mouth, I watched as Fuchs' men took their muskets from their shoulders.

'Maybe it's you who bought the help,' said their leader. 'No,' I replied.

'We know there are more of you,' added Fuchs.

'We left the others in Goslar,' said I.

'And you were here first,' said Hans.

I held up a hand, hoping that my old friend would say nothing more. 'Herr Fuchs, I take you at your word. And I ask you to do the same. In any case, I suggest we find out if we are being watched. One of your men and one of mine?'

My calm words had the desired effect.

Fuchs directed one of his men forward and I turned to Hans with a speculative look. The veteran unsheathed his sword and the chosen pair warily approached the trees, watched by the rest of us. Hans directed the other fellow to the left and soon the pair had disappeared from view. Not long afterward a cry went up and the two hunters exchanged a few shouts.

'What's going on?' demanded Fuchs.

'We've got him,' answered his subordinate.

'We're coming out,' added Hans.

And then they were there, brushing twigs off themselves, Hans holding a lad by the shoulder. The youth couldn't have been more than twelve and barely reached the adults' elbows. His terrified eyes took in the armed men before him.

'Sit down,' said I.

The lad complied without a word, still looking fearfully at his captors. I thought it best to take charge myself; who knew how Fuchs would handle this?

'Are you alone?'

The lad nodded.

'What's your name?'

He looked at the ground.

'I'm Christian. What's your name?'

'Walter.'

'What are you doing here, Walter?'

'I heard your wagon. Followed you.'

Fuchs moved closer so that he could hear everything.

I continued: 'What are you doing out here?'

'I live here.'

'Alone?'

'With my family. We live in the tunnels in the Old Mine.'

Another of Fuchs' men spoke up. 'I heard about that place. There are a few of them. Gypsies. A couple of miles from here.'

'I was checking my snares,' said Walter. 'We don't get many people around these parts. I was just curious.'

I looked up at Fuchs. 'All right to let him go?'

'That depends. Did you hear our conversation, boy?

Walter nodded.

Fuchs grimaced. 'Then he knows our names, who we are, and what we're doing. If he blabs to his people, could be trouble.'

'Gypsies,' added Fuchs' man. 'Always looking for ways to make money.'

'I'm prepared to risk it,' said I. 'He's just a boy.'

The man took a step towards Walter, musket in both hands. 'Easy enough to make sure he never blabs about anything again.'

'Herr Fuchs, please tell your voluble associate that unless he steps away and keeps his mouth shut, this meeting is over and you are stuck with product you can't shift.'

Fuchs evidently didn't much like my tone but he ordered his man to comply.

'Walter, go and stand with my friend Axel over there.'

The lad clearly understood his predicament and hurried away.

I continued: 'To my mind, we should be happy that it wasn't some soldier or spy watching us. Wouldn't you agree?'

'We've wasted enough time,' said Fuchs. 'Let's make the deal.'

The whole incident did little to ease the tension of an already fraught situation. But the money and the jars were exchanged without issue. We four stayed together – with young Walter – as Fuchs and his men mounted up and trotted out of the clearing.

'Bastards will probably try and ambush us,' muttered Hans.

'No chance,' answered Gunther. 'The chief showed them who's in charge.'

I didn't entirely share Gunther's confidence but neither did I think Fuchs would risk it. If he'd been planning a move, he could have attacked us on the way in. Hans suggested we wait an hour just in case and I agreed. We sent Walter on his way with a couple of pfennigs for giving him such a fright and I advised the lad to keep to himself from now on.

On our way back to the warehouse, we were forced to take a detour. A fire had broken out somewhere in Goslar and many were rushing to help, including the garrison troops. Unfamiliar with the town, we temporarily lost our way; but Hans' nose soon got us back on the right path and we reached the warehouse around midnight. Unfortunately, the day's surprises were not yet over.

***

I immediately knew something was wrong. The Beckers looked anxious and didn't ask us how we'd fared. As we climbed down from the wagon and the brothers shut the doors behind us, I saw a bizarre sight. Caught in the glow of the single lantern within the warehouse were two figures. The first was Wolfgang Schmidt, leaning back against the wall, arms crossed, a smug look upon his face. The second was a woman of about twenty-five, attired in a fine gown and shawl. She was sitting on a box, eyes wide with terror.

'What in God's name?' said Hans.

When no one answered him, he and I strode towards Wolfgang and the woman.

'Who is she and what is she doing here?'

The smug look became a grin. 'An opportunity Christian. I got bored – went to scout Zimmermann's before he closed. As I was coming out, I saw this young lady running away from a fire. I … came to her assistance and guided her back here. She's been no trouble.'

'He took me against my will,' she snapped, casting a hateful glance at Wolfgang. 'When I screamed, he threatened me with his blade.'

'I wouldn't have used it,' said Wolfgang. 'Before you say anything more, tell my friends who you are, Sophia.'

She sat up straight and raised her chin proudly. Princess Sophia Christine of the House of Thurn and Taxis. My father is Alexander Ferdinand and when he hears of this, he will have you all arrested and hanged. You will let me go at once.'

I was speechless.

Hans advanced towards Wolfgang until he was only inches away. 'Have you lost your mind?'

Wolfgang looked at the taller man then held up his hands. 'I understand your concern, Hans; and yours, Christian. Let us discuss this.' Sidestepping away from the ex-soldier, Wolfgang approached me and gestured towards the wagon. 'Please.'

I was still staring at Sophia Christine but at that moment, her appealing face was of no interest to me. I could not believe she was actually present in the warehouse.

'Come, Christian,' implored Wolfgang. 'Let me explain how we can all benefit from this.' He turned back to Sophia. 'I have explained to the young lady about cooperating and, so far, she's behaved well. I'm sure that will continue.' He caught the eye of Dieter Becker and waved him towards the captive. I was disturbed by the way Dieter obeyed instantly and admonished myself for this and many other oversights. I had seen the signs that Wolfgang's malign influence had spread to the brothers. I'd been foolish to ignore it.

Still unable to form a coherent sentence, I followed Wolfgang to the wagon. Hans reluctantly followed and Gunter and Axel joined us.

'We've not tried for a ransom before, I know,' began Wolfgang, 'but this girl's father is one of the richest men in all Prussia. They call her the Jewel of Regensburg. By God, she could be worth more to us than any jewel we've nabbed before. If we do this quickly, we can earn a fortune and be out of here by tomorrow. Of course, I wouldn't harm a hair on her head but Prince Alexander doesn't need to know that. I got quite a bit out of her before she realized my intentions. The family are staying with the Dietrich-Bormanns who have a townhouse only a couple of miles away. I suggest a ransom of two thousand thalers. What do you think?'

'I think you're a bloody idiot and we should never have taken you back.'

Not Hans but Axel, who had been listening in.

'No respect for your elders, lad, that's your problem.'

Wolfgang turned his attention to Hans and me. 'All right, perhaps I should have thought it through but she's here now. We can make enough on this to retire permanently. Plenty of people have done jobs like this before.'

'And they usually end in disaster,' said Axel.

Hans just glared at Wolfgang, that one eye boring into him.

'You are a fool. A bloody fool.' The veteran turned to me. 'What do we do?'

I had by now recovered enough to answer. 'We let her go. Let her go and get out of here as quickly as we can.'

'What about the chocolate?' asked Gunther, tapping the wagon.

'We'll have to forget it. We can't stay in Goslar.'

Gunther now struck the wagon with his fist.

'I'm not letting her go,' said Wolfgang. 'I took her. It's up to me.' Hans again touched his sword. 'I wonder if you know how close you are to being run through.'

'I'm not scared of you, Hans,' said Wolfgang. 'Never have been.' His fierce expression broke suddenly into a grin. 'Come on, where's the Lucky Thieves spirit? We can all do well out of this. Christian, aren't you the one who always wants to try something new? Give your share to the poor if you wish but don't deny the rest of us.'

The man clearly knew so little about me and how I saw the world that I could not even see the point in replying. The next voice within the warehouse was that of our captive.

'I know where we are,' said Sophia Christine. 'You tried to confuse me but I know where we are. I heard the bell of the Benedictine church.' She pointed in the correct direction. 'Please let me go. I can find my own way back to the townhouse.'

'She knows where we are,' said Hans, glaring once more at Wolfgang. 'You're no fool. You're a bloody idiot.'

Chapter Fifteen

Had I known how events would develop, I would have fled immediately. But Hans had made a good point about our captive's knowledge of our location and within an hour it became evident that the local watchmen and garrison soldiers were out searching for her. We locked the warehouse from the inside but heard at least two groups pass close by. The building had been rented from a man named Schaffer. I didn't believe he would betray us unless he discovered we were involved in the kidnapping.

I found the very word offensive. This was not how the Lucky Thieves conducted themselves. My anger towards Wolfgang was at least equaled by my anger towards myself. I had listened to my heart when I should have heeded my head. Even worse, the search parties were so close that we had to gag our poor captive. I reassured her that we intended no harm but was sure she didn't believe me and who could blame her?

If not for the immediate danger, I believe Hans might have attacked Wolfgang and I'll admit the thought crossed my mind. Worse still, his actions had driven a wedge between us. The Becker brothers believed we should make the most of the situation by exacting a ransom. Even Gunther seemed amenable to the idea, especially as we would now make a loss on the chocolate. I thought him better than that but I know he was tiring of the life. Perhaps the idea of one final huge payout was more important than his loyalty to me. At least I could be certain of Hans and Axel.

It clearly hadn't occurred to Wolfgang that even a wealthy aristocrat couldn't instantaneously produce thousands of thalers and there were numerous other problems with his 'scheme'. We didn't even allow him to outline further plans; we now found ourselves party to kidnap but we would not collaborate in a ransom.

The night passed with a terrible slowness, the tension borne not only of the dangers beyond the building's four walls but the enmities within. Wolfgang tried twice more to persuade us that his plot could still work but we would have none of it. I devoted my energies to deciding how best to escape and what exactly we would do with the young noblewoman.

As we'd planned to leave Goslar, we at least had our bags with us. Donning the latest iteration of my artisan outfit, I slipped out of the warehouse at dawn to learn what I could about our situation. I hadn't expected it to be good but I'd underestimated the influence a man such as the Prince of Thurn and Taxis could bring to bear. By the time I reached the city center, I had passed four pairs of watchmen and three sets of soldiers. I'd been questioned twice but used an old trick of mine: I pretended to be Russian. It was rare that a soldier or watchman would know any more than a few words of the language. In my shabby clothes and aged hat, I didn't look like an accomplished kidnapper or an accomplished anything for that matter.

Having seen so many soldiers and watchmen, I knew getting out of Goslar would be difficult. A town was far harder to escape than a city and there were only three main routes in or out. What I witnessed in the main square was even more alarming: an infantry captain briefing a group of soldiers that numbered at least fifty. I only caught the last few lines but he mentioned house-to-house searches and it seemed they would commence soon. I was minded to leave immediately but Goslar's mayor was next to speak. Standing with him was a finely dressed gentleman accompanied by two attendants. The mayor swiftly introduced the gentleman as Prince Alexander himself. He thanked the troops for gathering so quickly and announced that the prince was offering a reward of one hundred thalers for information leading to the capture and safe return of his daughter. By now, other townsfolk had gathered and mention of the money caused more than a few excited expressions. Within minutes, the entire town would be looking for us.

Endeavoring not to look like a man in a hurry, I hurried back to the warehouse. I was only a couple of streets away when I realized that the man I was about to overtake was none other than Ernst Schaffer, the fellow who'd rented us the warehouse. Schaffer also owned a tavern and his many customers had made him a well-connected individual. Though not an outright criminal like me, he was not averse to operating outside the law.

'Schaffer.'

He stopped but at first glance did not recognize me.

'It's me. Christian.' Schaffer did not know my true name but he knew we were the Lucky Thieves. In fact, he'd seemed almost in awe of us on the three previous occasions we'd collaborated.

'I was on my way to see you,' said he. 'You've heard about this kidnapping?'

'I have. Some bloody idiot bringing half the army down on us. Don't worry, we're leaving now. In fact, I have a deal for you.'

My motive was not solely to find a safe way out of Goslar. By giving Schaffer a bribe that could ultimately be connected back to the gang, I made it less likely that he would later betray us.

'A deal?' Schaffer was a plump man with a voluminous head of curly hair. He ran his fingers through it as we stood there, knowing soldiers or watchmen might approach at any moment.

'We're leaving presently. This kind of attention could be very dangerous for us.'

'Understood.'

'Inside your warehouse is sixty pounds of chocolate. We'll leave it. It's all yours – as long as you tell me the best way for us to get out of Goslar.'

'You have a deal.' The man fiddled with his hair again as he considered what to suggest.

'Herr Schaffer, time is short.'

When we went our separate ways, I told him that we would depart within the hour and leave the warehouse open. As I'd anticipated, the thought of this unexpected windfall had secured his cooperation. I didn't know if Schaffer would keep the chocolate there or hide it before some curious soldier came calling. That was his problem now.

My immediate problem was Sophia Christine, Princess of Thurn and Taxis. When I returned to the warehouse, I found the horses yoked to the wagon once more. The others were packed up and ready to leave but the unfortunate aristocrat was still sitting, gagged, watched over by Hans.

'What do we do with her?' asked Axel as I removed my disguise.

'We take her with us,' said Wolfgang. 'This can still work out well.'

My patience with the man had reached its end. 'Perhaps you could shut up for a moment. I need to think.'

'We can't take her, can we?' said Axel.

'Believe me, I don't want to, but if we let her go now, she can connect us to this place and this place connects us to Schaffer. And he's just provided me with the best way out of Goslar. We will let her go. But not now.'

'Very sensible,' added Wolfgang.

I walked over to him. 'Give me one reason why we shouldn't leave you here.'

'I'll give you three, Christian. Dieter, Roland and Gunther. They all agree that we should try for a ransom. What do we care for this spoiled bitch anyway?'

'That "spoiled bitch" is a perfectly innocent woman who you preyed upon like some gutter rat. You have dragged us all down to your level.'

'But you're outvoted, Christian. By my reckoning, it's four to three.' 'You're forgetting something. I lead the Lucky Thieves with Hans and Axel. Everyone else is hired help.'

In retrospect, it was not the right thing to say but it at least kept Wolfgang quiet.

The chocolate had already been removed from the wagon and now I told the others to load our gear. I then took another disguise outfit from my knapsack. Over the years, I have had numerous reasons to be thankful for these garments but they were never more important than on this occasion. I hurried over to Hans and quickly briefed him on our escape plan. While he informed the others, I spoke to the young princess.

Taking her by the arm, I helped her up off the barrel. I could not bear to see a woman so ill-treated.

'If you promise not to shout out, I'll remove the gag. Do you promise?'

She nodded. I not only removed the gag but also fetched her a flask of water.

'Please listen very carefully. As you'll have gathered by now, this was not my idea. Unfortunately, we cannot leave you here.'

'I won't tell them,' she said instantly, again showing her sharp understanding of her situation. 'I won't tell them *anything*. Just go now and I can pretend I got lost or something.'

'I'm afraid it's a bit late for that. But once we're clear of the town, we will set you free. You'll just have to be quiet for a while though. Can you do that?'

'Please just let me go. Now.'

'We will. I promise.'

'Please.'

I did not wish to say what I then did but I knew our survival might depend on it.

'Young lady, you're clearly bright enough to appreciate that not everyone here is as amenable as I am. You will be in their care for the next hour or two. Do as you are told and you will soon be free.'

'How can you be so cruel?'

I lifted the gag again and secured it. 'I am sorry.'

Leaving Hans to organize the final preparations, I put on the disguise, which I hoped would deliver us from peril. Once attired, I saw that the others were prepared. All except Axel were lying in the back of the wagon, including the poor princess. With his youthful, friendly face, Axel was the least suspicious looking of my compatriots. So it was he and I who pulled the cover over the others, leaving a space above their faces so they could breathe.

Axel then opened the doors an inch and checked outside. He waited for a pair of women to pass then opened the doors wide. I was already up on the wagon and now guided the two horses out onto the street. Axel swiftly shut the doors then jumped up beside me and took control of the reins.

'You have it?' said I.

Axel nodded pointed downwards at his cudgel. Like me, he did not enjoy wielding weapons but this at least gave us some defense if we needed it. I hoped my disguise would deter any inquisitors but with so many armed men around and that hefty reward on offer, anything was possible.

'Don't go too fast,' I added as the wagon rumbled loudly along the cobbled street.

I then adjusted my black robes and ensured that my white collar and golden cross were clearly visible. As always, I embraced the part I was playing and offered a heartfelt prayer that we would escape Goslar without incident.

It was not to be. When I'd told him of my disguise, Herr Schaffer had suggested we head south towards a church at the edge of town. Behind this was a large orchard and from there a clear path that led between two hills. Beyond lay the wilderness of the Harz Forest, which was fifty miles across at its widest. There could be no doubt that this was our best chance of evading capture. First, we had to get there.

We passed several townsfolk on our way to the church. I greeted them all with a friendly word but attracted some curious looks. Goslar was not a large place so the locals would know the priests. We also passed a soldier who emerged from a house, still buttoning up his jacket while holding a musket. He gave us no more than a passing glance and trotted away towards the town center.

I was beginning to feel less anxious as we neared the church. It was not a large structure but the tower at least gave us something to aim for as we negotiated the cramped, narrow streets. If not for the rattles and bumps and squeaks of a wagon in motion, I believe I would have heard the patrol approaching. There were around a dozen of them, marching behind a lieutenant; and they emerged suddenly from a side street. I nodded cordially but was met with a suspicious expression from the officer. Determined not to glance at Axel, I winced as we passed the patrol. I suppose we had traveled twenty or thirty feet when the lieutenant called out to us.

'Father, can you stop a moment?'

His hail was quite clear but I did not react, instead whispering to Axel. 'Keep going.'

'Father!'

'They'll come after us,' said Axel.

'If they stop us, they'll check the back. Keep going.'

'Stop that wagon!' ordered the lieutenant. 'Stop at once!'

Then came the loud crack of a musket shot.

Axel was already reining in when I told him to halt. We were no more than fifty feet away: well within range.

I turned to see one soldier still aiming at us and the others running down the street spreading out to surround us. And in my mind's eye, I saw an image that came to me often: the moldering corpse of a criminal hanged and left to rot on the Potsdam road. Apparently, it had been on the order of Lieutenant-General Von Munchow.

I was about to try and convince the lieutenant that he should let us go on our way when the cover was suddenly thrown aside. Gunther appeared first; sitting up and hauling Princess Sophia up beside him. Next to appear was Wolfgang, a dagger in his hand, which he swiftly placed upon our captive's shoulder, the tip only inches from her neck.

'Stop there!'

The lieutenant was not slow to appraise this new development. 'Men – do as he says.' The officer, who appeared no more than twenty-five, was holding his own musket in two hands. 'Now then, let's not do anything stupid.'

'I quite agree,' said Wolfgang. 'We wouldn't want anything to happen to the princess here.'

'You've no hope of getting away. Let the lady go.'

I suppose a moral man would have intervened. I suppose a true hero would have jumped into the wagon, disarmed the fool whose fault all this was. Then the innocent Sophia would be free and we criminals would have been arrested and executed, as we no doubt deserved. But one does not think in such terms when one knows that surrender means suffering and death. The truth is that I was grateful to my old mentor for his quick thinking. I doubt he would have injured her, but he gave the appearance of being entirely prepared to do so.

Hans was the next to sit up. 'Wouldn't want to be the man who gets the prince's daughter killed, would you, lieutenant? It would be the end of your career and a lot more besides.'

I didn't think it wise to wait for reinforcements to come and trap us. I turned back to Axel and gave him the nod. One horse was misbehaving but a couple of blows from Axel's crop secured its cooperation and we set off again.

'Not another step forward,' shouted Wolfgang.

As Axel urged the horses into a trot, I watched the troops. The lieutenant still had both hands up, keeping his men at bay. But he also gave an order and one soldier set off in the other direction – to alert his superiors, no doubt.

'That'll do.' This was an order from Hans and as we rounded a corner, Wolfgang lowered the knife. Sophia threw herself downward, crying.

'Steady,' said I as Axel shouted at the horses. But he nimbly guided them around two corners and suddenly we were at the church. There was only a single man present, who appeared to be weeding the graveyard. We all leaped off the wagon and Hans and Wolfgang helped Sophia down as carefully as they could. She stood there, head bowed, still sobbing. Had there been time, I would have felt nothing but shame.

'Christian, she's all that stands between us and the noose.'

These words were not spoken by Wolfgang but Hans. 'We have to take her with us.'

'We should let her go,' stated Axel.

'You saw what happened,' snapped Wolfgang. 'We need her.'

'But if we leave her, they might not …' Even Axel himself saw the futility of this argument. We were now hunted men and the truth was that if our enemies got close again, Sophia was our only bargaining chip.

There was no time for debate. Instead, I knelt by our captive and took off first one shoe then the other. Using the wheel of the wagon, I snapped off both heels before replacing them on her feet. There were no words I could offer the young woman. I had broken my promise to her.

The Lucky Thieves fled, our captive with us, past the church and into the orchard. I swiftly abandoned my priestly robes, which were not conducive to running. As was normal in such situations, Hans remained at the back to keep a lookout. And as I was the one who'd received the guidance from Schaffer, I led the way. Not wanting to add to the torment for Sophia, I told Wolfgang to stay clear of her.

Schaffer had told me that the path was to be found in the southeast corner of the orchard. After sprinting along the southern wall, I found the gate and was first through. There were in fact three paths in view but one was less overgrown and seemed to lead in the right direction. I knew we would eventually have to leave it to escape our pursuers but the priority in that moment was to put distance between us.

We must have covered two or three miles before we stopped. By that point, we had entered dense woodland and taken at least five turns. I was disturbed to discover that I am no long-distance runner. Axel and Dieter were both very fast and able to sustain that speed. Gunther was average and Hans did remarkably well, considering he was ten years older even than Wolfgang. But Wolfgang's age, life of excess, and heavy frame counted against him and Roland was very much built for strength. I performed better than those two but not as well as the young princess, who was clearly quite the athlete.

'Sweaty pig,' she said to Wolfgang who, like myself, was doubled over and sucking in breath. She said it in French, however, so he did not understand.

I could not help laughing at a brief comedic respite from an awful few hours.

'You speak French?' she asked me.

'I do.'

'You are no pig,' she replied, walking past me. 'You are a *snake*.' Though her pale gown was dirtied and torn, the captive princess had run with such ease and grace that she was breathing easier than the rest of us.

Hans was last into the small clearing where we'd halted. He was holding his telescope and also had to catch his breath before he could speak. 'Got a decent look back when we came over that rise. No one immediately behind us but I saw at least two groups of troops. Closest was no more than a quarter-mile.'

'How long until nightfall?' asked Axel.

'About three hours,' replied Hans.

'What if they use dogs?' said Gunther.

'Didn't hear any yet,' said Dieter.

'We have to get off the trails,' said Wolfgang. 'Even a small one like this.'

'And do what?' said Hans, 'blunder off some cliff or into a bog? You know these lands well?'

'As well as you.'

We had visited the Harz forest twice. The first occasion had been many years ago, a brief excursion into the western flank to elude some aggressive competitors. The last occasion had been three years before: There were several gangs that used the forest as a base of operations. It was said that they dwelt in caves upon the mountainsides or in remote groves far from any known path. We had dealt briefly with one such gang known as the Ghosts. I believe they came up with this exotic moniker themselves for in fact, they were a mediocre outfit that specialized in smuggling animal hides. They had insisted on meeting us at the edge of the forest and said not a word about their base. We were in dire need of their help but the forest was so enormous that we could have walked it for ten years and not run into them.

'We'll stay on this path for now,' said I, anxious to keep Wolfgang in his place. 'Leave it when Hans gives the say-so.'

Princess Sophia had found a log to sit on. She now stood and made a pronouncement, hands set proudly on her hips. 'You cretins are just making it worse for yourselves. My father is a very fair man. If I tell him you did me no harm, he will ensure you're spared the noose.'

Wolfgang scoffed at the idea.

‘Thank you for the suggestion,’ said I. ‘Hans, perhaps you should lead the way now?’

The veteran hurried past me, steadying his sword with one hand as he broke into a run.

I have never been so relieved to see the sunset. Just as twilight descended, Hans halted beside a stream that we had been following for some time. The ex-grenadier was convinced that we’d extended our lead over the troops and had decided to set a false trail. Ordering the rest of us across the stream, he told us to continue along that side, not straying far from the water. He returned to us some twenty minutes later, hopeful that his effort had been worthwhile.

Turning away from the stream, we continued up a shallow slope and passed through a patch of dense undergrowth until we emerged into an attractive glade. Though gloomy, it seemed a benevolent part of the forest, with moss-covered logs, sprawling ferns, and even a few pretty flowers. Hans took us to the center of the glade and declared that this was the best place to stay the night. Though clearly exhausted, he set off with Gunther to scout escape routes in case we were discovered.

It seemed only fair that the rest of us keep busy so I ordered the men to make a shelter. I knew the importance of keeping our provisions dry and wanted to give the princess somewhere to sleep. Using fallen logs and fern, we had the structure up by the time Hans and Gunther returned. Once the old soldier had detailed two escape routes, we settled down. We had filled our flasks at the stream and also had a little food, which we shared out. The princess drank but refused to eat anything; and when I offered her the shelter, she also refused that. As we others ate, she set about making a bed of ferns for herself.

A discussion began amongst the men and soon an angry exchange broke out between Axel and Wolfgang. Personally, I would still have been quite happy to take Axel’s cudgel and strike

Wolfgang with it but now was not the time for infighting. I stood up.

'Gentlemen, we are in a far better position than we were this morning. There is still hope. I'm sure we all have our own feelings about what's transpired but this is not the occasion for recriminations. Our only task is to survive, and we stand a far better chance of doing that if we work together. Do we agree?'

I did not move until I'd received nods from them all. As Hans detailed a system for sentry duty, I took a hunk of bread and some dried sausage over to our captive.

She was sitting on her ferns with legs and arms crossed. It was impossible not to admire the way she had dealt with the day's trying events.

'I told you – I don't want your disgusting food.'

'I'm afraid there's nothing else and I can't say when next we'll have something.' I placed the food on a clean-looking fern.

She brushed her hair away from her face. 'Are you going to tell me you're sorry again?'

For all my supposed charm and eloquence, I could find no reply.

'You're the Lucky Thieves, aren't you?' said Princess Sophia.

'We are.'

'And that makes you the King of Thieves.'

'I'm not particularly fond of that name.'

'I heard the servants talking about you once. They seemed to quite admire you. I wonder what they'd think of you now.'

Chapter Sixteen

For five days we played a tortuous game of hide and seek with our pursuers. Three times the soldiers got close enough for us to see them and on the third they had dogs. Hans again successfully used a stream to put them off the scent. Every mile south or east took us further into the vast forest and increased the search area for our enemies. We generally hid during the day and moved at night, and by the sixth day we felt considerably safer. The nights were chilly but we had enough blankets and coats to keep warm.

We'd initially survived on stream-water and berries but encountered an injured deer on the fourth day. Returning to a cave we'd earlier used for shelter, we cooked the meat and enjoyed our first hot meal. Princess Sophia devoured the venison with as much enthusiasm as any of the men. This will sound strange, ridiculous even, but it seemed to me that she grew more at ease with every passing day. Though still wary of Wolfgang, she mocked us when the opportunity arose and continued to demonstrate remarkable fortitude.

As we sat chewing on the last of the deer meat, she informed us that we all smelled disgusting and that Hans should find a body of water for us to bathe in. An odd rapport had developed between the aristocrat and the Lucky Thieves and Hans responded with a respectful bow.

'I shall do my best, your grace, though we must continue east.'

I had done whatever I could to make this ordeal easier for her; and, in private moments, we'd even begun to discuss each other's lives. Sophia seemed quite interested in mine and, though I was vague about details, I described some of our adventures and close scrapes. Though she never admitted it, I could tell she harbored some sense of curiosity – perhaps even admiration – for our unusual lifestyle. Even so, she regularly admonished me for thievery and seemed unimpressed by our charitable donations.

I can honestly say that Princess Sophia Christine was one of the most remarkable women I have ever met. She was willful, short-tempered, and possessed of a steel and tenacity I would never have expected from a lady of her class. I did at least solve the mystery of her remarkable physical health and love of the outdoors. Of the prince's progeny, it was only Sophia who emulated his pursuits and she'd spent much of her childhood riding, walking and learning about the wild within her father's sprawling estates. During the few relaxed moments, she had pointed out rare birds and animal trails. She was far more at home in the forest than the rest of us, including Hans.

We had spent the night trekking east and now found ourselves in a rocky hollow ideal for seeing out the day. Hans and Gunther were taking the first watch and the others were settling down for sleep. I had given Sophia my blanket, which she laid out beside a slab of lichen covered rock. The gown she had been wearing was long past use so she wore a pair of Hans' breeches and one of my spare shirts.

'What are you looking at?' said she, noting my interest. The truth is that, like my compatriots, I couldn't help looking at her. Despite the conditions, she possessed a natural appeal that I believe had entranced us all, with the possible exception of Wolfgang, who Sophia continued to insult at any opportunity. The rest of us did nothing to defend him, conscious that our apparent escape could be reversed at any moment.

Sophia was one of those lucky individuals who appears slender, almost frail, yet is in fact hardy and surprisingly strong. She was not strikingly beautiful but hers was an expressive, compelling face. Her hair was a shiny blonde and always looked wonderful when touched by the sun.

'Sorry,' said I, flushing as I sat on my coat. 'I was just wondering how a lady such as yourself would normally spend a Saturday morning.'

'Is it Saturday? I had no idea. I would be in bed, of course. One of the maids would wake me at nine. A bath perhaps, then breakfast with mother and father. Often some music before lunch.'

'What do you play?'

'Piano. But my little brother and sister are really the musical ones. I have no talent for it.'

'And a ride in the afternoon, I suppose?'

'Or a hunt, depending on whether we're entertaining. Honestly, I prefer it when it's just father and the staff. We don't have to observe all the social niceties.'

'You can shoot then?' I had not settled on an appropriate method of addressing our captive. 'Sophia' was far too familiar while the correct term – 'your grace' – seemed ridiculous given the circumstances.

'Of course. Mother tried to discourage it but I wore Daddy down. I can hit a pheasant from a hundred yards.'

'Is that so? And in the evenings?'

She rolled her eyes. 'Probably a ball. I am inevitably expected to dance with a succession of chinless idiots who probably took longer to dress and powder their faces than I did. Mother seems insistent that I'

It seemed to me that Sophia suddenly realized how odd our friendly exchange was. It wasn't the first time we had communicated in such a way but I suppose it was strange to act normally when the situation was anything but. She paused for some time before speaking again:

'This can't go on, Christian. You've escaped the troops. Let me go on my way.' She lowered her voice. 'Talk to your men. Persuade them.'

I did not answer.

'Perhaps you want to keep me here too.'

'It's not that I want to. When we've truly escaped, we will let you go.' 'Is that another of your promises?'

With that she laid down and turned away from me.

***

What came next was the closest encounter with our pursuers yet. Once again, we traveled under the cover of darkness. Spying a collection of torches in the early hours, we gave them a wide berth. As the sun rose, we found ourselves close to a lake. Though able to refill our flasks and quickly wash ourselves, we were far more likely to encounter our enemies in such a location.

And as we continued east, away from the lake, that is precisely what happened. Walking in single file through a rocky gully, we came across two young infantrymen dozing in the morning sun. Thanks to the quick thinking of Axel and Hans, who snatched their muskets before they could react, we instantly acquired two more prisoners. As soon as they saw Sophia, they realized who we were and exchanged an anxious glance.

'What the hell do we do with these two?' said Hans.

'Take what they have,' said Wolfgang, already delving inside one of the soldier's knapsacks.

'Including information,' said I, convinced we had to take advantage while they were still in shock. I didn't particularly want to inflict suffering on yet more victims but I was desperate for knowledge of the forces ranged against us. Taking Hans' sword from him, I held the tip under the nearest soldier's chin. Like his friend, he looked no more than eighteen, which perhaps explained their lax attitude.

'How many are there?'

'I'm not telling you'

Once again, I was called upon to employ my acting skills and I elected to channel a little of Wolfgang's vicious streak.

'Oh, you'll tell me,' said I through gritted teeth. 'Unless you want to taste the end of this blade.'

'Th-th-three platoons. The Prince is paying for the whole thing. And they say the general is arriving soon with a company of Jagers.'

'What general?'

'Lieutenant General Von Munchow.'

The news could not have been worse. We faced not only a man determined to avenge himself but a force of Jagers. These were military scouts who wore green and specialized in unconventional warfare. Most of them were hunters drawn from rural areas; if anyone could track us down, it was them.

My compatriots cursed and shook their heads.

'What else?' I asked.

'Th-that's all I know, I swear.'

'And the rest of your unit?'

'The command post is at the western end of the lake. We were sent out in pairs to search this area until noon.'

'Then I suggest you return there.'

'You're not serious!' snapped Wolfgang. 'They'll be there in half an hour.'

'No they won't – because you're about to hobble and gag them.' Wolfgang just frowned at me.

'What other choice do we have? Or are you keen to graduate from kidnapping to murder?'

Roland produced some rope from his pack and the pair of them set about following my instructions. We had at least acquired two muskets, some ammunition, food, and useful clothing to add to our meager supplies.

Despite the precautions we took with the hapless infantrymen, we continued east as swiftly as we could. We were of course more vulnerable in daylight but kept away from open areas and put many miles between the lake and ourselves before nightfall. As the sun set, it was clear to me that the spirits of the group had sunk even lower. The force now unleashed suggested that Von Munchow was committed to apprehending us once and for all. With the political influence the Prince of Thurn and Taxis was able to exert, I considered it possible that even the king's authority might have been invoked.

It was the coldest night so far and we sought shelter under an over-hanging ledge. After we had shared out the soldiers' food, Wolfgang spoke up:

'We're going about this all wrong. What's the point of keeping the girl if we're not using her?'

'What are you suggesting?' replied Gunther. Though he and the Becker brothers seemed to have sided with Wolfgang early on, they were also aware that he had landed us in this mess.

'Simple. We write a note and leave it somewhere for them to find. We state that every time we see a soldier, we'll cut off one of her fingers. As long as they leave us alone, we'll set her free within one week.'

Sophia was sitting quite close to me. Neither of us said anything.

'And you think they'll believe that?' replied Axel.

'The prince won't dare take the chance,' said Wolfgang with his usual confidence. 'Not for his precious daughter. Or we could try and get a ransom. We could keep it reasonable, let's say a thousand thalers.'

I scoffed at this idea.

'You still don't understand, do you?' said Hans in an unusually loud voice. 'You think we hold the upper hand? We'll be lucky to escape this forest alive, Wolfgang. And all because you couldn't turn down the chance of another get quick rich scheme. Almost fifty years old and you still haven't worked out that your judgment is bloody awful. Where did that judgment get you? Nowhere. Homeless, penniless, stinking and destitute. You arrogant bastard, we should have left you where we f-'

Wolfgang launched himself at Hans and in a moment the pair were trading blows and rolling across the ground. It took five of us – and some time – to separate them and when we did so, Wolfgang was still spitting and snarling. Hans pushed even me away.

To his credit, he was the first to realize our captive had disappeared.

'Where is she?' yelled Axel.

'Spread out,' ordered Hans. 'All of you.'

With the exception of Wolfgang, we obeyed. I headed back the way we'd come, blundering through high grass with nothing but moonlight to guide me. I stopped as I approached a stand of trees, to check if I could hear anything.

At first, there was nothing except a shout from behind me. Then I realized I could hear footfalls within the trees ahead. Stepping lightly but swiftly, I took ten paces forward. The noise had stopped but I sensed a presence close by. Once in the trees, I glanced in every direction but the moonlight barely penetrated the canopy. I saw only inky darkness.

Another noise. Close. Very close.

I fancied that I could hear the sound of breathing. I spun around, suddenly fearful of an attack from behind.

How far had I run? Had I accidentally crossed paths with some spy on our trail?

Again, the breathing. For once I wished I had a weapon.

Then a flurry of movement to my left. I turned, put my hands up to protect myself.

'Who's there?' A man's voice. A man I knew.

'Christian?'

'Gunther? By god.'

'Sorry, chief.'

'Not your fault,' I said. 'Let's keep looking.'

Before we could do so, a whistle sounded from our camp – a long whistle then a short. We both knew Hans' signal; we were to return at once.

Roland had found her and, judging by the marks on his face, Sophia had put up quite a fight. I assisted Hans as he tied her hands behind her back. I would have spoken to her but another matter now concerned me. Everyone was at the camp except Wolfgang and a brief search told us that he'd taken his knapsack with him.

'Can't say I'm going to miss the fool,' announced Axel.

'Surprised he abandoned his precious captive,' said Dieter.

'Probably thinks he has a better chance of escaping alone,' said Hans. And he may be right.'

As the minutes then hours passed, it became obvious that Wolfgang would not return. I was surprised but as glad as Axel in a way; his absence would at least keep our group unified. After Sophia's attempted escape, I was sorely tempted to simply let her go. But for all his stupidity, Wolfgang had shown us her value during our confrontation with the troops in Goslar. There was perhaps another, deeper, reason too: I was beginning to suspect I was in love with her.

With Axel on sentry duty, I lay out on my coat only two feet from Sophia. Her hands were bound and tied to a rock.

'Are you warm enough?' I asked, checking that my blanket still covered her.

'I am. But I can't sleep. You can still guard me but not like this.'

'What do you mean?' said I, the events of another trying day catching up with me.

'Come closer,' she whispered. 'If you put your arm over me, you'll know where I am.'

Though surprised and concerned that the others might realize what was going on, I could not resist this invitation. As quietly as I could, I maneuvered my way over to her and hesitantly reached out.

When I touched her arm, Sophia squirmed backwards until we were pressed tightly together. She turned her head and when our mouths found each other, kissed me as passionately as I had ever been kissed.

I reached down, untied the rope binding her wrists and cast it aside. She shared the blanket with me. Despite what had happened, I was concerned that this was another trick; another escape attempt.

And yet, lying there beside this aristocratic beauty, I fell asleep easily. And when I awoke at dawn, Sophia was still there.

The rain came in mid-morning and continued into the afternoon. Tired and miserable, we pressed on through a narrow gorge that at least took us directly eastward. The sides of the gorge were steep but partly covered with shrubs and shale. Axel was at the front of our little column, Hans at the rear; both with loaded muskets under their coats to protect them from the rain.

Though it was not yet winter, we had been wet for several hours and I believe we were all suffering from the cold. I wasn't sure if any of my compatriots had witnessed my sleeping arrangements. Nor did I particularly care if they saw now that Sophia and I held hands. I could still not quite believe what had happened the previous night but could also not deny my feelings for her. It was disorientating to simultaneously feel such fear and such hope.

As we approached the end of the gorge, she squeezed my hand and I returned the gesture. Seconds later, I heard a cry of alarm from Axel. Apparently from nowhere, six green-clad Jagers had sprung up in front of us. Each was armed with a heavy musket but as they would be unreliable in the heavy rain, the soldiers had drawn their swords.

I wanted to tell my compatriots not to fight but within seconds Axel, Gunther, and the Beckers had drawn their own weapons. I looked on in horror as the Jagers struck.

In moments Gunther and Dieter had fallen. Roland was wrestling with two soldiers while Axel traded sword blows with two more.

'More behind them!' yelled Hans. 'Christian, come on!'

Though I heard his words clearly, I could not drag my eyes from the battle. This was precisely what I had feared and I could do nothing to stop it.

Eventually, Hans wrenched me around. 'Come on!'

At last, I could move and with Sophia still in hand, I followed Hans back along the gorge at a sprint. It didn't occur to me at the time but of course, Sophia could have left me then. She did not take the opportunity.

The sounds of the clash were soon behind us. There was no need for discussion; all three of us knew that we had to reach the other end of the gorge before our pursuers could cut off the only route of escape. Hans had previously expressed doubts about trapping ourselves in the confined space but other paths would have taken us higher, onto hills with bare flanks where we'd have been dangerously exposed.

As we ran, I felt certain that the awful game we had played with our enemies had reached its conclusion. The expanses of the Harz forest had protected us for almost a week but Lieutenant-General Von Munchow had thrown considerable manpower at the situation. I tried not to think of the poor friends we had just left behind; if they were badly wounded – or worse. My fears for my own fate had now taken on a new dimension. My feelings towards Sophia had bloomed with impossible speed. Would I now lose her along with everything else?

The gorge was at least a mile long. We heard our enemies before we saw them and realized from their shouts that they were trying to intercept us before we reached open ground. We were at least fortunate that the rain had stopped, which allowed us to move quicker, despite the mud beneath our feet.

The race was a close-run thing. Just as we three left the high-walled trap behind and scrambled up a slope to the left, we found our way barred. Two Jagers, both wielding swords, were descending towards us. Hearing a shout, I looked over my shoulder and saw others a hundred yards away.

'Christian, keep going up,' said Hans as he reached beneath his coat. 'Stay in the trees wherever you can.'

The two Jagers had slowed to a walk. One fierce-looking fellow with a bushy mustache aimed his sword at us.

'Halt at once.'

Hans retrieved his musket and aimed at the man. The pan flashed and a moment later, the Jager fell to the ground, clutching his wounded thigh.

'Go now, Christian.' Hans dropped the musket, drew his blade and sprang towards the second man with surprising speed.

'Hans'

'Just go!'

I looked at Sophia, whose eyes were wide with fear and confusion. I asked no question and yet she answered with a nod and soon the two of us were pounding up the slope, Hans covering our retreat. The hill was steep and we were both exhausted but fear drove me on and not once did I let go of Sophia's hand.

From below us came the sounds of a struggle, then the shouts of the approaching troops. I told myself not to look back, terrified by what I might see. But as we reached the top of the slope, I could not help myself.

Hans had bettered the second man and now faced a line of advancing Jagers, some of whom wielded their own muskets. With a cry, the old soldier charged at them.

Even in that moment, I realized this was no attack but Hans' way of ending his life on his own terms. He could not face the shame of a trial or a prolonged incarceration. He wanted to die as he had lived: a fighting man.

Two shots rang out. Hit at close range, Hans was blown off his feet, landing in a pile of mud and leaves.

The Jagers walked towards him, two of their muskets now smoking. Hans raised his right hand for a moment but then it fell and he moved no more.

Chapter Seventeen

The rain returned and barely stopped for three days. I have no doubt that this is what saved us. On that first day, we slogged on across sodden ground, knowing that no dogs could track us and that no one would move much quicker. I had my coat and Sophia had one of those we had taken from the hapless soldiers. These peerless garments kept us dry and warm, and that night we found shelter below a fallen tree. We were so exhausted that we fell asleep almost immediately.

One might expect this to be the occasion on which Sophia abandoned the man who had caused her so much suffering. But she seemed to revel in our adventure and became almost as determined as I that we outwit our pursuers. Only then did I begin to realize that she was truly a kindred spirit; another individual who felt their true nature constrained by societal and familial expectations. On the second day and the third, as the loss of my friends struck home, it was Sophia that kept my spirits up.

On that third day, we reached the village of Hasselfelde. We were able to pilfer half a dozen apples and I also spoke to a young goatherd.

From him, I learned that we had in fact come much further south than east and were only eight miles from the western edge of the forest. As Von Munchow would expect us to continue in our original direction, this seemed a logical route of escape.

I have no idea if the goatherd was aware of the ongoing hunt for the King of Thieves and the Princess Sophia but he readily accepted my offer of two thalers to guide us. We, at last, left the Harz forest behind that evening. I intercepted a passing farmer and paid him well to drive us to the nearest town, which was called Nordhausen.

I booked us into two small rooms on the first floor and asked for as much hot water as could be spared. When the innkeeper's wife inquired about how we'd ended up in such a state, I spun her a tale. Even so, I had no intention of remaining this close to our pursuers for long; we would be heading south in the morning, whatever the weather. I was running low on funds and the closest of my all-important bank accounts was in the city of Weimar.

Once I'd used the cauldron of hot water to thoroughly clean myself, I hung out my clothes on a rack beside the fireplace. Other than a few scratches and bruises, I had escaped the pursuit without serious injury. Sitting there in my undergarments, still and safe for the first time in what seemed like an eternity, I gazed at the flames, my mind drifting back to those horrible moments at both ends of that gorge. How brave they had all been and how typical of my old friend to sacrifice himself for me. I confess that I cried for some time before reflecting on the irony that perhaps only Wolfgang and I had escaped the clutches of Von Munchow.

I was about to get into bed when there was a knock at my door. I covered myself with a cloak and opened the door to find Sophia there, hair newly washed, barefoot and wearing a shawl over a nightdress.

'Are you going to let me in?' she said after an awkward pause. 'Yes, sorry.'

Shutting the door behind her, I guided Sophia to the chair I had left in front of the hearth.

'I've never felt so happy to be clean,' she said.

'I know.'

The flames were dying so I added some coal then sat on a stool beside her.

'Look at this old thing' she said, picking at the nightdress. 'I had to borrow it from the wife.'

'On you, it looks lovely.'

She reached down and took my hand in hers. 'What are we doing?'

Despite the situation, I couldn't help chuckling. 'Good question.'

Nothing was said for a while. We looked at each other, searching our eyes for meaning but I suppose our thoughts were too confused for either of us to find clarity. Eventually, I broke the silence.

'I just want you to think very carefully, Sophia. There is nothing to stop us going our separate ways in the morning.'

'You want that?' she asked, leaning towards me.

'No. I want the opposite. But I know what it is to leave everything behind. Life can be very lonely.'

'I wouldn't be alone.'

'No.'

'And my life would be my own.' She gripped my hand tight, then looked into the flames.

'Your family will worry,' said I. 'They will fear the worst.'

'We could get a message to them.'

'We could.' I looked away; feeling at once buoyed by thoughts of the future but weighed down by a burden.

'I'm not … I'm not really sure what I can offer you, Sophia.'

She leaned further towards me and put her hand on my face.

I continued: 'I'm quite a bit older than you, a wanted man. We'll have to live a secret life. I'm not sure I want to do that to you.'

'I decide what I do,' she insisted. 'Do you know how many men my mother has tried to pair me up with? They tried to ingratiate themselves but there was nothing there, nothing between us. The happiest couple I know is our steward and his wife. I can see the affection, the passion between them. It doesn't have to be forced or created; it's simply there. My parents don't have it. Most I know don't have it. They are married because it is advantageous or … convenient. I know it's not been long but I feel it and I know you do too.'

That I could not deny.

'But I won't be a party to crime, Christian,' added Sophia. 'Not ever. You must leave all that behind.'

'I will.' I didn't make a promise, having broken oaths to her before.

She had been so open and frank, I felt obliged to follow suit:

'Even before all this, I have been thinking about … changing things. Changing everything. I have enough money saved and I'd like to buy an inn. I'd like to live a quiet life, not having to look over my shoulder every five minutes.'

Sophia smiled. 'An inn?'

I shrugged. 'Every day is different. You don't know who will walk through the door, what tale you'll hear. You'd have to work, though; and neither of us could really be ourselves.'

'But we'll be together,' said she. 'And we'll be free.'

My remaining coins were just sufficient to get us to the ancient city of Weimar. Even when we arrived, I could not help feeling that Von Munchow's reach might extend this far. I wondered still who had survived; and what they may have told him. Axel might have been able to make an educated guess about my three crucial bank accounts but only Hans knew the truth and he was dead.

Upon arriving in Weimar, I left Sophia at our rather decrepit inn – all I could afford – and visited my bank along with one of my many sets of counterfeit identity papers. The retrieval of my savings all went smoothly and I was soon departing with five hundred and sixty thalers. The bank offered to sell me a strongbox but I was just about able to carry the coins within my knapsack.

I lugged it to our room, where Sophia greeted me. I'd expected a more enthusiastic reaction when I showed her the coins but she simply handed me a newspaper. The *Wiener Zeitung* was an Austrian publication but circulated widely around central Europe. Taking up a quarter of one page was an article titled, 'The Lucky Thieves No More'. Two weeks had now passed since our flight from the Harz and to the newspaper's credit, most of the report was accurate. The article included an appeal for information regarding Sophia and a quote from Lieutenant General Von Munchow about his determination to see the King of Thieves brought to justice. There was also a list of my fallen comrades and I learned that only Roland had survived the fight in the gorge. There was also an unconfirmed suggestion that a gang member who 'turned traitor' had assisted the soldiers.

'Wolfgang. He must have told them where we were.'

'He turned himself in?' said Sophia. 'Surely that was too risky?'

'I expect he made some kind of deal, especially as he's not mentioned here. I doubt he told them it was him that kidnapped you.'

'He got the others killed.'

I didn't reply. It was I who had brought Wolfgang back into the fold; I who had defended him, even after he had put us all in danger. There was no escaping the fact that much of the blame was mine. Yet hadn't I known – hadn't we all known – that one day our house of cards would come crashing down around us? Couldn't any of those past operations ended our criminal career?

I put down the newspaper and held Sophia in my arms. I had lost so much but at least I had her. And my money.

'Tell me, darling, where would you like to live?'

Two more bank visits were required: to Wittenburg and Dessau. With the last of these completed, I was now in possession of over two thousand thalers. I purchased two horses and we traveled to the city of Kassel. Why here? Primarily because neither Sophia nor myself had any connection to the place. Also, it was one of the few cities in Prussia I had not visited and if we were to make a fresh start, why not in an entirely fresh locale?

Kassel is situated within the state of Hesse and is located on the banks of the Fulda river. It is known for its observatory and its theater but is otherwise an unexceptional place. But when we arrived there, our impressions were favorable. We admired the numerous parks and green spaces and discovered there was also a substantial population of Huguenots, whose antecedents had arrived as refugees from France half a century earlier.

Our main concern was finding a suitable inn. We had only seventeen hundred thalers remaining because I'd had to commission additional papers from the best forger I knew. I'd been wary of approaching him, for it seemed the whole of Prussia was aware of the missing Princess Sophia and the King of Thieves. We heard numerous rumors of our fate: that we had died fleeing the troops, that we had eloped to the New World together, even that we were setting up our own band of smugglers. Sophia sometimes laughed at these notions but I often saw regret and guilt in her eyes. It was still too soon for us to contact her family and we knew that they also would be speculating. The forger charged me a fortune, knowing that by assisting me, he had exposed himself to great risk.

I did not have enough to purchase one of the larger inns close to the town center but these were in any case unsuitable. We wanted somewhere busy but there was no sense taking unnecessary risks. We had both made a single but significant change to our appearance. I kept my hair very short and Sophia's was dyed brown but there was always the chance of encountering someone we knew.

After a good deal of searching, we eventually found a small inn named the Red Lion. It was on the outskirts of the city and faced the river. Consisting of a parlor, dining room, living quarters, and four guest rooms upstairs, the inn also had a small stable. The current owners were a middle-aged couple who ran the place along with a maid and a stable lad. Once Sophia and I had agreed on our choice, I approached the owner and asked him his best price. He proposed fourteen hundred thalers but said he wanted to continue until he was sixty, in three years' time. When I offered him fifteen hundred, he began to waver; sixteen hundred was enough to secure an immediate sale.

Three weeks later, at the start of July, the new owners of the Red Lion moved in.

Like most laymen, I suppose I'd imagined the life of an innkeeper to be one of relaxed banter with my patrons and a beer whenever I fancied it. The reality was somewhat different and even our small establishment required considerable work to keep it running. I found myself assailed by dozens of questions every day: from myself, from Sophia, from the staff, from the customers.

How many kegs do we need to order for his week? How many beef pies shall we buy, how much pork? Do we charge the same for a donkey as for a horse? Is there sufficient hay in the stables?

Should we paint the parlor? Who shall we hire to mend the bed in room two? Does this Dunkel taste strange?

And so it went on. Our maid was a woman of about thirty years named Lyse. Clearly dismayed by the swift sale and her change of employer, she was initially so reticent and unhelpful that Sophia and I considered dismissing her. However, she had been at the Red Lion for ten years and could answer many of the questions we could not. With this in mind, I gave her one last chance in the form of a pay rise. We couldn't really afford it but the measure had the desired effect. There remained some underlying tension between Lyse and Sophia but over the weeks even this was ironed out. Our stable lad, Bruno, was not the sharpest tool in the box but he fulfilled his duties well enough.

One of my most taxing tasks had nothing to do with the inn at all. This was the job of turning an aristocrat into a convincing innkeeper's wife. Outward appearance we dealt with by attiring her in pleasant – but unexceptional – dresses which she gradually became accustomed to. Although unafraid of hard work, Sophia retained the manner of one who issues orders and expects to receive the utmost respect at all times. Unfortunately, such respect is not always forthcoming from the patrons of an inn, who are often inebriated. Though rarely insulted, she endured the japes, rough talk, and colorful language typical of a public parlor. On several occasions, she delivered outraged rebukes that drew far too much attention to her refined voice. This I knew would be difficult to change but I at least convinced her not to raise that voice too often.

Before taking over the inn, I had spent a good many hours creating a convincing story for the pair of us: we were from the distant enclave of Minden, sweethearts who had escaped families resistant to our marriage due to our difference in age. Like most Prussians, the residents of Kassel were parochial, insular folk. My aim was that they should ascribe any perceived strangeness about the two new arrivals to our origins in Minden, a territory acquired under the Peace of Westphalia at the end of the Thirty Years' War.

Sophia did not have my experience in convincing others of elaborate falsehoods and was often put to the test by Lyse, who once on friendly terms, subjected us to a barrage of inquiries. There were a few stumbles – even the odd one by myself – but in many ways, our curious maid did us a great favor, for we solidified our false narrative and were better prepared for future interrogations.

For the first few weeks, there were many such inquiries but as summer turned to autumn, our new life in Kassel began to settle down. One fine September day, the previous owners returned and I was able to tell them – truthfully – that we were breaking even. The gentleman offered to look at the books with me and reckoned the local brewery was taking advantage of my inexperience. Armed with this knowledge, I visited them the next week and negotiated a small reduction that soon helped us turn a profit.

With the initial flurry of activity over, Sophia and I had time to reflect on the circumstances that had brought us here.

I still struggled with guilt. Time and time again I saw poor Hans fall back into the mud, his life extinguished in an instant. Almost as bad as that was what I imagined: my other compatriots lying bloodied on the sodden ground, flesh torn by the blades of the Jagers.

Any hatred I still felt for Wolfgang was subsumed within this guilt and I barely gave him a thought. In quiet moments, I sometimes found it hard to enjoy myself; for I knew that the other Lucky Thieves had found no such peace. It was I who had led them across Prussia for so long, taken risk after risk. And it was I who had signed their death warrants with one stupid mistake.

Sophia was not as used to swift changes of circumstances as I was; then again, who could be? I knew that she enjoyed our moments together and I believe she gradually began to exact some satisfaction from her new role. She told me as much, especially as I left many of the day-to-day affairs to her. But I watched her walking the banks of the river, or gazing from her bedroom window and I knew all was not well.

Again, how could it be? I don't believe there is any right-minded person capable of leaving their home and loved ones behind without great difficulty. From our discussions, I gleaned that she loved her parents but did not like them. But Sophia had also abandoned three brothers and a sister, and one of those brothers had fought illness for much of his life. Unlike me, she had not survived years of separation and isolation. She denied it, partly out of kindness to me, I suppose, but I could see she was not doing well.

We were in love – of that there was no doubt – and the happiest moments of my life were spent with my darling Sophia. But in my heart, I knew that we would not grow old together. For while our feelings were real our lives were not. I knew she would eventually leave me. Would it be years? Months? Weeks?

I doubt most would have been able to live like this. But uncertainty had dominated my adult years and I was often able to simply enjoy life at the Red Lion for as long as it lasted.

Winter is generally a difficult time for innkeepers. The roads turn to mud, travel becomes less frequent and most folks have fewer coins to spend on beer or wine. We'd been warned about this and had thankfully managed to put aside a bit to see us through. The winter of 1748 was a particularly harsh one in Hesse, and there were not many days in November and December when snow did not fall.

Personally, I enjoyed it. With fewer patrons and guests, we were easily able to cope with our workload. Even the streets of Kassel were often impassable; with the result that we all spent much of our time indoors. Evenings entailed a simple dinner with Sophia, and then retiring to our room, where we would sit together in front of the hearth. I had reacquainted myself with cigars and often enjoyed one after a meal. Like me, Sophia was a voracious reader and, when not engaged with a book, we would practice our French. I dread to think how many bottles of brandy we got through in those months. Though used to far more refined forms of alcohol, Sophia acquired quite a taste for it. We would often retire to bed rather tipsy, and more often than not we made love.

I did fear that Sophia would fall pregnant. Had I been assured of our long-term future, this would not have concerned me. Perhaps a child would have brought us even closer, but I did not wish to trap her in a situation that – whatever our feelings – was not of her own making. I also felt that I had enough responsibility in life. I did not feel cut out for fatherhood.

One evening, Sophia presented me with a bronze ring inscribed with the words, 'I love you.' It was a humble gift from a princess but by tradition, I was required to buy one for her. The following day, we exchanged them and, from that day forth, wore them with pride.

At that time, Kassel was known for its winter market. As Christmas approached, the weather improved and the roads cleared. Gradually, more visitors arrived. Our rooms were full and, even in our position on the edge of town, we benefited from the market's popularity. On the 20th of December, I found myself manning the bar. My interest in people had never left me and the experience of observing our many customers and guests was as intriguing as I'd anticipated.

And on this particular day, we were hosting a party of well-to-do farmers from the surrounding area. They had called in at the Red Lion on their way home from the market and were very excited about the party of nobles they had seen in the city. This group was apparently from Potsdam and included a high-ranking officer who had become famous for his crime-fighting escapades.

His name: Lieutenant-General Horst Von Munchow.

Chapter Eighteen

I could not resist the temptation to see the face of my nemesis. Despite an enmity that now stretched back many years, I had never actually set eyes upon the man. Knowing that Sophia would not approve, I retrieved one of my disguises from my trusty knapsack. Changing my appearance in the stable, I slipped away from the inn clad in the ragged robes of a vagrant.

Wishing I had at least brought some gloves, I tucked my cold hands into the pockets of my tatty smock and headed for the center of Kassel. The winter market took up most of the great square and there were countless stalls selling roasted meat, fruitcake, spiced wine, and other seasonal offerings. I walked between them unnoticed, peering out from beneath my hood for any sign of the general.

One could ask why did I care? What difference did it make to see the man's face? But Von Munchow's determination to see the Lucky Thieves brought to justice had cost the lives of my compatriots and best friend. It was more than curiosity.

Initially, I found no trace of the visiting nobles within the square. Expanding my search, I walked the surrounding streets, again with no success. At one stage, I spotted a well-dressed party attended to by many servants but these turned out to be a visiting delegation from Ravensburg.

The sky was beginning to darken as I stood on a corner, considering if I should head home. It was then that the door of a nearby church opened and a stream of people emerged. As with most churches, the worshipers were a broad mix from various levels of society. Once the initial surge had passed, a large group appeared at a stately speed. My eyes were immediately drawn to the blue greatcoats and yellow cuffs of several high-ranking army officers. Once beyond the church's arched entrance, they all put on their blue three-cornered hats. There must have been a dozen of them, some with wives and children in tow.

I subtly drifted towards the group, my eyes examining their upper arms, searching for the insignia that would mark out a lieutenant general. In fact, I never needed it. Despite the setting, the behavior of the officers made it quite clear who the senior man was. The group was deciding where to go for dinner, and I heard one man addressed several times as 'general'.

Von Munchow could only have been a high-ranking Prussian officer. Tall, lean, with a hawk-like nose and a monocle covering his right eye, he placed his hands behind his back and listened placidly to various opinions on where the best dining in Kassel was to be found. He appeared at first glance almost a bookish character but, looking closer, I noted his veiny, powerful hands and the angular hardness of his face. I guessed we were of a similar age. I imagined that he thought criminals like me the most detestable creatures in existence: those who dared to challenge and ignore the rigid strictures of the state in which we'd both been born.

I expected to feel more anger towards the man; an urge to lash out and seek revenge. It did not come; yet I was glad I had seen him, glad to lay this particular ghost to rest.

A decision seemed to have been made. The ladies – most of whom wore furs – took the arms of their husbands as they made their way to their destination. I noticed now that there were not only children but quite a number of servants.

I don't know why I continued to follow them but it was a fateful decision. Having led a conventional existence for many months, I made an elementary mistake: I forgot my disguise and how it might appear to others. The party passed two watchmen who I did not see until it was too late. Spying me not far behind the wealthy folk, they made the obvious conclusion.

'You stop there,' said one, while the other came forward and put a hand on my arm. 'Turn out your pockets. Quickly now.'

That might have been the end of it. The watchmen would have found nothing and Von Munchow's group would have continued on, oblivious. But fate had conspired against me and it was at that moment that my 'wife' also appeared.

'Leave him be,' said Sophia, hurrying across from the other side of the street.

'Stay out of it, miss,' replied one of the watchmen.

'He's my husband,' said Sophia, as forceful as ever.

'What?' answered the other man loudly. 'This filthy swine?'

Sophia turned her attention to me. 'What are you doing, Christian? Nobody knew where you'd gone. I was worried.'

'It's all right,' said I, trying to calm the situation. But as I glanced towards the general's party, I saw that some of the attendants and children had stopped and turned around. People do love a spectacle.

The most voluble of the watchmen seemed fixated on the idea that Sophia and I were married. 'This is your husband? Really?'

The argument did not get any further.

'Sophia?'

I looked over my shoulder and saw one of the richly attired noblewomen walking towards us, her fair face frowning. 'Sophia Christine?'

Eyes fixed with fear, Sophia turned away, which only encouraged the lady to come closer.

'Sophia Christine?'

An older woman spoke up from behind her. 'Not of the Thurns and Taxis?'

'It's her, I'm sure of it, though she's colored her hair. We attended finishing school in Paris together. Sophia, why won't you'

Von Munchow was already on the move, hand upon his sword as he marched towards us.

'Young lady, show your face!' But then he saw me, and when our eyes met, I knew the time for pretense was over.

Tearing myself from the watchman's grip, I sprinted away down the street.

***

I knew the center of Kassel well. Three swift turns along alleyways and I felt certain I had gained some distance. But as I burst onto another street, I looked back to see that Von Munchow's long strides had kept him close. I reckoned my best chance of losing him was to head for the nearby Schonfeld Park, especially as the darkness would come soon. I tripped on the cobbles and felt sure I would go down but with flailing arms I somehow kept my balance. I was lucky but my fortune did not last long.

Twenty paces along the street, I passed a pair of garrison soldiers on horseback. Other than shouting at me to slow down, they did nothing as I bolted past. But then I heard Von Munchow hailing them.

'Get down!' he cried. 'Give me your mount!'

Within moments, I heard the clatter of hooves behind me and I knew I had to once again leave the street. I passed an alley, another, and then one better suited to my purpose. For beside this one was a stack of four cages, each containing a chicken. As I entered the alley, I pulled the stack over, creating an obstacle. Realizing that the alley was probably too narrow for a horse in any case, I pressed on, determined to make the most of this advantage. But I could already feel myself tiring; my daily life of light work and drinking had done little for my physical condition.

Upon reaching the next street, I ran to the left, sure I was no more than a quarter-mile from Schonfeld Park. Darting around a group of children petting a dog, I sprinted between two carts and round a bend, now passing rows of houses on both sides. I could hear the hooves but they sounded considerably further away.

Breathing hard, the cold air bitter in my throat, I took two more turns before I could see the park ahead of me. I was onto the grass and heading for the closest trees when I heard a rider behind me once more.

Hooves on grass make considerably less noise than hooves on stone, so I did not notice the second horse until a few moments later. It flashed towards me from the left and before I knew it, had cut off my path to the trees. Glancing behind me, I saw the other mounted soldier now slowing to a trot.

Ahead of me, sword in hand was Lieutenant-General Von Munchow, a triumphant grin upon his face.

'The benefits of local knowledge – the corporal guessed you'd head for the park. You'll not lose me a third time, king of thieves.' He pronounced the term with hissing disdain and now aimed the tip of his sword at me. 'Turn and run if you wish. I am a cavalry officer – it would give me great pleasure to give pursuit and cut you down.'

Of that, I had no doubt. I raised my hands in surrender.

All that followed was hell.

I spent only one day in Kassel, languishing alone in a prison cell until I was dispatched to Berlin. I was transported inside a barred wagon along with two other prisoners and the three-day trip was as awful as I'd known. My criminal company, however, did not concern me; for I was wholly preoccupied by guilt at my remarkable stupidity. Several times I dashed my head back against the interior of the wagon to punish myself. My two fellow prisoners – both robbers – had initially questioned me, having heard I was the King of Thieves. When I hurt myself and drew blood, they left me alone.

All I could see was the panicked expression on Sophia's face as I'd fled. None of this was her fault. Why on earth had I felt this compulsion to see Von Munchow? To follow him? It was almost as if, somewhere deep inside, I wanted to be caught. Whatever had led me to this course of action, I felt sure that I would now pay for the choice with my life. My enemies had me in their possession now; and an opportunity to convict and execute one of the most infamous criminals in Prussian history.

Once in Berlin, I was taken immediately to an isolated cell. It was at least equipped with a bed and a small window, though this faced nothing more than a brick wall. I had been there less than an hour when four guards burst in. Handling me roughly, they dragged me along a corridor then down into a cellar illuminated by half a dozen lanterns. We descended a steep staircase and, once at the bottom, I shivered with fear.

Before me were two devices of torture. Though I had never seen either, I knew I was looking upon a wheel and a rack.

'Oh God no,' said I, unable to move under the fierce grip of the guards. 'Good afternoon,' said a voice from behind me. The guards shifted me aside as a small figure descended the stairs. I doubt he was more than five feet, dressed in the same drab attire as the guards.

'I am Assistant Warder Roth. You are Christian Gottlieb Mayer – a thief, correct?'

This was the pseudonym I had used in Kassel; one of many.

'They call him The King of Thieves,' said a guard.

'Do they now?'

Apart from his jagged, rotten teeth, Roth was an anonymous, bland presence; the type of man one would not normally notice or remember. I have never forgotten that face, for it is what I saw immediately before and after they hurt me.

'Well,' said Roth jauntily, 'as we are dealing with royalty, we must at least afford our guest a choice.' He gestured to the torture devices. 'Which is it to be, Your Majesty?'

The guards laughed.

I pleaded with Roth to spare me. I told him I had committed no violence; that I had stolen only from the rich and given to the poor.

'We do not deal with legal matters down here,' said he. 'Only practical matters. So, I ask again, which is it to be?'

Sweat poured from my back, my armpits, and my brow. I was utterly alone here; without defense. 'Please, you don't need to do this. I confess, I confess to it all. You don't need to

Roth stepped towards me. 'These measures are necessary to ensure the truthfulness of your confession.' His words sounded well-rehearsed. I was not sure if he believed them. 'And your suffering will help purify you in the eyes of God.'

'God?' said I. 'What god would allow this?'

Roth smiled. 'He has been allowing it for years. Centuries, in fact. I shall make this very clear for you – if you do not choose one, you shall endure both.'

'How? How can I decide?'

'That depends – what do you value more: your limbs or your back?'

I chose the rack, calculating that it was better to spread the load – and the pain – across my body.

All but my underclothes were removed and I was placed, face upward, upon the timbers of the machine. As they forced me down, I tried to resist but one of the guards drew a sword and held the tip close to my neck. My wrists and ankles were bound, the ropes attached to the rollers at either end of the rack. The guards followed the calm, precise directions of Herr Roth, who had clearly done this many times before.

I pleaded with them again, even began to list my crimes, but they paid me no heed. I suppose one can get used even to the desperate invocations of a terrified man.

It is impossible to describe that suffering in words but I know that I screamed so loudly and for so long that my voice cracked and I was reduced to a whimper. With every inch that the rollers turned, I felt sure that my limbs would be ripped from the sockets. I imagined my broken body resembling an abandoned puppet, limp and lifeless.

It was the muscles in my right ankle that tore first. The fiery agony shot up my leg and I passed out immediately. When they roused me with water, Herr Roth was still there, looking impassively down at me.

***

The rollers began to turn again, the machine creaking and groaning. Then my left shoulder tore. I passed out again. When I awoke, I thanked God that I was back in my cell.

My guards told me that I was lucky no bones had been broken. For the next few days, I simply lay on the bed. The pain did lessen, helped in no small part by a delivery of brandy passed to me with a meal. Though the individual responsible never showed their face, I guessed it was some sympathetic soul or another admirer of the King of Thieves.

Chair, table, and writing implements were then placed in the cell and I was ordered to write out a full confession, detailing my criminal offenses and admitting my guilt. I gave no second thought to doing so, fearing that any refusal would result in another appointment with Herr Roth. The process of writing it all down was an odd one. After describing each episode and crime, I paused to reflect on my choices. None had been as bad as the one that had led me here.

Having not seen a single other inmate, I realized I was being kept away from the other prisoners. When I asked for information, my guard told me only that I was to be held there while the crown prepared its case against me. He could not tell me how long this might take though he added, with a smile, that they were moving things especially quickly for me. I asked repeatedly if I could write to Sophia but was refused.

A week passed. Two. Though the pain in my limbs was bearable now, I was still hobbling around and my aching shoulder disturbed my sleep. My situation seemed hopeless and I suppose I could have hanged himself: they had left me my belt, after all. But for all my failings, I am not a man to ever give up hope. I had escaped so many dire situations; perhaps I could do so again.

Then came a visitor.

CHAPTER EIGHTEEN

I was given no warning and woke from an uneasy sleep to find the door open. A guard – armed with a cudgel on his belt like all of them – beckoned me forward then stopped me at the doorway. Two more guards were stationed just outside and there, sitting casually on a chair, was Lieutenant General Horst Von Munchow.

'Good afternoon, to you, Christian.'

I stood there, still dazed, gazing past the officer at the corridor behind him. Even that dour tunnel of stone seemed appealing. I had never been imprisoned before and only now was I beginning to understand the brutal power of incarceration.

Von Munchow adjusted his monocle and crossed his legs, his polished leather boots gleaming under lamplight.

'I would say Herr Gottlieb Mayer but, though you signed your confession as such, we both know that's not your real name.'

I was determined not to give it. I did not want my family involved.

'No matter. The end result will be the same. It's interesting – one seldom hears even the chattering classes speak of you in glowing terms these days. That tends to happen when one is responsible for abduction and murder.'

'Murder?'

'What else would you call it?' Von Munchow's expression darkened.

Two of my men killed by your cohorts, another has lost his leg – simply for fulfilling their oaths to uphold the law. Only god knows how many others have suffered at your hands.'

My weariness left me suddenly. For all my many faults, I could not tolerate such falsehoods and misrepresentations.

'And how many have gained?' said I. 'We took from those who could afford it and gave to those who had nothing.'

'Those who could afford it? Does that include my soldiers? Men who were about to risk their lives for their country while cowards like you skulked around the countryside?' Von Munchow suddenly leaped to his feet. 'How dare you lecture me, you thieving dog!' He advanced as close as the doorway, one gloved fist now clenched.

I replied quietly. 'Lieutenant-General, I know I have led a criminal life; and I suppose I should have known that this day would come. But I am no murderer.'

Von Munchow drew in a long breath through the wide nostrils of his prominent nose. 'Tell me something. What were you doing in Kassel? Why were you following my party?'

'I was curious. Our paths had crossed at Altenburg. You hunted us in the Harz. A stupid mistake.'

'Your last one, I should think. By god, man, buying an inn with the poor princess – what have you done to the girl?'

'Nothing,' said I. 'She remained with me of her own free will. It was not I that abducted her but Wolfgang Schmidt, the man who betrayed us. I suspect you know that. I also suspect he won't be seeing the inside of a courtroom.'

The general gave a thin smile. 'Your lecture extends to the use of underhand tactics? You wrote the book.'

I couldn't think of much to say to that. I had more pressing concerns than trying to score points against my foe.

'The princess. Might I send a letter?'

The officer shook his head in disbelief. 'What makes you think she wants to correspond with you?'

'Does she?'

Von Munchow cleared his throat. 'If I were you, I would concern myself with my own fate. Do you not realize that, as we speak, a wealth of evidence is being assembled? From myself and many, many others.'

I felt sure the crown had more than enough to guarantee a verdict of guilt; in fact, I suspected I could have been convicted solely on the evidence of the man standing before me.

'I have given my confession. I will continue to give the court whatever it asks for. Does that not deserve some small gesture in return? Sophia is … all I have in the world.'

For once, I saw a glimpse of uncertainty – perhaps even humanity – on the general's face.

I continued: 'General, will you allow a letter from me to be delivered? If Sophia does not reply, if she wants nothing more to do with me – so be it. But if she replies, I would like to correspond. Is it really so much to ask?'

'I'll have to consult the presiding judge and the king's representative.'

'I understand. Sir, my men – those killed in the forest. What happened to them?'

'They were buried out there. Unmarked graves. But I ensured a priest was present. All was conducted properly.'

That at least gave me a little peace of mind. 'Thank you. Do you have any idea when my case will be called?'

'No. But you will be assigned an advocate soon. By the way, I've asked His Majesty for you to be tried in a military court. I shall see you there.'

Lieutenant General Von Munchow did not get his way. Fortunately for me, the king was at that time seeking to modernize our antiquated system of justice, much of which had not changed in centuries. One of these changes was to reduce the influence of the army over judicial affairs and, when my advocate was eventually assigned to me a month later I learned that I would be tried in a regular provincial court in Berlin. The date was set for the first week of March.

By that time, I had exchanged half a dozen letters with Sophia. I often found myself gazing at the ring she had given me and I was immensely touched to find that she wished to stand by me. That did not stop me from trying to persuade her to do otherwise. Nobody could expect any outcome other than my execution and I suggested that she return home to her family at once. She had closed the Red Lion and refused to admit anyone, though she had communicated with her parents.

I realized that I'd underestimated her love for me, which only worsened the guilt over my senseless act of sabotage. I was profoundly grateful to have at last experienced true love in my life but I did not wish to further Sophia's suffering. In every letter, I advised her to give in. She was still a young woman with much to look forward to. As the trial approached, I sensed that her resolve was beginning to weaken.

My advocate was a lawyer named Herr Fischer. He was an experienced man, well-practiced in defending criminals, and I appreciated his frankness regarding my chances. He listened patiently to my pleas about stealing only from the rich and always avoiding violence where I could, but we both knew the judge would be under tremendous pressure to declare me guilty. All my offenses could be proven (including by my own confession) and I faced more than two dozen counts of theft, several of assaulting officers of the law, and one of kidnapping. Herr Fischer had at least succeeded in persuading the judge to remove the charge of conspiracy to murder. This was related to the two soldiers killed by my men, the advocate successfully arguing that I had fled the conflict and not drawn a weapon. In agreeing, the judge ruled that the assault charges would remain. Such are the vagaries of the law.

CHAPTER EIGHTEEN

Arriving at the courtroom on March 3rd, 1749, I was escorted through a substantial crowd several hundred in number. There were numerous soldiers present but that did not stop some cheering my arrival and shouting greetings. A few brave souls even offered their support:

'Keep up your spirits!'

'You're a hero to the working people!'

'Spare the King of Thieves!'

Though buoyed by these sentiments, I took care to react only with solemn nod: I could not give the court another reason to make an example of me.

The courtroom itself was an austere, high-roofed, wood-paneled chamber. At the near end were rows of benches, and then came the tables for advocates, officials, and the accused. Raised several feet above us all was the judge's position, upon the wall behind it the royal seal of the Hohenzollern house as well as municipal and provincial flags. I already knew from Herr Fischer that the trial would be closed to the public, yet every seat was full. It seemed that my case was not only of interest to the common people, for I noted many high-ranking officers and administrators.

Hands chained, I took up my position beside my lawyer at our bench. The guards sat just behind me and the walls were lined with at least two-dozen soldiers – perhaps they feared the King of Thieves would attempt yet another escape. Despite my low spirits, old habits had led me to look out for opportunities but I'd seen few at the prison and none here. The state of Prussia was not taking any chances.

'Is the general here?' I asked Herr Fischer.

'I didn't notice him,' replied the advocate quietly. 'I believe I spotted Eichel though – a cabinet secretary and one of the king's most trusted men. I imagine he will report back personally to His Majesty.'

I could not help feeling a tinge of pride that King Frederick was interested in my trial. The feeling faded rapidly when I reflected on what I knew of his character: a ruthless, aggressive leader who demanded discipline and order above all else. Surely a popular criminal like me was a dangerous flame he would be happy to see extinguished.

My expectations were not improved by the opening remarks of the judge: a man who appeared to be at least seventy and regarded me with a withering glare. He gave me one final chance to admit my true name and date of birth and, when I refused, declared that this would count against me. I felt sure that the only person who could have revealed my true origins was Wolfgang Schmidt and, as he had not yet done so, I hoped this would remain the case. I wondered if part of his arrangement with Von Munchow involved him disappearing – in order not to detract from the glory of the general's victory.

The trial then commenced and for four consecutive days I heard evidence against me. Much of it was presented in the form of written testimony but there were also personal appearances from selected witnesses. These included Von Munchow and some of his staff and the now aged Countess Zulich, who had of course never recovered her emerald.

In total, over thirty cases were discussed and I must concede that the chief prosecuting lawyer and his subordinates did an impressive job of corroboration and proving my guilt beyond doubt. He was also clever in not trying to associate me with violent offenses until he came to the events that transpired in Goslar and the Harz forest. At this point, none other than the Prince of Thurn and Taxis was called to offer his testimony. The poor man was moved to tears as he described the fear and uncertainty that he had suffered for days, weeks, and months. The prosecutor accurately contended that I'd had several opportunities to free Sophia but that I'd been more interested in saving my own skin.

I wondered if she would hear of all this back in Kassel.

The Prince concluded his statement by claiming that I had turned Sophia against her own flesh and blood; manipulated a poor girl who had been abducted and intimidated. When dismissed from the stand, the Prince stood and pointed his finger at me, eyes raging.

He was not the last witness, for my accusers had one last card to play. She was the wife of one of the soldiers killed by my men in the gorge: a young soldier with a newborn daughter he would never see. I wept at her every word.

By that stage, I simply wished for the trial to end and for the judge to pass the sentence. When the time came for Herr Fischer to offer my defense, he sensibly made no attempt to deny my crimes. What he did do, with some success, was to compare me with other notorious robbers who'd left a trail of violence and death in their wake. He'd decided not to mention the Lucky Thieves' charitable efforts because he felt any attempt to distract from my proven guilt would anger the judge, not to mention the wealthy, influential victims observing the trial.

Herr Fischer had informed me that I was entitled to speak briefly in my own defense but advised me strongly not to do so. Yet when he sat down, I felt a need to say a few words, if only for my own satisfaction.

The advocate tried to dissuade me but I would not be denied. He passed on the request to the judge who was compelled by the law to grant it. I cleared my throat and stood.

'Your honor, I thank you for allowing me to address the court. I have confessed to my crimes of robbery. I have not confessed to assault or murder for I have never owned a weapon nor struck another man in my life. But I have caused great suffering: of that, there is no doubt, and I offer my profound apologies to all those affected. Beyond that, I wish only to say this: in religious terms, I have sinned. In moral terms, I have done much that is bad. But I have also done some good – helped many less fortunate than myself. If I am … allowed the opportunity …I will endeavor to lead a better life, continue on that path, and leave criminality behind forever. Your honor, I ask for clemency.’

Chapter Nineteen

Alone in my cell, awaiting the verdict, I prayed for the first time in many years. I admitted the very sins I'd mentioned in court and repeated my pledge to change my ways. Yet I suspected I was long lost to the Almighty – what reason did he have to heed me?

I knew the very best I could expect was life imprisonment. A terrible prospect and yet now, with the verdict and the knowledge of my fate so close, I was not ready to die. Perhaps I held out hope that I would one day be freed, or that I might find some way to escape. Beyond that, I could not stand the thought that I would never see my loved ones again: not Sophia, not my mother. No one.

My fear drove me on. I remained at prayer all night, and I repeated my pleas again and again until finally a shaft of morning light speared my cell.

March 13th, 1749. The crowds outside the court had increased in number and again there was not a spare seat to be found within. Exhausted by my sleepless night and gripped by fear, I could not stop my hands from shaking, which caused the chains to rattle. Herr Fischer did his best to calm me but I simply could not help myself. Thankfully, the judge did not tarry. Fingers held together like a steeple, eyes cold, he looked out at the court and delivered the verdict.

'Let it be known that I have considered all the evidence and testimony presented to this court. In the name of our Lord and His

Majesty King Frederick of Prussia, I now pass sentence on Christian Gottlieb Mayer. The defendant is charged with twenty-eight counts of theft, one of kidnapping, four of assault. In all charges, the defendant is pronounced guilty. The sentence is to be execution by hanging on the last day of this month.' The judge turned calmly to the chief of guards. 'Take him away.'

***

Three hangings were to take place on a single day. Lieutenant General Von Munchow was not present but I detected his hand in the way proceedings unfolded. For I was made to wait in another holding cell that faced directly onto the prison's rear courtyard. It was here; in this cold, empty square that Prussia eliminated traitors, spies, and criminals.

My execution was scheduled for eleven o'clock; two others would occur at nine and ten. In the minutes before nine, I could hear the preparations being made for the first hanging. My cell was entirely bare and I sat in one corner, determined not to witness what I would soon face.

In my pocket was the last letter I would ever receive from Sophia Christine. Tear-stained and written in a chaotic hand, the princess explained that she had at last given in and returned to Regensburg and her family. I was glad to learn that she did not blame them for the sentence, for, in fact, her father was not one of the many influential figures (all victims of mine) who had petitioned the judge. It gave me great solace to know that Sophia would enjoy the support of her family as she attempted to rebuild her life.

She ended her letter by declaring her love and telling me we would meet again in heaven. That was all I could hope for now. Folding the letter carefully, I placed it in my shirt pocket with Sophia's bronze ring.

I heard shouted orders from the courtyard. Despite my determination, a morbid fascination drew me to the small, barred window. Looking out, I saw the first prisoner being escorted towards the gallows. I knew from the guards that he was a murderer. The second man to die was not only that but a rapist. I could not stand the thought that I was considered the same as these men.

Watching on from in front of the gallows was a small party that included Assistant Warder Roth. He seemed unperturbed by the occasion, and now blithely bent down to wipe something from his boot.

The prisoner did not resist as he was taken up the steps. The executioner was a white-haired fellow who positioned the condemned man above the trapdoor then placed the hood over his head. When the noose was put around his neck and pulled tight, the prisoner clasped his hands. I guessed he was praying.

When the executioner was satisfied, he left the guards and walked solemnly down the steps towards the lever that would open the trapdoor.

I could not watch anymore. I returned to my corner and a few seconds later heard the thud of the trapdoor. Then came silence then the mundane, chilling sounds of the aftermath. I imagined them removing the body, preparing the noose and the gallows for the next man.

I heard footsteps outside my cell, the clink of the key in the door. Was it my turn? Had the order changed? Would I be the next to hang?'

When the door opened, I was surprised to see Herr Fischer standing there, a single guard accompanying him. The advocate was holding a piece of paper, which he showed to me as he stepped into the cell.

'From Eichel. One was sent to us, another to the chief warder.'

Looking down, I saw the letter was marked with the official stamp of King Frederick.

'By God, Christian, His Majesty has intervened. We can only thank the Almighty that the post reached us in time.' Herr Fischer gripped my arm. 'It seems that King Frederick has followed your career and that your speech moved him. You have been spared, Christian. You have been spared.'

The realization that I would live had just begun to sink in when I was transferred. Perhaps only a condemned man could feel relief upon learning that he will spend the rest of his life behind bars. My destination was Stettin, capital of Western Pomerania, and a city some eighty miles northeast of Berlin. Chained to five other prisoners, I endured the week-long journey inside another covered wagon. The vehicle was airless and stuffy but, after only my first day at Stettin, I longed for such cleanliness and security.

The building was in fact an old fortress dating back to the Thirty Years' War, not a place designed to house over three hundred inmates. Within dank, stonewalled cells crawling with rats and lice, dwelt some of the toughest, most vicious, and venal individuals in all Prussia. There were no individual cells, but a series of dark, poorly ventilated dungeons. None of these was wider than twenty feet yet most contained a dozen men.

Upon arrival, every prisoner gave up his existing clothes and was issued with underwear, socks, two pairs of trousers, two shirts, and one smock, all of the most inferior quality imaginable. I now arrived with only three objects to my name: Sophia's ring and my two good leather boots. Once attired in my new clothes, I was also issued with a single blanket.

News of my arrival had preceded me and as I was escorted down into the dungeons by the guards, one of whom announced me as, 'The King of Thieves'. I knew a little of what such places were like and did not react with any enthusiasm to the shouts and welcomes that greeted me. I suspected that for every man that considered me a hero, there would be another jealous of my infamy, and another who wondered what I'd done with all my treasure. Yet I was also aware that I would need friends, and that I couldn't afford to entirely forgo the goodwill afforded me by my reputation.

There were, I believe, twenty-six 'cells' spread across three floors of the dungeon. The bottom floor was below ground; and therefore, the darkest, coldest and most beset by vermin. It was traditional for the most dangerous and disruptive prisoners to be housed there. The other two floors were broadly similar though the highest did have shutters upon the windows, which kept out a little cold in the winter months.

I was initially accommodated on the middle floor and the guards chose the cell purely based on the current number of inhabitants. The front consisted of iron bars sunk into the stone and a single wooden door. Once this was unlocked, I was shoved inside to meet my cellmates. Fortunately, the sun had not yet set and I could at least see my fellow prisoners.

A more filthy, wretched, and frightening group is difficult to imagine. Everyone one of them stank and all were clothed in attire fit only for burning. Razors were not allowed and so every man sported a beard to match his shaggy head of hair. All in all, I'm not sure that a tribe of prehistoric men would have looked much different.

'Good day,' said I, feeling that, whatever the audience, a cordial greeting was never wasted.

There were frowns and stares and grunts. But one man, a tall, slender fellow, came forward.

'The King of Thieves.'

I waved my hand dismissively, 'A ridiculous term. Especially in current circumstances.' This at least raised a few smiles so I continued. ‘Then again, assuming the guards are prepared to act as my servants, perhaps we can arrange a banquet for this evening. Roast pig anyone? French champagne? Dancing girls?’

Quite a few laughs though some were evidently resistant to my charms.

The tall fellow offered his hand. ‘I suppose I shouldn’t be surprised that you don’t recognize me. Name’s Richter. Curt Richter.’

The other occupants of the cell were all watching. I was very glad to have an associate here but I simply did not remember the man.

‘Perhaps you recall the name of my chief – Fuchs. Remember the mine? The chocolate?’

‘Ah yes, of course.’ I shook Richter’s hand. At that time, we had been near-enemies and yet, in this forsaken place, he counted as a friend. ‘And what brings you here?’

‘Fuchs made a mess of things. A month or two after Goslar we ran into an army patrol while moving some iron. The others were killed. I got ten years. We heard you’re here for the duration.’

This was still not a concept I could really grasp but I nodded nonetheless.

‘Got any money? Anything for the guards? We can buy and barter food.’

I wanted to be very clear on this point so I turned out my pockets. ‘The bastards at Berlin took everything from me.’ I did not, however, mention Sophia’s ring, which I kept in a boot.

Another man came forward. ‘Weren’t they going to hang you?’

‘They were. The king intervened on my behalf – saved me from the gallows.’

'Why?'

'Honestly, I have no idea.'

I was fortunate to find Curt Richter in that cell. There were eleven of us; and while a few seemed ambivalent, a few interested to hear of my past adventures, there were also four who offered no friendly signal and seemed to eye me as a predator does prey.

I doubt the cell was more than eight paces from corner to corner. In one of those corners was a filthy hole, which functioned as a toilet. There were also four wooden pallets, which were claimed by the hostile inmates and positioned directly below the windows. The worst sleeping positions were of course close to the hole, and as Curt Richter and I were the newest arrivals, we were allocated them. After spending several hours exchanging news with him, I learned that there was no such thing as dinner at Stettin, only a single meal delivered in mid-morning.

There were only two lamps positioned just outside the cell so when the sun set, the chamber was cast into inky darkness. Despite the season, the stone of the fortress was eternally cold and seemed to sap any warmth from the body. The blanket made little difference. Having noted some jealous eyes upon my boots, I used them as a pillow and lay down beside Curt on the hard, icy floor, not expecting to sleep. But despite the occasional – and thoroughly unpleasant – interruptions of those using the hole, I somehow achieved a few hours' rest.

At dawn, we could at least get on our feet and move away from the stinking latrine. I put my shoes back on and soon found myself in a group with Curt and some of the other friendly fellows. In fearful whispers, they told me to stay well clear of two of the tough men in particular. This pair were acolytes of a man named Olbrecht, who was currently housed on the floor above. He had been an inmate at Stettin for more than a decade. He had a loyal brother in the nearby city who was able to exert some influence on the warders; and the members of his gang numbered at least a dozen, including the two in our cell. I was reliably informed that both were 'lifers' who had killed other inmates during their time. Apparently, the guards and some of the warders often turned a blind eye to most disputes and outbreaks of violence.

During my period of imprisonment in Berlin, I had in some way been able to prepare myself for isolation and boredom but not deprivation, disease, and danger. This was like being thrown into a bear-pit.

That first morning, I sampled one of the disgusting meals that somehow had to sustain me. When the cell door opened, the guards deposited a cauldron of soup, a pile of bowls, and a plate piled with bread. The majority of the prisoners held back for the four thugs to take their share, then divided up what was left. This meant that Carl and I received only half a bowl each and a piece of bread only three inches across. The crust of the bread was green with mold and the 'soup' was more like vegetable-flavored water. But I was hungry and I ate it all.

According to the long-term residents, Stettin prison rules iterated that we were permitted two hours of 'outdoor time' every day. But on my first day, we were not allowed out at all, and on the second day only for an hour. I learned that the warders and guards were paid an absolute pittance; hence their reluctance to work harder than was necessary. One lifer, who had apparently spoken to the chief warder a couple of times, said that he seemed like a decent man but always complained about a complete lack of funds from Berlin.

'Outdoor time' consisted of a walk around the prison's central courtyard, overseen by a dozen guards armed with muskets on which the bayonets remained attached. Though dirty and surrounded by brick, the octagonal courtyard was a veritable paradise compared to the dungeon cell. I spent a pleasant time gazing up at the clouds, imagining them floating south to Regensburg, perhaps over the residence of the Thurns and Taxis family.

I just hoped Sophia was doing well. In my discussions with Curt and the other prisoners, I had not mentioned my idyllic time with the princess.

After all, they would never have believed me.

On my third trip to the courtyard, I had the dubious pleasure of meeting the much-discussed Herr Olbrecht. It was the habit of most inmates to stretch their legs and four of us – Curt included – were pacing around at some speed. Diseases such as scabies and rickets were common at Stettin; and we knew our only protection against illness was our physical health. I have always been a comparatively slim man, but I had much more flesh on my bones than most of the malnourished inmates.

This could not be said of Olbrecht, who was short but quite plump. He was also bald, clean-shaven, and possessor of beady, keen eyes that instantly appraised me when his thugs ushered me to the corner where he sat. My two friends from the cell made themselves scarce but I was grateful to Curt for remaining beside me. I cannot claim to fully understand his motives in befriending me, nor that I particularly liked the man, but I believe we both understood the value of alliances during our early weeks at Stettin.

At least half of Olbrecht's gang seemed to be present, including the two thugs from my cell. There were guards on duty but they habitually left Olbrecht alone. I had previously seen other prisoners summoned to his bench – the only one in the yard – and it was always he that seemed to be doing the talking.

I was surprised when he shook my hand. 'Good day to you. Christian, isn't it? Werner Olbrecht.'

'Good day.'

'Do not be fearful,' said he, offering me a seat beside him. 'I daresay you've heard all manner of stories about me from some of these imbeciles. Small minds, every one – they don't think in grand terms like you and I.'

I chose not to point out that – despite his status – he dwelt within one of the most hellish holes in all Europe.

'Here.' Olbrecht took a clean-looking cloth from his jacket pocket. Contained within it were three small, juicy-looking apples.

'Take them. A welcome gift.'

I wasn't about to refuse the man and swiftly placed the fruit in the pocket of my shabby smock.

Curt looked on anxiously, flanked by the enforcers.

Olbrecht said, 'You don't look particularly wealthy.'

'That's because I'm not.'

Olbrecht grinned. 'It's certainly clear that you wish to give that impression.'

He was not the first to raise the question of my wealth. By now, newspaper reports of the trial had spread far and wide. There had always been well-known tales concerning the Lucky Thieves, particularly incidents like the theft of the Udaipur Emerald. But now anyone who could read, or knew someone who could, was aware that our earnings over decades amounted to tens of thousands of thalers.

'Not at all.' I gestured to my clothes. 'Unfortunately, this is all I have.'

Olbrecht nodded neutrally. 'Barring some unforeseen circumstance, you and I are stuck in this place until we die. Not good. But there's not good, and then there's terrible. Which would you prefer?'

'I would have thought that's fairly obvious.'

'Indeed.' Olbrecht tapped his hand against my knee. 'And I can make things better for you. A better cell. Better food and drink. A proper pallet with a straw mattress. Protection.'

'I understand. And I appreciate the offer but I'm not sure what I can offer in return.'

'I have contacts. People on the outside. I'm sure a man like you would have put a little away for a rainy day. Now's the time to use it.'

'Unfortunately, I've already used it. I spent every last pfennig on an inn. I've no idea who even owns it now.'

Olbrecht cleared his throat. 'I heard talk of bank accounts. *Dozens* of bank accounts. And all those gems – the emerald, for example.'

'All long gone, I'm afraid.'

I had spent much of my life telling lies. Now I was struggling to convince someone of the truth.

'But I am a man with a few skills. If you need anything and I can help, I'll be glad to do so.'

Though his disappointment was obvious, Olbrecht gestured for me to stand. 'We'll talk again, Christian. But do remember, you're a king no more.' He gestured around the yard. 'My kingdom is not much to look at … but it is mine.'

Chapter Twenty

The inescapable truth was that Olbrecht and I were on a collision course. Nothing more was said to me for some time but barely a minute passed in the dungeon cell when I felt free to speak. The two thugs, Huber and Neubold, were always watching me and they also used intimidation to wear me down. There was no direct violence but they seemed to enjoy standing close to me, knocking my bowl when I was eating, disturbing my sleep. No doubt their master had ordered all this.

Another week passed before he again requested my presence. Once more I suffered no actual violence but Olbrecht made it very clear that I needed to reconsider my response. No matter what I said, the man simply wouldn't accept that the King of Thieves did not possess some hidden fortune that he could now share in. I considered inventing a secret stash or a wealthy associate just to get him off my back but worried that the inevitable disappointment would enrage him.

In the meantime, I also came to understand the true extent of Olbrecht's reach at Stettin. One night we were woken by the sounds of a disturbance in an adjoining cell. The guards took an age to intervene but we all looked on as a man was eventually dragged past us, his face a bloody pulp. We later learned that he'd claimed a bottle of brandy intended for Olbrecht's men. The prison was equipped with an infirmary but there were no permanent staff; only a local surgeon who attended when required. The guards informed us that the poor fellow was in an awful state, with many bones broken and his face swollen beyond recognition.

Brandy was what made Olbrecht most of his money. The prisoners were allowed to spend their own funds on such extras and, while only a few had any of their own coins, many received visitors who would pass on a few groschens. In theory, drinking was not permitted but Olbrecht's tame guards delivered it and he charged the inmates three times the going rate. They were happy to pay, after all, a quarter bottle of strong liquor allowed them to temporarily forget the horror of their surroundings.

Weeks became months, and while the situation with Olbrecht did not improve, I at least became used to Stettin. There was so much to despise: the cold, the smell, the food, the lack of space. And yet, I did admire how the other 'lifers' made the best of such an awful situation; and their ways helped Curt Richter and me to cope. Most inmates had a small bag of possessions containing blankets, clothes, and other bits and pieces (many of them still had a pillow from the famous occasion when a group of nuns had delivered one for every man). Some had sets of cards and dice, which were cared for as if fashioned from gold. Stones or chips of cement were used as counters and, as well as the usual games, there were many imaginative variations. We prisoners spent countless hours so occupied, often recounting old adventures and comparing notes on places we'd visited.

There were also a few books in our cell and most of their owners were prepared to share them. In my first month, I read a German translation of Robinson Crusoe (for the third time) and an illustrated version of The Arabian Nights. There was even a favored location in the cell reserved for readers where, during certain hours, the light was favorable. More than once, I found myself displaced from this location by Olbrecht's enforcers.

Criminals are not generally great linguists so, from the more curious inmates, there was considerable interest in my language skills. I don't suppose many of them would have made the effort had they been elsewhere, but with so much time to kill, I found a few willing students. French seemed to be the most popular and I began to instruct a small group for about an hour every morning. The lack of writing materials was not a serious disadvantage because the majority of my students could not read or write. However, it seemed to me that we all benefited from the sense that this was not time entirely wasted, for the great boon of education is the element of progress, even for the least talented student.

But as winter approached, we had less time to concern ourselves with leisure and education. When the first snows came, the temperature dropped rapidly and it became utterly impossible to enjoy even a moment of warmth. At night, every man put on every single item of clothing he owned and wrapped himself in his blanket. Yet even though we were so covered and so densely packed, there was simply no defense. The old fortress seemed a single block of ice, every stone freezing to the touch; and it drained our strength by minute, hour, and day. Hot soup and shafts of winter sunlight were a blessing but we were so exhausted that we could barely summon the energy for conversation.

We lost two men from our cell to the cold that December. They had become coughing, shivering wrecks who could not get up or feed themselves. Others were also taken to the infirmary and a week later we heard that inmates had been assigned to a digging detail in the prison graveyard. Five had been buried and it had taken an entire morning to cut through the frozen soil.

That same day, I was summoned to Olbrecht as snow whipped across the courtyard. I'd begun to think he'd accepted the truth as his men had left me alone but I could see from his expression that he was in no forgiving mood. He sat on his bench in a fur-lined coat and I could not help jealously eyeing his leather gloves. Despite the clothes, his rotund face was as pinched and whitened by cold as the rest of us.

'I'll keep this brief, Christian. You have one last chance.'

'Herr Olbrecht, I do not know what more I can say. If I had *anything* to offer you, I would have done so long ago. My money is gone, my gang dead. There is *nothing*!'

'Not a single friend nor relative?'

'My only friends were my compatriots. I left my family decades ago. I have not spoken to a single one of them in years.'

Even in that perilous moment, I wondered if now was finally the time. Prisoners were permitted to send letters. I could address one to Kasebier's in Halle. Perhaps my parents would even answer.

But I could not bear the thought of going to them like this, begging for help, even though I was in dire need. I suppose it was pride.

'You have one week,' said Olbrecht.

My pride did not immediately cost me but there was a terrible consequence for the unfortunate Curt Richter. We were still on good terms but I was now as friendly with several other men in our cell, particularly those who enjoyed my language lessons. And yet Olbrecht clearly believed Curt was my main ally.

The day in question began comparatively well. The chief warder decided that we needed to be cleaned up before a Christmas visit from the Pietists. There was a large and very active community of these Christians in Stettin, as there was in Halle. They were committed to a practical form of Christianity and noted across Prussia for their charitable efforts.

Each cell was emptied in turn and the prisoners escorted down to the seldom-used washhouse, where we were stunned to discover cauldrons full of hot water. To a man we stripped off our filthy clothes, washing not only them but also our dirty, lice-ridden bodies with the brushes and soap provided. Unfortunately, we were not allowed to wait while our newly cleaned clothes dried. The guards had by now been faced with several sets of naked men ready to return to the cells and had solved the problem in a novel way.

There was a rare moment of hilarity as we trooped back to our cell, each man clad in a sack with holes cut out for our arms and heads. We were also glad to have acquired a new garment – something else to cover us at night. Spirits were so high that we almost forgot about the cold.

It was some time later that I realized Curt had not returned with us. And when I checked the rest of the inmates, I realized Olbrecht's two thugs were also missing. Then a guard arrived to ask if anyone had seen what happened. I hurried over to the bars and questioned him.

'What do you mean?'

'Richter was badly beaten – we found him outside the wash house.' 'How is he?'

'Didn't look good.'

I knew this guard to be one of the more honest fellows but he was in a minority. It was perfectly possible that some of his compatriots had turned a blind eye while Olbrecht's men did their work.

'Warder Strauss says that Huber and Neubold were responsible. They've been put into the hole.'

This was the deepest, darkest dungeon at Stettin. I was glad that justice had been done and that I would not have to share a cell with my enemies. None of that would help poor Curt.

'Please, find out what you can. If there's no one else at the infirmary, I can care for him.'

This was not permitted but Curt and the rest of us benefited from the arrival of the Pietists that Christmas. Their leader was a very forceful man who reminded me of some of the Pietists I had known back home. He soon succeeded in persuading Chief Warder Strauss to allow his people to assist in the infirmary and deliver very welcome gifts from their congregation. I do not believe I have ever seen a happier group of people than my fellow inmates when the guards delivered wicker baskets full of woolen blankets, gloves, scarves, and socks. Each man also received his own Christmas treat: a package which included fresh bread, a cut of roast beef, and – best of all – fruit cake.

Even better than all this, however, was the news that Curt was recovering well. We later heard from the guards that the pious visitors had even asked to preach to us but here the chief warder drew the line. I believe the only prisoner who didn't welcome their presence was Olbrecht, who now found his alcoholic monopoly temporarily broken.

For all the relief and merriment delivered by the Pietists, I knew my time was running out. If I wanted to avoid suffering the same fate as Curt, I had to give Olbrecht something. While my fellow inmates enjoyed their presents, I was busy planning.

Two days later, I went to see my enemy. He did not admit any involvement in the attack on Curt but I gave him the impression that I'd, at last, caved in to his demands. I told him that there was a single source of money still remaining, claiming that I'd left it as a final reserve in case I could escape prison. I passed on a long, complicated series of instructions that would purportedly lead to a strongbox buried at a remote location outside distant Weimar. The instructions did indeed lead to such a box but it had been dug up and emptied by the Lucky Thieves three years earlier. I told Olbrecht that the prize was worth at least a hundred thalers and made him swear to ensure I received a third of that money. I knew that the search would take a while to organize and execute, buying me precious time.

A week after our meeting, Curt Richter was at last released from the infirmary. I learned that the Pietists had cared well for him and though his face was still marked, he indeed seemed largely recovered. Despite my profound and repeated apologies, Curt kept his distance from me, for which I could not blame him. My other cell-mates did likewise, even though Olbrecht's enforcers had not yet returned.

I was fully aware that my deception might not save me. If my enemy wanted me killed, all it would take was the quick slice of a blade in the courtyard. No one would mourn me, nobody would investigate, and my body would join the others in the frozen ground of that bleak graveyard.

What I did have was a little time, and I used it constructively. I needed to give Olbrecht a problem that would distract him from me when he inevitably learned that there was nothing of value in Weimar. I had now been at Stettin for four months, and with more time on my hands, I was more observant than ever. When I could see into another cell, I did so. When I could get close to groups of inmates, I listened in. I hoped to identify another inmate who could provide a threat to Olbrecht and engineer some dispute that might prove sufficiently distracting. Unfortunately, his domination of the place seemed near complete and I was also concerned about landing some poor swine in a similar fix to my own.

When he disclosed to me – with a smug grin – that his associate had arrived in Weimar, I realized time was running very short. So, as I hadn't discovered an enemy for Olbrecht, I decided to invent one.

Though the Pietists had now moved on to other charitable causes, they had doled out some writing materials, which now became of use. I pilfered a pencil and paper and created two notes.

Both were identical: a list of those inmates I knew to be in Olbrecht's gang. There were over a dozen of them, and I randomly underlined four. I dropped the notes on the same day: one inside, one in the yard, reasonably confident that word would eventually reach my opponent. The next stage was designed to sow further confusion and suspicion. A day later, I dropped two more lists, this time listing ten guards. In this case, I underlined three, including Assistant Warder Steiger, who was known to be Olbrecht's main collaborator on the prison staff.

I could soon see that the lists had taken effect. Not only did I note intense discussions among Olbrecht's gang, but I heard numerous rumors of a spy in our midst. Now was the time for the next step of my subterfuge.

Some observant fellow on the higher level of the prison had reported seeing an army patrol passing by and this gave me another opportunity. Olbrecht's two thugs had been re-located after serving out their punishment in the hole. But there was no cell at Stettin without one of his cronies and ours was named Weber. I needed him to play a role; he and a talkative individual named Schulz.

I planted a few subtle suggestions with my fellow inmates, allowing three of them to separately reach the conclusion that the army had planted the fictional spy to uncover criminality. I knew that Olbrecht had grown used to flourishing under the poorly paid warders but all Prussian criminals lived in fear of the army, for this was who the courts turned to when they took action. It is an inescapable truth that many criminals are not all that bright and my task presented no great challenge. As expected, Schulz was soon passing the 'theory' onto Weber, who would in turn brief his master.

Within two days, the whole of Stettin was in an uproar. I had to stifle a smile when Schulz revealed to us that Olbrecht had suspended all smuggling and other transactions indefinitely. He no longer held court in the yard and talk of his paranoia spread widely.

In fact, it was eventually I that sought him out, pretending to be eager for news of our buried treasure.

'There was nothing there, you idiot,' said he.

'What?' said I. 'That's impossible.'

Where previously, the man might have had me beaten or worse, he simply cursed and went on his way.

I suppose he had other things on his mind.

Of course, it couldn't last forever. As the sense of crisis died down, the risk to me grew once more and I could see Olbrecht's old confidence returning. Would he now decide that he could risk a reckoning with me?

Fortunately, the weeks I had bought myself proved crucial.

One day in March of 1750, we learned from the guards that, following complaints to the state authorities by the Pietists, Chief Warder Strauss was to be replaced. Two weeks later, every man was summoned to the courtyard, where we were introduced to the fearsome Colonel Hamann, a former grenadier who'd been charged with whipping the prison staff and inmates into shape.

Hamann duly informed us that we would now spend our days working instead of idling: we were to construct a new church beside the prison. We would devote ourselves to labor and religion, not gambling, idling, and drinking. The colonel said he knew that criminality was rife but that he would offer those involved a chance for a fresh start. However, anyone who crossed him could expect a quick trip to the gallows. I do not believe I was the only one who turned to see the expression on Olbrecht's face. He already looked beaten.

As Colonel Hamman continued, I resisted the impulse to run forward and embrace him.

Chapter Twenty-One

1753, Kustrin

Four years, three months and six days after I entered Stettin prison, I was transferred. The erstwhile Colonel Hamman was still in charge, and he'd concluded that the ancient fortress could not function as a prison in its current condition. The authorities agreed; and the three hundred or so inmates were divided up among other institutions. Along with several dozen others, I was sent sixty miles south, to Kustrin. This building was also a former fortress, but nothing like as old and in a far better state. In the weeks leading up to the temporary closure of Stettin, the talk was only of where we might go and what conditions might be like. None of Prussia's prisons were pleasant but almost all were superior to Stettin, and I considered myself very fortunate to have escaped that place alive.

Though I have spoken of the terrible winters, it was in fact during spring – and an outbreak of influenza in 1751 – that I came closest to death. In all, a third of the inmates succumbed, including poor Curt Richter and my old adversary Olbrecht. The disease spread quickly through the packed cells and I suspect Colonel Hamman's speedy actions saved us. He confined already-ill inmates to the fortress and moved the rest of us into a hastily erected camp in the grounds. We were still watched over day and night and – despite concocting several schemes – I made no attempt to escape.

Weeks later, when we returned to the dungeons, I admonished myself for not making a greater effort and wondered at the cause. First, it must be said that – like all the prisoners – I was physically weak and lacking the sharpness and energy for such endeavors. Second, I was no longer a young man. At forty-three, I was well into middle age, my hair thankfully still thick but now tinged heavily with grey. The third potential reason troubled me more: perhaps I simply did not know what I'd do if I could escape; where I would go.

I still had Sophia's ring and while I occasionally thought of her, those few precious months seemed almost a fanciful dream. The distance between myself and my family in Halle now appeared to me an uncrossable chasm. I had not seen one of them in more than fifteen years and their faces were lost to me. If I indulged myself in thoughts of my mother and father and siblings, I sometimes became emotional, but for the most part, I concentrated on getting through each day, and I believe this practical approach helped me survive those awful years at Stettin.

In my time there, one hundred and thirty men perished. Seventeen took their own lives.

The key advantage of my new location was the cells. The main body of the fortress had been divided by wooden partitions, leaving the prisoners in pairs or fours. As a new arrival, I feared the worst but my cellmate was an elderly fellow who suffered with his bones and gave me little trouble. Each prisoner was also given a decent pallet to lie on, each equipped with a straw mattress. There was a large latrine within each of the four cell blocks, which included a wash house manned by prisoners.

It is impossible to convey in words what such small things mean to a lifer: I could sleep in peace at night; I could stay moderately clean; I could avoid the constant fear of who was suffering what ailment and whether I would catch it.

Still, all was not easy at Kustrin. The city was the capital of wealthy Neumark and possessed sufficient funds to properly pay the warders. This meant that there was very little corruption and laxity but the regime was utterly brutal. The chief warder, Major Von Castro, was another military man and he responded to any hint of resistance with violence. Prisoners were expected to keep their cells spotlessly clean and fulfill their duties in the wash house, kitchen or grounds. Slovenliness and tardiness were Von Castro's particular obsessions and any man who didn't meet his standards could expect a swift, vicious beating. His subordinates were all armed with wooden rods a yard long and an inch thick. A blow from these could easily break an arm or leg and the guards were not slow to use them.

It soon became obvious to me that his methods were effective. The whole place ran efficiently, and at least we were kept occupied. I had amassed a collection of a dozen books and – when I could get hold of ink – continued writing a text on teaching languages to the less able. But like all at Kustrin, I spent a majority of my time working; and this is how I experienced not only my first beating but my first encounter with Chief Warder Von Castro.

One of the duties I undertook in my first weeks involved supplying firewood to the wash house. The wood came in on wagons and was dumped in a corner of the prison yard. We moved every piece by hand into a store within the wash house (I could not help recalling the same chore I'd undertaken as a young man in Halle). The firewood was then used to heat great vats of water so a considerable amount was required.

Typically, prisoners worked a certain detail for two weeks, usually from eight in the morning until six at night. Within one of the four towers at each corner of the fortress was a bell, and its chimes dictated our every move. There were two meals a day – one at noon, one at seven in the evening. On Saturdays, we were generally left alone and on Sundays, we attended the prison chapel in four shifts, one for each cell block.

One of my fellow wood carriers on this occasion was a familiar face from Stettin – a former highwayman named Hempel. Though fortunate to be in Kustrin, we were unfortunate in the reputation we brought with us. Von Castro's guards had convinced themselves that we were lazy and feckless, to be watched especially carefully. I have always possessed an ability to get on with most people and this helped me negotiate those first weeks. The guards were always on the lookout for infractions but I paid attention to every rule, addressed them correctly, and did every job to the best of my ability. I also made it my business to observe slight differences in their character. Some wanted us to work in silence while others weren't averse to a friendly greeting or even a brief conversation. Some considered every last one of us to be worthless wretches; others saw us as fellow men.

By the third day of shifting wood, I had acquired not only a number of painful splinters but also some insight into our guards. There were four, and the most senior of them was named Ossenfuss. The other guards referred to him simply as 'Oss' and even they seemed wary. Ossenfuss was in fact the smallest of the four but he paced around with eyes narrowed as if determined to find fault. On the first two days in the yard, I'd already seen him kick Hempel and insult almost every other inmate except myself.

It was summertime, so we labored with sleeves rolled up and a constant film of sweat upon our skin. Though the work was not easy, the regular meals and improved conditions had allowed my body to renew itself and I coped with our task as well as the younger men. There was, however, an issue, which had already caused some tension. We had been permitted to fill a pail of water, which we left in the shade and drank from during our breaks. The guards could see how tough our task was in the relentless sun and permitted us to drink every two hours. I would have preferred every hour but if prison had taught me anything it was patience, and I could cope.

Hempel could not. I knew from our time at Stettin that the man suffered terribly with headaches. These were often exacerbated by heat and his only method of alleviating them was to drink a great deal of water.

On the third day – the hottest so far – he had asked for a drink between our allotted breaks. At that particular moment, Ossenfuss was absent, having been summoned by one of the warders; and Hempel was able to refresh himself. But when he made the same request on the fourth day, Ossenfuss refused, and none of the other guards contradicted him. I could see that Hempel was struggling: his work had slowed and his eyes had become bloodshot. As I passed him on my way back to the huge pile of wood, I saw him stagger and drop half his load. I stopped to help.

Ossenfuss was leaning against an empty wagon in the shade.

'Careful there, idiot.'

I was glad he did not intervene but a quarter-hour later, Hempel simply stopped working, hand gripping his head. I was close by and watched as Ossenfuss approached.

'What's all this, Hempel?' he barked. 'You'll get your water at eleven. Move!'

'Sir, please – I need water now. I beg you. My head.'

'What about your head? Have you been drinking?'

'No sir, but I suffer from'

'You think I care!' yelled Ossenfuss, slipping his rod from his belt. 'Remember your bloody place or I'll give you a painful reminder.'

Hempel ambled away. Ossenfuss didn't seem to care that the prisoner's eyes were now weeping and he could barely coordinate his movements.

'Sir, may I say something?'

The guard looked over at me, as did the other three, who were still in the shade.

'What?' snapped Ossenfuss.

'Hempel – his condition. I've seen it before. It pains him so much I've known him to bang his head against the wall to relieve the agony.'

'Is that so?' said Ossenfuss with a grin. 'Maybe we should try it now.' 'Sir, if he can drink, he can keep working. If he faints, he'll end up in the infirmary.'

What's your name?'

'That's the King of Thieves, Oss!' said one of the other guards. 'He used to be famous.'

'Ain't king of much now, are you?' said Ossenfuss as he approached me, rod already swinging. 'If there's one thing I cannot abide, it's bloody prisoners telling me how to do my bloody job. Give me a reason not to give you the reminder.'

'Tell him one of your jokes.' This came from another guard.

I kept a supply of little jests on hand as they sometimes helped defuse tension and win opponents over. At the time, it seemed like a good idea.

I forced a grin and delivered the joke: 'A man goes to the doctor, tells him, "Doctor, my bowels move every morning at seven o'clock." "Very good," says the doctor. "Not for me," said the man, "I don't get up until eight."'

The other three men chuckled at this and Ossenfuss broke into a smile. I felt confident that the tension had eased sufficiently for me to help poor Hempel. 'Sir, might I fetch some water for him? It'll only take a minute.'

Before I could get out of the way, the thuggish swine swung his rod, striking me a weighty blow on the upper arm that almost knocked me off my feet.

'Still trying to tell me how to do my job! Get back to work.'

I was not slow to respond, even though the pulsing pain of the blow coursed through me. I knew nothing had been broken but that was scant reward as I returned to my labors, the pain worsening every time I lifted something.

I was at least glad that Hempel made it to the break and was able to refresh himself. Once recovered, he thanked me.

It was customary for miscreants to be paraded before Chief Warder Von Castro on Friday evenings, before the second meal. Even though my offense had not been recorded and no punishment sanctioned, Ossenfuss made sure I was there. Thankfully, by keeping my head down I'd avoided further confrontations. I had suffered no fracture but my arm was discolored from elbow to shoulder. As I stood there in the courtyard that Friday, every inch of that arm ached.

Von Castro – a stern, grey-haired man with a barrel chest – made his way along the line, listening to the guards outline the prisoners' offenses. Where no punishment had been given, he ordered a lashing, solitary confinement, or half-rations. When it came to my turn, he listened blankly to Ossenfuss' explanation, which was far from entirely truthful.

'Show me your arm,' said he, upon hearing of the blow.

He did not react to the bruising, which was the worst I had ever experienced.

'I suppose that will do. We're watching you, you know.'

'Sir?'

'The King of Thieves. If you couldn't get out of Stettin, I'll make damn sure you don't get out of Kustrin.'

'I won't be trying to escape, sir. Nowhere to go.'

I cannot be sure if I meant that, though there was certainly good reason to say it.

'I've been here five years,' said Von Castro, 'and no one's managed it yet.'

I suppose I took it as a challenge; and as soon as he said those words, the plotting began. Looking back, I suspect it was my renewed mental and physical strength that allowed me to contemplate an escape bid. I waited for three months before instigating my plan, long enough for any initial suspicion to fade. And in that time, I did nothing whatsoever to draw attention. My aged cellmate died in August and no replacement arrived, giving me time to plan and, crucially, to work.

That work echoed my early years at Kasebier's. It took me weeks to assemble the right amount of grey and black cloth, not to mention all the sewing materials. Stealing a guard's uniform would have been more straightforward but they washed their garments at home so I had to assemble my own. This involved creating a pair of grey breeches and a black jacket from discarded items. The guards also wore cloth caps and pilfering one of these did not present a difficulty. Once the outfit was complete, I instigated my plan on the evening of September 15th.

The best opportunity to escape my cellblock was during the evening meal, which was eaten on benches outside the kitchen. As the prisoners cooked and served the food with numerous guards in attendance, there was sufficient movement and mixing for me to make my attempt. Because I was not actually on the serving detail, I needed a distraction to get into the kitchen. This was achieved by placing a handful of corn kernels around the glass of a lamp. Once heated to a certain temperature, the corn popped, causing quite a scene.

With all those around me preoccupied with the explosions, I collected some bowls and made my way into the kitchen. Retreating into the pantry, I discarded my brown prisoner's fatigues, revealing the guard outfit I was wearing underneath. Once I'd added the cap, my transformation was complete. However, though there were hundreds of prisoners and scores of guards, we were all familiar with one another. I needed to do more.

Slipping unseen out of the pantry, I grabbed a knife and sliced it across my forearm: a slight cut but enough to draw blood. This I smeared on my fingers, then placed both hands over my face. I left by the rear entrance and hurried past the two guards I knew would be there.

'Where you going?' one asked, unable to see much of my features.

'Infirmary. A scuffle. That idiot Ossenfuss hit me instead of the prisoner.'

'Cretin,' said one, while the other laughed. I was not armed with a rod but hoped they surmised I'd lost it in the 'scuffle'.

This same method and excuse were enough to get me past two more sets of guards on my way to the infirmary. Unlike Stettin, Kustrin had two medical officers, who alternated the duty. I of course had no intention of entering, so instead crept around the rear of the cell block to the closest tower.

I knew that if I could access an outward-facing window, I had a chance at escape. Unfortunately, I'd been unable to gain much intelligence regarding the interior so, not for the first time, I'd have to improvise. Unlike the doors within the cell blocks, the main tower door was not locked. Having wiped the blood off my fingers, I crept inside.

There was one door to my left, one to my right, ahead a spiral staircase. The door to the right was slightly ajar. Peering inside, I saw three senior warders studying some papers. Also present was a guard, who was lighting a lantern.

Hoping there would be fewer people on the higher levels, I tiptoed up the stairs to the first floor. Here I discovered a locked door and another room containing only wooden racks stuffed with documents and a collection of old-looking furniture. I cursed when I saw there was no window.

From below came the sounds of movement but I looked down and saw that it was simply one of the warders leaving. Continuing to the second floor, I found myself facing a door with a plaque upon it: this was the office of Chief Warder Von Castro. I had no idea what hours the man kept so stood close to the door and listened. I heard nothing so gently tried it. Locked.

Circling around the staircase, I came to the other room and was relieved to find it open. There was a single lantern hanging beside the stairs but this room was shrouded by darkness. From what I could tell, it contained racks of clothing but the small, square window at the far end immediately took my attention. Once there, I opened it and looked downward.

I felt a surge of excitement when I realized that I was directly above grass and well beyond the prison wall. Judgment was difficult in the dark but I reckoned I was forty feet up. For all my skills, I am no cat burglar and so the hunt for a rope began. Rifling through the room in the near dark I found only racks and boxes full of clothes, nothing I could use to lower myself. I had covered most of the room when I heard bells ringing below.

My escape attempt had been discovered. I didn't have long. Hoping to find something on the third floor, I sprang up the staircase. Here, neither room was locked. One was empty, another used for storage; and I shoved my hands into barrels and boxes, desperate to find salvation. No solution presented itself until I reached some low boxes lined up against a wall. My fingers felt cold metal and I heard the clink of a chain. I pulled out a length of it: the chain was no more than eight feet long but there were several more. If I could connect these lengths, I'd have enough to reach the ground. Recalling the garments I'd discovered below, I realized I could use them to knot the chains together. Throwing four lengths over my shoulder, I hurried down the stairs, wincing at every noise.

Hoping that my pursuers would take some time to search the tower, I told myself to remain calm. I still had a chance.

I was almost at the door when I heard a steely voice.

'Good evening, Christian.'

I turned to see Chief Warder Von Castro halfway up the staircase below. Upon his face a satisfied grin, in his hand, a flintlock pistol.

One might assume that I was punished terribly, which is precisely what I expected. But for some reason, Von Castro chose solitary confinement instead of the usual violence. The cell I spent the next three months in gave me chilling reminders of Stettin but, in the last month, things improved. Why? The visits of none other than the chief warder himself.

During his first trip, he stood outside the barred door and informed me that he'd attended a dinner party where several guests were excited to learn of my presence at Kustrin. It seemed Von Castro had not fully grasped the extent and infamy of my criminal career and he was apparently intrigued. During the ensuing discussions, he was always careful to show disapproval of my crimes but clearly enjoyed my tales and the way I told them. I'm sure the chief warder would not have acted in this way had I been in the main block but in privacy, we spoke almost as – dare I say it? – equals.

As we got to know each other, I concluded that, like me, he was adept at playing a role. Beneath the grim, efficient facade, was a pleasant character and an inquiring mind.

In all, Von Castro visited me nine times, on each occasion requesting a new 'adventure'. On the last few occasions, he bought a chair to sit on and a pipe to smoke. Perhaps the man was just bored.

On the last day of my confinement, I made a request. For all the hard labor undertaken by the inmates at Kustrin, nothing was done for their minds. I asked the chief warder whether he would be prepared to allow me to reconstitute my language instruction if there was sufficient interest. Von Castro clearly took pride in the prison, and I suspect he considered this another way in which he might set his institution apart. He also shared my view that occupying the men was its own form of discipline. And so, he agreed.

Within weeks, I was teaching small groups for an hour a day. Within months, a room was set aside for my instruction and, to my astonishment, some of the guards even joined in. I taught Russian, English, and French. I was not entirely excused from duties but more of my time was spent teaching than laboring.

Chief Warder Von Castro did not formally soften his regime but I began to see that my classes were quite effective in civilizing this most uncivilized place. For once in my life, I had achieved something that brought only gain to others, not cost. I suppose it gave me some direction. I felt proud.

After two years at Kustrin, I became a regular visitor to the very tower from where I'd once attempted to escape. Von Castro often inquired about the classes and on one occasion introduced me to a party of visiting dignitaries.

Though always careful to remember my place, I used my influence to win small concessions, and in the spring of 1756, work began on turning a section of waste ground behind the prison into a vegetable patch. This provided another variety of labor for Von Castro and a variety of diet for the inmates. In fact, once established, the vegetable patch became more like a small farm and so productive that the chief warder actually saved money. I did not care that he claimed credit for the idea.

In the summer of 1756, Prussia again found herself at war. King Frederick was now allied with Great Britain and, in great fear of an Austrian/Russian axis, launched a strike against the Habsburgs. Information was always scant within prison but I tried to keep abreast of developments. As ever it seemed that our king was doing well against superior numbers and, by the following April, he was attacking the great city of Prague.

On the third day of that month, I was summoned to Von Castro's office, where I found an immaculately presented officer standing beside the chief warder.

'It seems you will be leaving us, Christian,' said Von Castro, who was holding some papers. 'This is Colonel Danneburg, attaché to His Majesty King Frederick.'

Utterly surprised and confused, I couldn't even articulate a greeting. The colonel addressed me in the clipped, cold tones typical of his class.

'You are the man known as Christian Gottlieb Meyer – sentenced to life imprisonment in Berlin in the year 1749?'

'I am.'

'His Majesty requires your assistance with a military matter. We leave for Prague immediately.'

Chapter Twenty-Two

Prague, 1757

I have never traveled at such speed. Colonel Danneburg didn't even allow me to return to my cell; I was instead conducted directly to the prison stable. Two junior officers and a squad of cavalrymen with many spare horses accompanied the colonel. The distance to Prague was over one hundred and fifty miles yet – by barely sleeping and changing mounts regularly – we reached the city in three days. I of course had not ridden in years and every part of my body ached.

Colonel Danneburg evidently had instructions to deliver me at maximum speed yet if he knew anything of the reason why he was not letting on. I simply could not imagine what possible use His Majesty might have for me. I was now a man of forty-seven years, whose previous life of adventure had been replaced by one of captivity and routine. One might be surprised that I was not filled with joy at a chance for freedom. The truth is that I was scared.

Having ridden through the third night, we arrived at dawn. All I had learned from the colonel was that the king commanded a great force of over a hundred thousand and that he had met a similar-sized Austrian army in battle east of the city. Apparently, the king's brother, Prince Henry, had outdone himself, bravely leading his men forward until the depleted Austrian ranks retreated to the gates of Prague. Over fifty thousand of them had withdrawn behind the formidable walls under the command of Charles, Prince of Lorraine, an old enemy of King Frederick.

Though the battle had concluded almost a week ago, its remnants were everywhere. We passed ruined buildings, trees felled by artillery, and the bloated bodies of dead horses. There were many burial parties, and an officer by the roadside informed us that the Prussian forces had lost twelve thousand men. One of them was the famous Field Marshal Von Schwerin, who even a prisoner like me knew to be one of Prussia's ablest commanders. Field hospitals were overflowing with casualties and I lost count of the walking wounded: many limping, many bandaged.

Upon seeing a regiment of what looked like uniformed giants, I was told by Danneburg that these were the king's 'tall boys', a specially selected unit of grenadiers. Apparently, every man was between six and eight feet in height.

As we rode on, I lost all sense of number or scale, for I could not have ever conceived of such a gathering of men and horses and weaponry. Assembled here in Bohemia was the bulk of the entire Prussian army. I saw fields packed with artillery pieces, row after row of tents, line after line of horses; units of hussars and cuirassiers and dragoons and Jagers. I saw a band practicing amid a meadow of yellow flowers and a young preacher addressing what looked like an entire regiment.

Reaching a high point, I, at last, gained a clear view of Prague itself. The army had surrounded the city but Frederick's forces were concentrated to the west. Prague was famed for its one hundred spires but what struck me were the walls. They looked to be at least thirty feet high and several yards thick. Many sections boasted triangular bastions, which gave the defenders a further advantage. Here and there, the black noses of artillery pieces poked out through the battlements. Those walls had not been seriously damaged though I could see numerous impacts from the Prussian artillery. Within my view were five bridges, all of which were eerily empty. The city was protected by the Vltava river to the west and north, and a deep moat to the south and east. I was not surprised the enemy forces had withdrawn here.

I believe Colonel Danneburg was almost as exhausted as I, for he had to ask directions to the command headquarters three times. Upon arriving there and dismounting, I fell onto my backside and had to be helped to my feet by one of the colonel's men. He hurried away and returned with a young soldier.

'This man will help you get cleaned up,' said Danneburg, who was now sporting his own light beard. 'The king will see you presently.'

Still in a daze, I followed the soldier to a small tent. Inside were three chairs and a table with a mirror. Once I had slumped down, my new assistant fetched some hot water and produced a blade. Shaving was an infrequent affair back at Kustrin but I set to work with fingers sore and stiff from gripping reins.

'I'll put some clothes out for you, sir,' said the soldier. 'And bring more water. Some soap and perfume too.'

I had not changed since leaving the prison and could only imagine the odor I was giving off.

'Very kind. I don't suppose you could rustle up some coffee? Might wake me up a bit.'

'Of course.'

He was about to leave when I realized I could hear a surprising sound.

'Is that a violin? Somebody plays well.'

'That's His Majesty,' said the soldier. 'He plays almost every morning. He composed that piece with Herr Bach.'

I halted my shaving for a moment. 'Herr Bach? Johann Sebastian Bach?'

'Why yes, sir. Who else?'

Though I felt a good deal better once clean and freshly clothed, my legs and backside still ached terribly and I felt my fingers shake as Colonel Danneburg escorted me towards the king's tent. It was an enormous affair, thirty feet across at least. Outside were numerous officers, several of them gathered around a great map table. I received suspicious looks from them, and disconcerting glares from the two immense sentries that guarded the tent's entrance. A staff officer appeared and ushered us in immediately.

The tent was divided into four sections by partitions and we found ourselves in one corner that contained six chairs and as many small tables. Sitting, clad in a rather shabby blue officer's coat and currently sniffing from a snuffbox, was His Majesty, King Frederick. He took a moment to enjoy his inhalation, after which the staff officer introduced us.

I emulated Colonel Danneburg, who bowed low before slowly straightening up.

King Frederick wore a white wig of the type favored by all men of his class but I was surprised by the youthfulness of his face, which would have appeared delicate if not for his piercing blue eyes and strong nose. Ever the tailor's son, I was shocked by the state of his clothes. The well-worn jacket was stained by mud at the hem and snuff at the sleeves. He was wearing only socks on his feet but close by were a pair of tired riding boots that looked at least ten years old.

'Where's that Prowler?'

I had no answer to this question but one was provided by the arrival of a whippet, which trotted through from the rear of the tent. The dog sat obediently beside its master, who stroked its head while appraising me.

'You look tired, man. I do hope you're ready to take your chance.'

'My chance, Your Majesty?'

Instead of answering, the king waved a hand towards the entrance. 'You're dismissed for the moment, colonel. Tell them to ready my horse.'

With another neat bow, Danneburg withdrew.

Of all the bizarre turns my life has taken, I'm not sure any compare with the surrealness of that moment. I was alone with the king.

'Perhaps you should sit,' said he. 'Save your energy.'

I sat opposite him, hands clasped in my lap, still bemused about what was expected of me.

'I recall your trial,' continued the king. 'It was quite the event. Eichel sent me very detailed reports. I'll admit I was impressed by your escapades, despite your lack of moral fiber. The last report included the speech you gave to save your skin. It has always seemed to be that most men are so very … mediocre. I felt you were deserving of a little mercy.'

'Your Majesty, I was most grateful for your intervention. I have done my best'

'And you only tried to escape once? Disappointing. But when I was reminded that you were still alive, the thought occurred that you might be of use to me. Let us hope that you can rediscover some of your past form.'

'Your Majesty, I'm still not entirely'

'Behind the city walls are fifty thousand men. Victory in Bohemia is not possible until I have them and the city. We have tried bombardment but Charles of Lorraine is standing firm. Worse, my scouts report that Von Daun is gathering his troops to the east.'

This too was a familiar name – an Austrian field marshal of some repute.

The king pulled on his left boot. 'And reinforcements are coming up from the south. I cannot afford to simply wait here for the Austrians to recover themselves. I need a way into Prague. We have no decent spies, no way of knowing what is going on behind those walls. If there is a weakness in the defenses or the defenders, we can exploit it. I need intelligence. If you get it for me, I will pardon you. You will be a free man.'

King Frederick pulled on his right boot. 'Now, I am going to inspect the troops and watch the first bombardment of the day. We must at least keep up the appearance of the upper hand, after all. By the time I return, you will tell me your plan. Ask my officers if you have any questions.' With the dog close on his heels, the king departed.

***

And that is how I found myself up on the hill that day, trying to think of a way to infiltrate the city and win my freedom. Even a short time by myself showed me the value of this unexpected opportunity. True, I had become used to prison life; but if it meant never returning there, I would do what I had to. Hurrying back down the hill, I questioned the officers just as the king had suggested. They gave full, frank answers and I was not surprised to find most of my ideas unworkable. One, however, seemed to have a slim chance of success.

I was surprised that, upon his return, the king did not wish to hear the details. It was Colonel Danneburg who was summoned inside the king's tent, only to swiftly reappear.

'We are to go ahead, Christian. Come, let's assemble what we need.' An hour later, after a rushed but welcome breakfast of bacon and bread, I found myself crawling through the undergrowth on the eastern side of the city. Any approach to the west was far too exposed for what I had in mind. On the eastern side were two gates that could be accessed by shorter bridges that crossed the moat.

The Prussian lines were a thousand paces out, to protect them from the defenders' artillery. This left a wide tract of 'no man's land' and I'd learned that several Austrian units had found their way through the lines before being admitted to the city. Despite the great number of Prussian troops, they had to cover a perimeter of many miles and could not hope to stop every man. Although there were few reports of stragglers in recent days, I believed there was a good chance I could get inside – especially as I was now wearing the uniform of an Austrian soldier. After 'liberating' the uniform from a similarly sized prisoner, we'd circled around to the east in the company of one Captain Volland – an intelligence officer who briefed me on the Austrians.

I have met many Bohemians in my time and felt confident about approximating the accent. I would also have to hope that my briefing from Captain Volland would equip me for the debrief I would likely face if allowed into the city. He had escorted us as far as the outlying Prussian pickets but only Colonel Danneburg and went on from there. We first negotiated an abandoned hamlet, then cut through a copse of trees before entering the undergrowth we now crawled through.

Despite my exhaustion, I could appreciate the benefits of our difficult path. I was now suitably grubby and – with my genuine tiredness – hoped to resemble a soldier who'd been on the run for several days. Indeed, the striking white and black uniform was now heavily marked.

Danneburg was a cold character but I couldn't fault his professionalism and I was surprised when he shook my hand.

'All the best, Christian. Learn as much as you can, try and get out tonight if possible. Every hour counts.'

I felt it equally likely that I would be discovered and hanged but there seemed little point in saying so.

Once free of the undergrowth, I ran for the closest bridge as if in fear of my life. I believe the uniform prevented me from being shot but, as I neared the walls, I spied the barrels of cannons and muskets, and men looking down upon me. The road that led to the gate was paved but covered in mud and detritus, including a broken cartwheel and a child's doll. Once across the bridge, I halted in front of the imposing gatehouse and the immense wooden doors.

'Identify yourself!' demanded an unseen individual from the battlements.

'Corporal Christian Wahl, Breysach Brigade! I've been on the run for two days. Please let me in.'

'Your immediate superior?'

'Sergeant Otto Thorwald.

We had not selected the Breysach brigade at random. According to Captain Volland, we had eleven prisoners from this unit and he had used bribes to obtain the name of the sergeant. The brigade had been intercepted while fleeing south but the majority had escaped. We could therefore assume that there wouldn't be many others within the city to contradict my cover story.

I waited. After the run, my tiredness had only increased and – seeing an opportunity to convince as a desperate man – I simply sat down and bowed my head.

After several minutes, the defender spoke up again. 'Raise your hands and keep them there.'

As I stood, I heard movement beyond the doors, then the clang of metal bolts. One great door opened slightly and I found myself staring at the lethal head of a lance. An officer who beckoned me forward accompanied the grim-faced soldier holding it.

'Keep those hands up,' said the senior man.

Once I was inside, others shut the gate, securing the bolts and adding an enormous locking plank. I found myself amidst a motley crew of haggard soldiers, clearly from many different units. Directly ahead was a broad street that led to the heart of the city. I could see hundreds more people upon it, many of them in uniform.

'Search him,' ordered the officer.

His men found only a few pfennigs; I had already checked the uniform's pockets.

The officer ordered me to sit on a nearby step and I did so with the lance still aimed at me.

'You say you're with the Breysach Brigade?'

'I was,' I replied. 'God knows where the rest of them are. I was trapped in a village just to the east. I saw some men heading this way yesterday and decided to make a run for it this morning.

'The commander of your battalion?'

'Harrach.'

The officer looked to a nearby fellow whose uniform bore the same markings as my own. I felt a shiver of fear. With no more than a few telling questions, this fellow could expose me. But his head was covered with a blood stained bandage and he looked unsteady on his feet.

He nodded. 'Harrach. That's right.'

This seemed to be enough to satisfy the officer, who ordered my guard to shoulder his lance.

'Is there any food?' I asked.

'Not much,' said the officer.

I looked to the man who'd been asked to corroborate my story. 'Any others from the brigade, friend?'

The injured man shrugged and ambled away.

When the officer also wandered off, I realized I had passed this test with some ease.

Is there a latrine?'

The man with the lance pointed at a nearby inn. 'Use theirs.'

Again affecting the behavior of an exhausted man, I hauled myself off the step and plodded over to the inn. The parlor was busy, mostly occupied with soldiers. But this was no typical scene: many had laid out on the floor, heads upon their knapsacks. Others were playing cards but there was the same quiet tension here that I'd observed outside. I saw not a single mug of beer nor glass of wine.

I had not been followed by my 'guard' so instead of finding the latrine, I simply walked out of the rear of the inn and continued into the middle of Prague. I hadn't gone far when I saw the first damaged building: a warehouse with two walls blown into piles of bricks. Dozens of locals were at work in the rubble and I saw three bodies covered by blankets. One was too small to be an adult.

As well as the many thousands of troops, the inhabitants found themselves in great peril, with no clue of what might unfold. I saw many gazing out from darkened windows; others in groups, deep in discussion; a few pressing the Austrian officers for news. Some were making the best of the situation: selling their wares to a huge captive market, but I saw precious little on the stalls, for supplies were surely running short. One soldier was arguing with a baker regarding the cost of his last few loaves. Apparently, the occupiers had ordered a freeze on prices. The only ones who seemed unconcerned by their predicament were children, many of whom were amusing themselves with ball games or songs. I envied them their innocent ignorance.

Once at the center of the city, I began my observations in earnest. Nobody gave yet another Austrian soldier a second look, and I first concentrated on locating the commander. By masquerading as a messenger, I was directed to the city hall, which Charles of Lorraine had occupied. There I found quite a crowd, with dozens of residents – common and distinguished – attempting to petition the man now in charge of their fate. Realizing I had no chance of getting inside, I followed my orders and began as full a survey of the occupied city as I could undertake.

Captain Volland had suggested that I complete a circuit of the walls and this I did, beginning at the bridge facing the king's position. Volland had also told me not to write anything down in case of capture but I knew my powers of observation and recall would serve me well. I noted the placement of the artillery, the relative strength of forces at each gate, even the location of the various brigades. There were a few dragoons and cuirassiers but most of the soldiers were infantrymen. The majority were from various Habsburg provinces fighting under noblemen in divisions named after count this or duke that. I was surprised to also find several hundred Irishmen present. These tough-looking fellows fought under a Habsburg general of Irish descent named Von Browne.

Despite the cramped, difficult circumstances and what appeared to me a severe shortage of food, I saw little evidence of disorder. There were simply so many troops that, as long as the officers kept them under control, the city was theirs. One man in particular seemed determined to do so:

While in the central square, I watched several soldiers being flogged for the offense of looting. I wasn't there long but found myself beside two officers who clearly approved of the measure, and the man overseeing it. I imagine he was a subordinate of Prince Charles, for he had a French name – Major Bisset. Unlike many of the other officers within the beleaguered city, Bisset still appeared immaculate, and he supervised the flogging with a steely countenance.

As for armaments, I'd seen few soldiers without a weapon and considerable stocks of cannonballs and canisters for the artillery. I could see no obvious weakness for King Frederick to exploit but at least I had considerable intelligence to pass on; it was he and his staff who would now have to make their decisions.

I concluded my survey of the defenses as the sun set, staying well clear of the eastern gate where I had entered. I wondered if it was worth trying again to infiltrate the city hall but the prospect of learning anything crucial seemed remote, unlike the prospect of capture. Knowing I could reach friendly forces on any side, I now considered the best location to escape once darkness fell.

As I was doing so, an unexpected obstacle presented itself. The time was around seven o'clock and as dusk approached, the Austrian officers began to round up their troops for inspection. It was the job of corporals and sergeants to whip their men into shape and I soon realized that a lone man such as myself would be noticed. I was not prepared for such military efficiency and within minutes was forced to hide in a church.

Here I found several families and a priest trying to calm a group of elderly women. I sat upon a pew well away from the nearest lamp and considered what to do next. I had to go over the wall; the question was how. I'd originally considered the southern side but my current position was far closer to the west. I did not want to risk a long flight across the city and realized I would not need a rope if I simply jumped into the river. I am a fair swimmer and had seen that the Vltava was no more than a quarter-mile across.

This was not something I particularly wanted to do but I knew the king would expect a prompt return. Leaving the church, I made my way carefully towards the walls, evading several voluble men rounding up soldiers. I headed for the nearest bastion, reckoning that I would have less distance to cover once in the water and more distance from the defenders.

Once I'd reached the battlements, I affected a busy manner and passed several groups, including officers smoking pipes. More remarkable than the lights within the city behind me were the campfires of the Prussian troops; there seemed as many as there were stars in the sky.

Close to the tip of the bastion, I reached a section of battlements some twenty feet from the nearest soldier. Leaning over the cold stone and peering down at the water, I felt a moment of fear. Knowing hesitation might stop me, I swiftly removed my shoes and jacket. I climbed up onto the battlements and jumped.

The fall could only have taken a second or two but it seemed far, far longer.

I at least kept my body straight and it was my feet that struck the water first. I plunged deep, the chill water almost shocking me into opening my mouth. Fortunately, I had enough presence of mind to take a few strokes, ensuring that I came up several yards from where I landed.

The crack of a musket persuaded me to steal a breath and dive again. I'd wondered how the defenders might react but I suppose they assumed I was a defector, deserter or spy. Staying underwater for as long as I could, I only remained on the surface once sure the defenders could not see me.

My spirits fell when I realized how distant the campfires seemed but I concentrated on a steady stroke and plowed on, despite the slowing effect of my shirt and breeches.

When my right hand struck something, I stopped instantly. Whatever it was drifted closer and when I pushed it away, my fingers touched hair – human hair – and then the softness of the dead man's face.

Cursing with revulsion, I swam away and onward with a renewed vigor, trying not to think about the body.

I felt ground under my feet before I saw the far bank and was soon wading through thick weed. Glancing back, I could make out the silhouette of the wall and could hardly believe how far I'd come. Soon, I was clambering up a muddy bank.

I had taken no more than fifty steps on solid ground when I was approached by a patrol. One man had a lantern; the others had muskets, all now aimed at me.

I raised my hands. 'I am an ally. A spy in the employ of His Majesty King Frederick. He will want to see me. Immediately.'

Chapter Twenty-Three

I in fact saw nothing of the king that night. Once back at the command post, I was again in the hands of Colonel Danneburg. He provided me with some clean clothes then conveyed me to a large tent where the senior officers had assembled. They sat me down in front of a map of the city and debriefed me. I was thankful for the colonel's presence for he at least grasped how weary I was and ensured that the questioning proceeded in a logical fashion. As I spoke, counters representing troops and artillery were placed upon the map and two junior men took notes. I have no idea of the hour when I was finally allowed to retire. Possessed by a raging thirst, I downed half a flask of water and collapsed onto a camp bed.

I was woken by the drums of reveille and my first thought was that I had endured a nightmare. Though warm below a blanket, I shivered from head to toe when I recalled the body in the water and my escape across the river. I felt as if I'd been trampled by a horse and threw back my blankets to check for injuries. But other than some bruises on my arms from all the crawling around in the undergrowth, I was in good condition. Covering myself once more, I lay back and wondered what the day might hold.

When Colonel Danneburg entered the tent and handed me a plate of food and a mug of steaming coffee, I had some questions.

'Has His Majesty been briefed?'

'He has.'

'Were my findings useful?'

'I'm sure of it. Honestly, I doubt there's any man here who could have done a better job. And to get out unscathed ...'

The colonel watched me sip my coffee, which had been sugared and to me tasted like nectar.

'Between you and me, Christian, I'll confess I thought my mission to fetch you a foolish one but I see now that your reputation is well-deserved.'

'Very kind, colonel. What happens now?'

'I suggest you enjoy your breakfast.'

With that, Danneburg left me alone. As I ate the bread and cheese on my plate, the first bombardment of the day began.

The hours passed. Under the summer sun, the tent became hot so I moved outside and sat on a wooden chest. Some thirty yards away, the command post was still busy, with numerous officers of various ranks coming and going. I felt sure that the intelligence I'd passed on had been of use, that an attack was being planned.

I suppose it wasn't far off midday when I was again summoned before the king. He was now sitting in the shade of a sprawling oak tree, accompanied by three men, two of them in civilian dress. As we approached, I asked Colonel Danneburg who they were.

'Closest to him is Eichel, his private secretary.'

I recalled the name from my trial. The man looked like a bureaucrat, a sharp-faced fellow with a thin mustache. He seemed perturbed by the whippet nosing his leg.

'The man in uniform is Prince Henry.'

Frederick's younger brother was very similar in appearance, his white wig identical. He sat now with his legs crossed, one hand at rest on a cane, gazing contemplatively at the walls of Prague.

'The last fellow is Algarotti, the king's … companion.'

I knew from conversations during our journey from Kustrin that this Italian philosopher and poet was a great favorite of the king's. Another such man was the influential Frenchman Voltaire, whom I had first heard of so many years earlier. It was said that Frederick greatly preferred their company to that of his wife.

As I neared the king, Eichel, Henry, and Algarotti rose to bid farewell to an injured man on a wagon who could barely lift his arm.

'General Winterfeldt,' added Danneburg. 'I do hope the surgeons can save him. We cannot afford to lose both he and Von Schwerin.'

As we passed under the shade of the oak, the colonel and I bowed low.

The king had an open book upon his lap, which seemed to contain several diagrams. He tapped a thumb upon it and looked down at the city.

'I won't say that what you provided was useless but my officers and I are no nearer to a solution. It appears that the southern side offers our best chance but I haven't the ammunition to bring down those walls. In fact, it sounds like Charles has twice as many cannonballs as I do. Frankly, I was hoping for something a little more … original.'

His next words were heavy with sarcasm. 'After all, he is only a prince. Can a king such as yourself not outwit him?'

'Your Majesty, I'm not entirely sure what you expect from me.'

King Frederick slammed his book shut. 'Cunning! Trickery! Deception! Something my straightforward, honorable, conventional subordinates would never think of. If I am to strike, it will have to be tomorrow at the latest. I need an advantage. If you cannot provide it, you will find yourself back behind bars. You have two hours.'

With that, the king stood and walked back to his tent. He didn't seem at all concerned about his stricken general.

It took me some time to absorb what I had heard. Colonel Danneburg walked with me as I wandered to the shade of another tree. I gazed blankly at my surroundings: saw a group of soldiers erecting a tent, others polishing their boots.

'His Majesty is a hard taskmaster,' said the colonel eventually.

'That is an understatement. Why in god's name does he think I can summon some magical solution where he and his officers have failed?' 'He is desperate. Time is running short. The news from the east is not good. The Austrian force under Von Daun grows by the hour. Most of these men have already been in one terrible battle. The king cannot be sure they will win another.'

I leaned against the tree and returned to an idea I had briefly considered the previous day. It was bold, audacious, and very risky. But despite the trials I had endured since being liberated from Kustrin, I had once again experienced the thrill and joy of freedom. I was not returning to a cell. Not ever.

'Is it possible that a messenger has got through from Von Daun to Charles?'

'Probable. If not through our lines, then the tunnels.'

'What tunnels?'

'The city has always had problems with inundation from the Vltava. It is not only the walls that have grown up over the centuries but the very buildings themselves. They say most of the center is a full story higher than the original foundations. There are hundreds of cellars and tunnels, even under the city hall. Much is flooded but some come out beyond the walls, even beyond the moat. We've covered the ones we know of but there may be more.'

This revelation added fuel to the fire of my plan but I still needed more information if it was to have any chance of success.

'Colonel, I need to speak to Captain Volland.'

Three hours later, I approached the city again, but in a rather different fashion: I strode across the long, arched bridge that led to the western gate, now dressed as a senior Prussian officer. I was in fact masquerading as a certain individual: Lieutenant Colonel Johann Von Mayr, who led one of the Prussian free battalions – a mercenary outfit King Frederick had raised in his determination to match his numerous enemies. I had only learned of the man in the last hour from the well-informed Captain Volland and I reckoned Mayr's history and reputation might serve my purpose well. Mayr and the Free Battalion were in fact currently located in Franconia; I would have to hope that Charles of Lorraine was unaware of this.

As before, the king had listened to my second proposal and, after making a few suggestions, given his approval. Volland and Danneburg had continued to assist me, yet I sensed a profound doubt on their part that I could make this work. I understood their concerns entirely but I have spent much of my life proving people wrong. Despite my many fears, I felt a surge of confidence as I traversed the bridge, boots tapping on the stone, thousands of eyes upon me.

Once halfway across the bridge, I began to see the defenders on the battlements congregating to observe my approach. To reduce the possibility of a musket ball striking me, I removed my only weapon, my sword, and placed it – with theatrical exaggeration – upon the broad surround of the bridge. I was also holding a leather case, ostensibly containing a written declaration from the king that I represented him, though I had another purpose in mind.

Upon reaching the gate, I identified myself as Lieutenant Colonel Von Mayr and declared that 'I was present to negotiate with Prince Charles on behalf of His Majesty King Frederick.'

The delay was longer on this occasion but I was once again permitted to enter. Having been thoroughly searched by the officer on duty, I was handed over to a young captain who escorted me towards the center with a platoon of troops. I was watched every step of the way by soldiers and residents alike. It was a warm afternoon, and I soon found sweat dripping down my face from under my three-cornered hat. Once at the city hall, I was surprised by the haste at which I was conveyed to a small but well-appointed room. Among the many Austrian officers, I passed was Major Bisset, the stern fellow I had observed the previous day.

Inside the room stood five men. The prince was not difficult to identify; he wore a superb red jacket and a silken cape of white and gold. Below his wig was a long, rather shapeless face and heavy jowls that didn't match his slender build.

'And you are?'

I felt sure he would have been told but answered with a bow.

'Lieutenant Colonel Johann Von Mayr of the Free Battalion.'

'May I, sir?' interjected one of the others, who were all in military dress.

Charles nodded.

'Why in God's name would the king send a man of such low rank?'

I answered swiftly: 'Perhaps you are not aware, good sir, that I have fought for the Habsburg empire – under Field-Marshal Von Seckendorff, no less.'

'That is correct,' said another man. 'I remember the name.'

'You are a mercenary,' said Charles, with no little disgust.

'Indeed. But I was able to convince the king that my experience fighting alongside the forces of the Emperor would assist my mission.'

'And what precisely is that?' demanded Charles. 'He wants us to surrender, I suppose?'

'That is what he wants, yes.'

'Explain yourself,' demanded another officer.

'I'm happy to, for I believe, your grace, that you will be very interested in what I have to say.'

I requested that we speak alone but Charles and his officers would not agree. It was eventually decided that a single advisor, an older general who had not yet spoken, would remain with him. After searching me once more to ensure I possessed no hidden weapon, the three other officers left. Charles invited me to sit opposite him in a well-lit corner of the room. The general stood by his side.

'Well then,' said the prince. 'What can you offer me?'

'A proposal. A way to end this war right here, right now.'

I can only assume that a man in charge of a besieged city would struggle to feel hope. My job was to give him precisely that.

I continued: 'You may be aware that Field-Marshal Von Daun is assembling a large force to the east. That is why the king wishes to force the issue here: so that he can take the city first, then turn his attention to Von Daun. I told him I would come here on his behalf, engage with my former allies, learn what I could in an attempt to give him an advantage. That was not my true purpose.'

'Go on.'

'Old Fritz has lost his way. You might think you did badly but he's lost twenty thousand men, not to mention Von Schwerin and Winterfeldt.' The prince and the general exchanged a satisfied smile upon hearing these half-truths.

'Even his brother is beginning to doubt him. Several units have deserted already.' I leaned forward, eyes locked on the prince. 'What if you could entangle him here, keep him occupied until Von Daun can strike in the rear? Most of the Prussian army is camped out there. You could take them in one piece.'

I could see from the prince's reaction that he was intrigued.

'How would we "entangle" him?'

'I will inform the king that the situation here is desperate – imply that you might surrender. When I know Von Daun is close enough, I will return here. You will appear to offer your surrender and open one gate. You will allow the Prussians to enter, then spring your trap. If all goes well, you will keep him engaged until relief arrives.'

Charles considered all this for some time before answering:

'How do we know we can trust you?'

'You don't. But where is the great risk? Can fifty thousand men not contain one gate?'

The pair offered no answer to this.

'Why now?' asked the general. 'What's in it for you?'

'I am a realist. I can see which way the scales are tipping. Why have a free battalion if you are not free to switch sides? It's not the first time. What's in it for me? Two hundred golden ducats. I'm sure you'll be able to find the money somewhere. There's no hurry, I can collect it when I return. Shall I give you some time to consider my suggestion?'

Two hours after crossing the bridge, I walked back the other way. Charles had privately consulted with the general for some time before tentatively agreeing that I proceed. As I'd made clear, he indeed had little to lose and a slim hope of a famous victory. I knew from Volland that he was a man of tremendous ambition and it was this trait I'd depended on.

I could do nothing more now. Charles might easily change his mind, or be persuaded to do so by his advisors. As I marched onward, I told myself to put all thoughts of this first half of my scheme behind me. I had to concentrate on the second half now.

I'd had enough of being a puppet of the king. True, I owed him my life. But I had seen enough to know that, for all his immense gifts, Old Fritz had brought great suffering to his allies and enemies, with what seemed to be apparent indifference.

While I had awaited Charles' decision, my king had unleashed another bombardment. When I again passed through the streets, I saw mothers weeping over dead children, their little bodies bloodied and ripped apart.

I would not assist Frederick, for I wanted no part of a war.

He was a king, and I a criminal, but I'd never harmed a hair on another's head. This man challenged empires, ruled millions, commanded tens of thousands but I tired of being his plaything.

He had called on me to employ my gifts in his service. Now I would employ them as I had throughout my adult life: in the service of none but myself.

***

Upon my return, I at least enjoyed a more pleasant reception than the previous occasion. Colonel Danneburg had a horse for me and we rode swiftly back through the lines to the command post. King Frederick was hearing the latest from his pickets and we waited a good half hour before I was summoned once more.

I found the king standing over a table, gazing down at various maps and plans. The tent was airless and stuffy and he stood there without his jacket, the top button of his shirt undone. Prowler lay at his feet, dozing. Without a single glance at me, Frederick grabbed his snuffbox, took a pinch and drew it in. Then, using his finger for scale, he measured out several distances on a map marked by pencil. I also noted a pile of small pieces of paper with brief notes scrawled on them.

'Well?' said the king, hands resting on the table as he, at last, looked up.

'I believe Prince Charles took the bait, sir. I think we've got a good chance of getting the bridge gate open.'

The king's eyes narrowed as he rounded the table. 'Is that so? You know the majority of my officers consider this plot of yours harebrained. I approved it because my other choices are limited. But perhaps they're right.'

'Your Majesty, I cannot guarantee success. But the prince believes he is taking no great risk. If he does concentrate his forces to the west gate and I can get the eastern gate open, you will have a great advantage.'

'And how do you propose to do that?'

'As you'll recall, I was there previously and saw a rather disorganized scene. I feel certain that I can recruit enough men to help me. I will, however, need a considerable amount of bribe money. At least two hundred golden ducats.'

The king's eyes widened.

'Your Majesty, I will not get a second chance. If I have any skill at all, it is in seeking out and persuading men who can be bought. But what I offer them must be enough to buy their immediate and full cooperation.'

King Frederick rubbed his hands together and drew in a long breath. He then aimed a finger at the table.

'Von Daun is on the move so we must try it tonight. As soon as it's dark enough, I will shift my artillery and assault units to the east. We must agree on a signal.'

'Tonight?' This I was not prepared for, though in a way I was glad that all would be resolved swiftly. 'Very well, Your Majesty.'

The king stepped closer. 'I still cannot help but wonder if this is some plot designed to benefit you.'

I don't suppose I was the first to observe that the king was an exceptionally perceptive man.

'Your Majesty, you have saved my life once; and now you have given me a chance at freedom. I do not intend to waste it.'

The king nodded then gestured for me to leave. 'Make the arrangements then. You will return to the city at dusk.'

I bowed low and retreated. My acting skills had rarely been so tested but I felt sure I had passed.

I was almost into the daylight when the king spoke again.

'Christian.'

I halted and turned. 'Your Majesty?'

'I am a king but also a man; a man who has been betrayed many times before. But I ask you: do not betray Prussia. Do not betray your country.'

I bowed again before leaving, a solemn chill coursing through me.

Chapter Twenty-Four

When night came, I stood at the landward side of the bridge, accompanied by Colonel Danneburg once more. Though not a single light within the Prussian lines moved, we had already seen the soldiers beginning to do so. In groups no larger than platoons they would shift around to the east in a wide arc before reassembling. Later, the artillery would follow and it was Prince Henry and his battle-hardened grenadiers who would lead the assault. I was supposed to give my signal – a fire atop a spire – close to dawn, giving the king's forces the whole day to take the city.

I felt little guilt that no signal would appear, that no attack would take place, only resentment at being so involved in such great events; given a role I had never asked for. I did not wish to harm the king's chances but neither did I wish to improve them. My only goal was to escape the besieged city alive.

'I suppose I should get going.' I had left the sword at the camp but still carried my case, now made considerably heavier by two hundred golden ducats.

Colonel Danneburg and I shook hands once more. 'Best of luck, Christian. There's no faulting your courage and resourcefulness. May the Lord watch over you.'

Like most Prussian officers, Danneburg was fiercely religious. I had heard no such comments from the king, for it was widely known that he had no interest in the divine. I suppose a man who could begin or end a war with a single order did not want for influence.

'Thank you, colonel, for everything you've done. May he watch over you too.'

'Farewell.'

'Farewell.'

I made some final adjustments to my uniform then looked about me. It was another clear night with only a few thin wisps of cloud in the sky. The encampment and the city seemed quiet, the dark water eerily still. I set off across the bridge for the last time.

The city seemed very different at night. There were only a few lanterns lit and I found myself watched from every window, doorway, corner, and nook. The ordeal of the last week now seemed to catch up with me and my legs felt leaden as I walked to the city hall, again surrounded by Austrian troops. Discussions – some shouted, some hushed – followed us as the locals and the troops tried to deduce what my return might signify.

My fingers were clammy on the handle of the case. When it had been opened at the gate, I'd calmly stated that the two hundred golden ducats were a matter solely of interest to the prince and myself. My nerves were not aided by the presence of Major Bisset. He wasn't in charge of my escort but strode along with us and more than once I saw his eyes upon me.

I endeavored to put aside my fears and take in my surroundings. I had already absorbed much about the city but of primary interest to me now was the proximity of any inns or taverns. If I was to escape Prague, I would need the assistance of a certain type of man; and I knew precisely in what type of place I would find him.

Fewer people were gathered outside the city hall than in the daytime and I was again conveyed inside at speed. There was to be no intimate meeting this time, however. I was searched once more, then shown into a long hall with great paintings and crests displayed upon the walls. Sitting in the middle of the hall around a circular table, illuminated by a quartet of huge candelabras, sat Prince Charles and at least a dozen of his staff.

I was held back until the prince signaled that I should approach, then offered the last seat at the table. Trying to appear calm, I glanced at the assembled faces and saw a good deal of suspicion, perhaps even hostility.

'What have you to tell us, Mayr?' asked Charles.

I was glad at least that my identity was not under question.

'Speak up, man!' snapped one of the generals almost instantly. 'Do you think we have time to spare?'

I kept my eyes on the prince. 'I shall be happy to answer every question, your grace. But my cooperation is conditional upon payment. We agreed two hundred gold ducats, did we not?'

'By god, this is an outrage!' thundered the general.

'With respect,' said I, 'if all goes to plan, my battalion and I will be coming over to your side. They will follow my orders but I shall need to keep them happy.'

'Get his money,' said the prince.

As two officers trotted away, Charles leaned forward over the table. I'm told you already have two hundred in your possession.'

'I informed the king that I would need it for bribery money. Please, gentlemen, try not to look so shocked. I am a mercenary, after all.'

Fortunately for me, the money arrived swiftly, one of the officers placing a heavy-sounding bag beside my chair.

'Earlier today I met with His Majesty King Frederick, who is currently planning to strike the eastern gate at my signal. He believes your forces are poorly organized, that morale is low and that the populace will turn against you if given the opportunity. This signal is to take the form of a fire upon one of the high spires. He is expecting it close to dawn but I of course will leave the precise timing to you.'

The aggressive general had another question for me. 'Why would the king risk an attack?'

'Two reasons. Firstly, because I have convinced him that he can make a breakthrough. Secondly, and more importantly, Von Daun is moving quickly. It has to be now. If not, the king will have to abandon the city.'

'This we can corroborate,' said another officer. 'The messenger that got through this afternoon told us as much.'

The fierce general was still not convinced. 'You have admitted deceiving the king. Why should we believe that you are not deceiving us?'

'Time will tell, general. If we do not give the signal, the king will not attack. In that case, the likely outcome is that he will then turn to engage Von Daun. He has the numbers to win. If, on the other hand, you keep his force – or at least a portion of it – tied up here, the Prussians are badly exposed. It is not my place to dictate tactics but what if you leave only a token force at the gate, allow it to be breached? The attackers will have no way of knowing that every surrounding street is barricaded, that fifty thousand men will stop them progressing any further.'

No one spoke but I could tell that the idea was an appealing one. I doubted there was an Austrian officer alive who wouldn't want part of a victory over Old Fritz.

Charles spoke up. 'Leave us, Mayr.'

'Of course, your grace.'

I cannot recall a more tense wait. I sat outside the hall, alone on a row of many chairs, watched by a pair of guards. I felt far from certain that the decision would go my way and knew that, if it didn't, I could well be in danger. My intention was to make my escape later when under less scrutiny but, as the minutes ticked past, I considered my options in case I had to flee.

The two guards were armed with swords and standing only feet away. Directly opposite me was the main door, and I knew several soldiers and officers were outside. To the right was another door where I had seen a few civilians going in or out; I assumed this was some kind of office. To my left was another door, which I'd not seen used. If unlocked, this was probably my best chance.

I was once again unarmed so looked around for any other object that might be of use. Nothing obvious presented itself. My only slight advantage was the soldiers themselves. As grenadiers, they were encumbered not only with their swords but tall, heavy miter caps. Given their prestigious duty close to the prince, I daresay they'd been instructed to keep them on. My three-sided hat now sat on the chair beside me and I intended on leaving it there. As for the case now containing four hundred ducats, that I would be holding on to for dear life.

I was still racking my brain for an idea when the main door opened. In walked Major Bisset with an older man of lower rank.

Bisset cast a suspicious glance in my direction as he and his companion strode past me to the door of the hall. He was too far away for me to hear the conversation but the officer stationed there agreed to admit him. Gesturing for the older man to remain outside, Bisset entered.

Once the door had closed, I turned my attention to the older man, who was now talking to the officer. I am no expert lip reader but I have spent my life observing people and I watched intently as the old soldier shrugged then spoke. I clearly saw him mouth 'Von Seckendorff' and knew instantly that I was in trouble.

That determined swine Bisset had somehow found an aged soldier who had fought with Von Seckendorff: the field marshal the real Johann Von Mayr had served under. No doubt he intended to use this man to check my identity. I had to leave now.

When I stood up, the guards turned. But I did not look at them, instead staring hard at the new arrival. 'Gentlemen, I don't wish to alarm you but does that fellow look suspicious to you? See the bulge under the jacket. Is he not concealing a weapon? A flintlock, perhaps?'

They both looked, and one even took a step. Knowing this was as much of a chance as I would get, I grabbed the case and sprinted for the door. Relieved to find it open, I knew I had a few paces head start.

Hauling the door shut behind me, I ran on through a darkened room, crying out but not slowing down as I caught my shin on some hard object. There was enough light coming from the windows to guide me to the far side of the room and another doorway. I could hear shouting behind me and the footfalls of several soldiers.

Once through the next door, I spied the angular shape of a table and grabbed it. Dragging it in front of the door as an obstacle for my pursuers, I glanced around. Finding myself opposite a broad chimney, I realized I was in a spacious kitchen. Reaching the only other visible door, I twisted the handle and pulled. Locked.

Scrambling past barrels and chairs, I reached the nearest window, lifted the latch and wrenched it open. Once up on the ledge, I realized how small the space was. I first dropped the case onto the street, then maneuvered my legs downward. I had to twist awkwardly to get my shoulders through but was soon on the ground.

As I looked around, I heard thuds and cracks from behind me as the soldiers struggled to get through the door. Away to my right was the city hall's main entrance. The important building was set apart from other structures but there were numerous side streets away to my left and I set off towards them at a run, tripping again as I struck a curb.

I have never been so grateful for darkness. Better still, there were very few lanterns alight, for I imagine oil was at a premium. However, there was not space to billet all of the soldiers and many were still gathered in the open spaces. I knew the alarm would go up swiftly; I had to get well away from the city hall.

The first street I reached housed a tavern where a band was playing. Staying in the shadows on the other side, I hurried past but had not gone far when I heard the shouts and boots of my pursuers. I was now at the corner of a square and did not dare risk crossing it and exposing myself.

Noting an unusual silhouette to my left, I trotted over to what I soon realized was another damaged building. Instead of venturing inside, I clambered over rubble to a high pile of bricks where I could seek cover. Squatting low and bowing my head, I watched as troops flooded the square, many wielding lanterns; all wielding weapons.

As they spread out, I realized I had time to ditch my wig and jacket, which I duly buried under some bricks. Now clad in a white shirt, I would not attract attention unless someone appraised the quality of my breeches and boots. At one stage, a pair of soldiers came perilously close to my position but once they moved on, I decided I had to clear the area entirely.

My old skills and instincts were very much put to the test: sometimes I crept along murky alleys, sometimes I walked brazenly along the street. Once I used the rooftops to bypass a platoon of troops, twice I used wagons to cover me as I passed even larger concentrations of soldiers. And on one awful occasion, I felt a hand on my shoulder and spun around, half-expecting to be confronted by Major Bisset. The interloper turned out to be an aged woman who uttered nothing but nonsense.

Now close to the northern walls, I had to look into the windows of several inns and taverns to find one without troops. Once inside, I realized why this particular tavern was so quiet: it was a dingy, dirty place, thick with the scent of ale and sweat. There were no more than a dozen patrons, most of them playing cards. I had already used one of my ducats to purchase a knapsack from a passer-by. Twenty of the coins were now in my pocket, the rest on my back. Though the leather case helped mask the noise, I didn't want to alert anyone to my fortune.

Taking a stool at the counter, I ordered some wine from the barkeep. When he offered me the drink in a very unappealing glass, I slid a ducat across to him.

'For your assistance. And discretion.'

The barkeep, a rotund man around my age, brushed some errant strands of hair from his face and nodded. Affecting a casual air, he leaned onto the counter.

'Assistance with what?'

'Getting out of Prague. The tunnels.'

The barkeep gave a smile of disbelief. 'You and every other poor sod on this side of the walls.'

'Not every poor sod has as much gold as me.'

This maintained his interest. 'The Austrians know most of the tunnels. They've got the local officials in their pocket.'

'Most? What about the others?'

'I believe there are a few but I don't know where.'

'Who would? Smuggler?'

'Maybe.'

I leaned closer. 'You find someone who can get me out of here, there's another nine coins in it for you.'

'I might know a man. But there are no guarantees.'

'I'll pay you in any case.'

The barkeep straightened up and walked to the other end of the counter. Sitting close by was an elderly fellow nursing a mug of ale.

'Anton, watch the bar for a bit.'

My new associate insisted on receiving four more of his ducats before guiding me to the home of a man named Jiri. According to the barkeep, this fellow had used the tunnels for smuggling in the past, though he'd apparently turned his back on criminality in recent times. This choice had apparently not brought him great wealth because his home was a rickety wooden construction built beside a stinking waterway. His wife answered the door, handing a slender candle to him when he summoned her back inside.

Seeing the barkeep, the former smuggler frowned. 'Perlich, what are you doing here?'

'This gentleman is looking for a way out of Prague, preferably via the tunnels.'

'*Definitely* via the tunnels,' added I. 'And I can pay you well.'

Perlich offered a confirmatory nod.

'I've not been to Hades in a while,' said Jiri.

'That's what they call it,' explained Perlich, 'as in the underworld. Not for the faint-hearted.'

Can you help me or not?'

'The Austrians will be guarding the tunnels,' said Jiri.

'The ones they know about,' said I. 'There must be others.'

'That's not my life anymore.'

My patience was beginning to wear thin. 'Who would know then?'

The two locals exchanged a look.

'What is it?'

'You mentioned payment,' said Jiri.

'By God! Ten golden ducats if you get me to someone who can get me out.'

'I can tell you where to find him but I won't be joining you.'

'Why?'

Jiri sighed. 'His name is Romberg. A smuggler, a thief, and … worse. But he knows Hades better than anyone. He's usually a hard man to track down but his wife runs a brothel above the Black Ox.'

I handed Jiri the coins then turned to the barkeep. 'Can you take me there?'

'For another ten ducats – absolutely.'

Half an hour later, I found myself alone in an empty bedroom. Business was obviously good in the brothel because I could hear passionate noises from the rooms on either side. I had paid off the barkeep and slipped another coin to the proprietor, a well-preserved woman of at least fifty. I was relieved to hear that her husband was currently playing cards in the Black Ox and that she would happily fetch him.

Seeing flickering light outside, I moved to the window and spied a platoon of troops carrying flaming torches. I recognized the uniforms of the Irish soldiers and hoped that this was some random patrol, not a search party. However, only a minute later I saw another platoon pass by. Leading them was the now-familiar figure and resolute expression of Major Bisset.

Instinctively ducking away from the window, I cursed. Could this be a coincidence or had Perlich or Jiri given me away? Creeping to another window, I was relieved to see Bisset and his men continue past. They hadn't tracked me down. Yet.

My optimism lasted only as long as it took for the door to open. Romberg wore a long, black coat that I felt sure hid all manner of nasty surprises. He was at least fifty, his face lined and scarred in several places. His lank, grey hair was tied back in a tail. His voice was a disconcerting rasp, with an accent I could not place.

'Not normally one to leave a card game when I'm winning. Gold coins are always liable to change a man's mind.'

'Can you get me out of Prague?'

He kicked the door shut with his boot. 'Depends how much you're willing to pay.'

'Fifty golds to get me through the tunnels and out the other side. Half now. Half when I'm safe.'

'That'll do me,' said Romberg with a grin. 'Here's the bad news. Usually six ways out of the city through Hades. Three of those the Austrians know about. Of the other three, the Prussians are guarding two. That leaves one. Fortunately for you, I can get you there. Worse news – we've had a wet few months. Hope you can swim.'

I nodded and took the twenty-five coins out of my pocket. I'd already prepared them, not wanting this rogue to see just how much I had.

Romberg continued: 'The entrance is below a warehouse owned by the Dvorak gang. They'll want ten just to let us use it. Not coming out of my end.'

'Very well.'

'We best get moving then,' said Romberg. 'You know my name. What do I call you?'

'Christian.'

Chapter Twenty-Five

I believed I had done well to move around the besieged city without detection but I was a mere amateur compared to Romberg. Hidden beneath a peaked cap and that black coat, the man seemed to know every dark corner of Prague. On the rare occasions he was spotted, those who saw him stayed clear. I simply trailed along in his wake. The initial burst of energy following my escape had now faded and I felt very tired. The considerable weight of the golden coins on my back did not help; and the thought that my fate was now in the hands of this sinister character was a second burden.

The warehouse was a long, low structure built opposite a grand church. We were now some way from the northern wall and, thankfully, there seemed to be few troops in this area. Two watchmen guarded the warehouse. One was sent to fetch his master while the other waited with Romberg and myself. I imagine the prospect of gold was a factor in their haste because the watchmen returned with another man in less than ten minutes. As they approached, Romberg confided that this was one of the four Dvorak brothers.

'This better be good,' said the new arrival. 'The army is combing the streets, looking for some spy. You two, go watch the corners.'

The watchmen hurried away.

'Wish they'd find the bastard,' said I.

'Maybe you are the bastard,' countered Dvorak.

'Come now,' said Romberg. 'We're all businessmen here. Long as Christian pays his way, where's the problem?'

'No problem,' said Dvorak. 'But maybe we can get more by selling him out to the army.'

'And bring their attention on your affairs?' said I. 'Not to mention your warehouse and this precious tunnel. I think we all know you're not going to do that.'

'Let's see your money. Twenty.'

'Romberg said ten.'

'Romberg shouldn't have said anything. Our tunnel, our price.'

'Even though it's half full of water?'

'More than half,' replied Dvorak with a chuckle. 'But beggars can't be choosers. If it was easily passable, we'd be taking people out and bringing brandy and tobacco in.'

As before, I had surreptitiously retrieved some coins so as not to betray my true haul, of which I had now given up a considerable portion.

'Very nice,' said Dvorak, examining a handful of golden ducats under a lantern.

He brought out a hefty set of keys and attended to the three separate locks needed to open the warehouse door. I followed Romberg and was almost inside when one of the watchmen ran along the side of the warehouse.

'Patrol. That tough bloody Frenchmen in charge, by the looks of it.' 'Inside, everyone,' ordered Dvorak. 'We'll lock up and hope they pass by.'

I made no mention of Major Bisset but it was clear that he was almost as well known in Prague as Prince Charles. This was clearly not a man to accept defeat.

Once we were all inside and the door locked, the single lantern was half-shuttered and we filed across the building. Much of the space was unoccupied but I glimpsed several stacks of barrels and wooden chests. We then entered a convoluted path between these stacks until I had completely lost my bearings. While Dvorak held the lantern, the two watchmen shifted one particularly large barrel. Underneath was a trapdoor.

One man grabbed the loop of rope around the handle and heaved it upward. In the grainy light provided by the lantern, I could see only a set of steep steps, slick with moisture and green with mold.

'I'm assuming the twenty includes the lantern,' said I.

'Indeed,' replied Dvorak, handing it to Romberg. 'I daresay your guide has some oil and a few candles in one of his many pockets. That and a good deal more besides.'

Romberg removed his hat and stuffed it into his coat. 'Don't go scaring the gentleman, Dvorak.' With that, he turned around and started downward.

I looked at the others but their faces were now no more than dark shapes. I tightened the straps of my knapsack and followed Romberg. There was nothing to hold onto and more than once I thought I would slip and fall. At the bottom of the twenty steps were several inches of water. Hearing noise from above, I looked up and could just make out a lighter area. It abruptly disappeared when the trapdoor was shut.

'How will you get out?' I asked Romberg.

He did not reply; but was looking upwards, listening to what I now realized were several raised voices.

'Sounds like the soldiers are inside. Come on.'

Romberg sloshed away along a narrow tunnel and I swiftly found myself in darkness once more. Desperate to stay close to him, I now realized how stupid I'd been not to arm myself. I was alone down here with this man. He had every advantage.

My suspicions were partially eased by the obvious knowledge of my guide. The narrow tunnel gave way to a series of old cellars. We must have passed through a dozen, sometimes crawling under a half collapsed ceiling, sometimes climbing a pile of rubble. Beyond the last of them was an ancient cistern, complete with ornate columns, many inscribed in Latin. Here the water was deeper – well over my knees and the tops of my boots.

Halfway across the cistern, Romberg stopped to refill the lantern with oil and I was entrusted with a taper to keep the flame alive. When he lit the lantern once more, the orange light illuminated a nearby column and the eerie, grotesque faces etched in the stone.

Hades, indeed.

We had just reached the far end of the cistern when we heard voices behind us. Then came a trace of light.

'Not giving up easily,' said Romberg. 'You are the spy then, Christian?'

Even now, I saw no reason to admit the truth. 'Actually no. Though they may think I am.'

'Don't worry. They will not move quickly through the rat trap.'

The place was well named: a low ceiling but broad sewer with many sloping tunnels leading down into it. The putrid water was two-feet deep: stinking and thick with what I knew could only be human waste. Romberg had already put a handkerchief over his mouth and nose and fortunately I had one too. As we waded through the muck, I saw rats entering and exiting the tunnels and some swimming brazenly past.

Thankfully we did not follow the sewer for too long but the way out was via one of the smaller tunnels. From it came a trickle of water and, where it passed over the lip, detritus had accumulated.

'Not easy, this section,' remarked Romberg. 'Least the rope's still here.'

Holding the lantern in his teeth, my guide climbed into the tunnel and fed the rope back to me. As he set off up the incline, I wiped my hands on my breeches to try and improve my grip. I was a second away from following Romberg when I glimpsed something far to my left. Back where we had entered the sewer, flickering torchlight now illuminated the water.

I found it hard to believe that the soldiers had followed us so far; and now wondered if Dvorak or someone else was assisting them. It mattered not. Romberg had told me we were three-quarters of the way through. If he was intercepted on the way back, so be it. Nobody would stop me.

'Come, Christian.'

'Coming.'

As the end was near, some instinct told me to take two precautions. Firstly, I removed my knapsack and retrieved five coins. These I slipped into the tops of my boots for safe-keeping. Once the knapsack was back on, I felt around in the litter upon the tunnel lip. My fingers found a jagged chunk of rock that fitted my hand well enough. This I placed in my pocket before following Romberg. It was not much of a weapon but it was better than nothing.

Though the incline was not great, the water and slippery stone made the climb surprisingly difficult, especially as there was little space to maneuver. I have no idea how Romberg managed to do it so quickly and with the lantern in his mouth.

By the time I pulled myself clear, panting with exertion, my guide was breathing normally. He stood in a narrow corridor of stone, lantern tucked into a niche, drinking from a flask.

'Not far now. A refreshment?'

'No thank you.'

'On we go then.'

This corridor was so tight that we could only negotiate it by shuffling sideways. I consider myself a good judge of character but I remained utterly unsure about Romberg. He had so far treated me well; and if he planned to attack and take all my treasure, why escort me so far? I wondered if – like many within the criminal fraternity – it suited him to cultivate a ruthless reputation. Or perhaps it was entirely well-earned.

There was little time for further thought as the corridor now widened out and Romberg stepped over a hole in the ground. He turned towards me and pointed downwards. 'The remains of an old well. Then it's the last cellar – we'll see if we can actually get through at all.'

'What do you mean?'

'We're almost at the end – under the moat. The last cellar is the deepest point. Always flooded, just depends how badly.'

Again hanging the lantern from his mouth, Romberg sat on the side of the hole then lowered himself down. I saw that someone had installed a rope ladder that looked in reasonable condition and indeed he negotiated it quickly. Upon reaching the bottom, I reckoned we had descended another thirty feet.

I again found myself in a well-made cellar with walls of brick. It was the first of several, each connected by a doorway. Water dripped from countless locations in the roof and the foul smell was more than dankness: it was horribly bitter and made breathing difficult.

The fourth cellar was entirely flooded to knee-height. Romberg now moved very carefully to the right wall and held the lantern up. He only stopped when he came close to a clear horizontal line rendered in chalk. Close to the line was a metal hook, from which Romberg hung the lantern.

He gestured forward. The furthest edge of the light only just reached the far wall.

'Not good.'

I came up beside him.

'I'd stop there if I were you,' warned Romberg. 'Take another step and you'll be in over your head.'

'What?'

As with all the water I had seen in Hades, this was thick with dirt and utterly impenetrable.

'From the chalk line is a set of steps leading down to the last cellar. The roof is submerged.'

'You mean the whole cellar is underwater?'

Romberg nodded. 'It's no more than twenty feet across but I'm damned if I'm going to try it.' He turned away. 'Should have bloody well known.'

I just stood there, gazing down at the water. All my efforts to escape the city had come to this: an impassable obstacle. Or was it?

'Twenty feet's not so far.'

'Try it then,' said Romberg. 'It'll be easier without the gold.'

I turned to see him grinning at me. Light gleamed upon the long, slender knife now in his hand.

'Rather honorable of me, wouldn't you say? I could have just stabbed you in the back.'

'I'm paying you fifty ducats. That isn't enough?'

'That bag of yours looks very heavy, Christian. Guessing you've got a least two hundred in there. You don't seriously think I'm going to let that slip through my hands? I'm taking it all.' Romberg gestured to the water. 'You still get a chance to be free. Swiftly now – hand it over.'

He had barely finished speaking when the sound of falling rubble echoed through the cellars. As his head turned in that direction, I pounced, circling his wrist with both hands.

Romberg threw a punch. I saw it coming and turned so that he struck only my shoulder. Now he put his spare hand on both of mine as we struggled for control of the blade.

We seemed to be matched for strength; no one could find an advantage. He hooked his foot behind my ankle but when I tried to twist away, we both overbalanced and fell into the water.

I felt the knife fly free but my relief was short-lived, for Romberg swiftly pinned me with his knees. His hands were instantly around my throat and, while submerged, I could do nothing more than keep my mouth closed.

Then I remembered my weapon. With my right hand, I reached down and pulled it out of my pocket. Using my left to locate my foe's jaw, I clubbed him with the rock.

I knew I had struck an effective blow, for Romberg's hands let go and I was able to struggle clear. The thief crawled away through the water, blood dripping from his face.

Now came shouts from the cellar and I could hear the soldiers splashing towards us. With Romberg still on the floor, I turned and looked at the water.

Twenty feet. Easy on the surface.

But here – in pitch-black water? Beneath solid rock?

'He's there!' came the shout. 'I see him.'

Romberg looked up but hadn't the strength to move.

The light from the soldier's lanterns grew brighter.

It was a stark choice. But I knew capture meant imprisonment, torture, and probably death.

No. No more.

I reached back and tightened the knapsack's straps then drew in several long breaths. I walked up to the chalk mark and looked back over my shoulder.

The relentless Major Bisset was first into the cellar. He drew his sword.

'You there, halt! Halt!'

I dived into the water and swam for the wall. With a final breath, I plunged deeper, kicking hard with my legs and pulling myself along with broad strokes. Eyes shut, I told myself to stay calm and concentrate solely on my progress.

For the first few strokes, this worked well. Then, with an awful suddenness, the reality of my predicament struck me. I reached up, touched only slimy stone. I kicked and kicked and tried to pull myself along but the smooth surface could not be grasped. I stretched out my arms, longing to touch the edge that would mean salvation.

Some fearful spasm struck me and again I almost opened my mouth. I had stopped moving and had to tell myself to keep going. I dived again, kicked and pulled myself through that deathly oblivion.

At last, I opened my eyes. Ahead was something fractionally lighter than the darkness surrounding me. I summoned one last effort, turned over as I swam and my fingers at last found the edge. I hauled myself forward and under the roof.

Moments later I broke the surface, sucking in breath after breath until I could finally give thought to moving. Around me was only more darkness but I swam onward and eventually found another set of steps beneath me. Soon I was dragging myself out of the water. I collapsed onto my knees, coughing and spluttering.

There was so little light that I could only feel my way forward. I reached a dead-end but by moving first left, then right, came to a hole that seemed to have been cut out of the wall. I found myself in another low tunnel reinforced by wood and crawled on across sodden mud. This tunnel met another at right angles, and here were solid steps leading upward. As I, at last, began to inhale fresh air, I knew I was close to the surface and sure enough the steps led me up to a narrow shaft partially covered by a sack. I moved this aside and clambered up onto dewy grass.

Once I'd recovered a little, I examined my surroundings and found I was in a tiny copse of trees only a stone's throw from the moat. Around me were numerous campfires. I could hear several conversations.

I took another few minutes to regain some energy, then drained the water from my rucksack and boots (without losing the gold pieces). Though it was not a cold night, I was already shivering. Yet I had to move; only the hours of darkness would allow me to escape the Prussian lines.

Extricating myself quietly from the trees, I crouched low and set a course between campfires. This path took me dangerously close to a row of tents – and snoring soldiers – but I covered at least half a mile before nearing a road where I could see several wagons parked. Knowing that troops sometimes slept inside or under the vehicles, I steered well clear.

I was beginning to feel hopeful as I approached a low wall. Only yards away, my right foot fell into a hollow and I tripped, landing noisily. By the time I was back on my feet, I saw four immense figures rise up and clamber over the wall. One had a lantern, and I saw a tall, broad soldier in the blue coat of a Prussian infantryman.

'Who goes there?' demanded another man.

The quartet closed in quickly and when I saw that two had muskets, I realized there was no chance of escape.

After all I had been through, a moment of sheer bad fortune had cost me dear. From their great height, I knew these were some of the king's 'tall lads' regiment. I was entirely at their mercy. I raised my hands.

'Who are you?' repeated one of the giants, who appeared the oldest of the four.

'No one. Just a man trying to get home.'

The words came to me without thought.

'He's wet,' said one of the soldiers.

'Did you come across the moat?' asked another.

'Not exactly.'

'What have you got there?' asked a third, pointing at my knapsack.

Perhaps I was too tired to think or attempt deceit but I simply took it off and dropped it in front of them.

'About three hundred golden ducats.'

The soldiers chuckled. But then one knelt down and opened the sack and satchel. The coins glinted appealingly under the lantern light.

'By God,' said the man as two others knelt beside him and grabbed handfuls of gold.

The older man gave me a sharp look.

'You better tell your officers,' said I. 'The treasury is always on the lookout for funds. Wars are very expensive. Or I suppose you could keep it: divide it amongst yourselves, hide it until you get home. I've no doubt you deserve it.'

The other three looked up at the older man, who remained silent.

'Your choice.' Again without a thought, I walked around the soldiers and clambered over the wall. As I strode away across the field, not one of them said a word.

Chapter Twenty-Six

I walked on through the night, only stopping at the first trace of dawn. Exhausted and afraid that I was still being pursued, I stole into a barn and slept the whole day there, thankfully without being disturbed. As soon as the sun set, I departed, staying away from main roads, using the stars to guide me north.

On the following morning, I walked into a sizable town and found the nearest inn. The proprietor eyed me suspiciously – no surprise given my ragged condition – but overcame his doubts when I offered him a golden ducat. Having bathed, I used another coin to purchase two sets of clothes and a new knapsack.

On the third day after my flight from Prague, I bought a seat on a coach heading north to Drezno. From here, I traveled on to Leipzig and it was there I heard news of the war. King Frederick had met the army of Von Daun east of Prague and suffered a telling defeat at a place called Kolin. The siege of the city was now over and the invasion of Bohemia in disarray.

I felt a little guilty upon hearing this, though I was not convinced that my actions would have influenced the eventual outcome. I didn't wish to see either my king or my country defeated but the Austrians were protecting their land from invasion. Was it my duty to help my king? After how he had treated me, I did not feel so.

There was no telling how long I might have to enjoy my freedom and therefore only one choice of destination. Thirty miles east of Leipzig was my family and my home. I was bound for Halle.

A full twenty years after my last visit, I walked along the Fleisherstrasse towards Kasebier's.

Nothing could have kept me away, for my unlikely survival and escape had prompted me to return to my loved ones. I did not plan on staying, for while it was still possible that no one had connected Christian Kasebier to the King of Thieves, I was now guilty of high treason, and could not allow my family to be dragged into the consequences of my misdeeds. This would be a brief visit.

Without a moment of hesitation, I walked up to the door and knocked. Though it was late in the evening, I could see clothes displayed in the window and the family name still rendered in bright yellow paint above.

Yet it was a stranger who answered: a young man of about eighteen.

'Yes?'

'Johann Kasebier? Margaretha?'

'Mistress Margaretha is here. What name shall I give?'

'Christian.'

'Family name?'

'She knows me.'

'Very well.' The young man departed only to return swiftly, a concerned look upon his face. 'She says you better come in.'

He led me through the hall and to the kitchen. It is not possible for me to describe accurately the mixture of emotions and sensations that I experienced.

My mother stood there, one hand on the kitchen table, watching wide-eyed as I entered. She had a white shawl over her shoulders and, though her hair was grey and her face lined, she didn't look so very different.

'Martin, would you leave us?' she said quietly.

'Of course.' The young man retreated towards the shop.

I approached my mother so that she could see me better; know it was truly her youngest son. She came forward until we were close, reached out and touched my arm and my shoulder. I bent over so that she could touch my face.

In my thoughts of this meeting, I had imagined her overcome with emotion but it was I who cried, who threw my arms around her and held her close.

We stood in that embrace for many minutes, her head against my chest, mine on her shoulder, sobbing until no more tears came. I then escorted her to a seat and offered her a handkerchief.

'You need one too,' she said, dabbing her eyes. 'And what about some brandy? I must settle my nerves.'

I was faintly amused to find that my mother still kept the brandy hidden in the same corner cupboard. I poured us both a glass and sat down. She gripped my hand as we drank.

'I didn't expect to ever see you again, Christian. Why did you not come back? Why did you leave us?'

At that, I was overcome. Twice I tried to speak but my throat was tight, my eyes wet again with tears.

'It … it is so very hard to explain, Mama. I … did not follow a good path. I was … I am a criminal. They called me the King of Thieves.'

'You? I know that name.'

'Many do. But I am not proud. It is true that I stole, and for that, there is no excuse.'

'You truly gave to the poor?'

I nodded.

There was no comment, no judgment, and for that I was grateful. Some time passed in which neither of us spoke.

I knew my questions might cause my mother pain but there were things I needed to know. 'Father?'

'Twelve years ago. A rupture of the heart. He was still working so very hard, even in his old age. He died here, in his bed. A mercy from the Lord.' Mother now placed both her hands on mine. 'In his last hours, he told me … if I was ever to see you … he forgave you, wished you only well.'

I was overwhelmed once more, for though I knew now he was gone, I was so relieved to hear Father hadn't always thought ill of me.

'Is there any news from the New World; what of Johann?'

'You do not know?'

'Please tell me.'

'He is lost to us, Christian. Before your father. Not long after they crossed the ocean.'

Now I felt true agony and I knew this had been the hardest burden Margaretha Kasebier had borne.

'I had always feared such a thing,' she added, eyes gleaming as she gazed down at the table. 'Johann was stricken by a terrible illness and died. Your nephew, Gottlieb was struck upon the head and killed by the native Indians.'

Perhaps I am a natural optimist, for, in all my thoughts of my family, I simply imagined them getting on with life. The march of time made it likely that my parents might have passed on but Johann? My kind, courageous, dutiful brother had been dead for more than a decade and I hadn't even known it.

Had I been present, I might have been able to ease my mother's suffering. What had I been doing? Gallivanting around the countryside with a gang of rogues, feathering my own nest.

'I can never make this up to you, Mama. I have let you down terribly.'

'I just wish you'd kept writing, Christian. I have every one of your letters.' She stood and went through the door that led to father's study. I saw now that she did not move well, no surprise as she was not far from her seventieth year.

Mother returned with two bundles, each bound with twine. I could see that my letters were very precious by the way she handled them but it was the second pile that caught my attention.

'Those are from Maria. She writes every year. They live in a place called Philadelphia.'

'They?'

'She and her brothers – they traveled there to help her. There are still many dangers – Maria tells me it is not possible to follow a pacifist path. But the city is constantly growing and the business with it. Don't worry, it's still called Kasebiers – five stores, would you believe?'

Mother reached across to me. 'Do you have any money, Christian?'

'I did.'

'Maria sends a banker's notice along with her letter every year. Johann wanted a quarter of their profits to go to us. I've never touched a coin of it.'

'Business is good here?'

'Very good. We have a contract for breaches and shirts with the Halle division. Lucian and Martin run it all now with Isaac and Jacob.'

'Good for Lucian. Who's Martin?'

'Lucian's son. Your nephew. So are the others – your sister's sons.' Somehow, she summoned a smile. 'We always were a family business.'

Mother and I spoke long into the night. I spared her the worst of my ordeals but she heard something of my many travels, my time in prison, even my recent service for the king. She asked if I had found love in those years and I told her the unlikely story of my precious time with Sophia. She smiled when she saw the humble ring given to me by one of the richest women in Europe.

I learned all the other news and, though she asked if she could call Lucian in and fetch Martin, I had to say no. My confession to her was one thing; I could not face a reunion with the others.

She understood that I was not back for good but asked me to stay the night. In the morning, the two of us walked to one of the Halle banks and Mother withdrew a thousand thalers. Incredibly, this was only a fraction of the funds she'd received from Philadelphia.

Perhaps I should not have taken the money but Mother was insistent and I was in desperate need; for I knew I had to escape Prussia once and for all.

I escorted Mother home and we parted outside Kasebier's. I promised to write once I was settled. There were no more tears and few words but there was one thing more I wanted to say:

'Mother, I don't know what else you might hear about me but it will likely not be good. Whatever people say, please know that I never carried a weapon, nor struck a first blow. I have seen enough to know that I was very fortunate to be born to this family. You raised me well and I always knew that I was loved. It was only my own weaknesses that led me down the wrong path. I went so far that I could not find my way back.'

'But you did eventually,' said Mother. 'And I'm thankful for it.'

At that, we parted, and I left Halle for the last time.

Chapter Twenty-Seven

Bratislava, 1758

My first stop after Halle was a particularly skilled forger I knew in Freiberg. This man created a completely new identity for me as a Hungarian, for I knew I had to travel far to be safe. I had once visited the city of Bratislava and admired it. Close as it was to the Danube and the Carpathians, there were also a number of choices if I had to flee.

This I hoped to avoid because I sought only a simple, settled life. Once in Bratislava, I began to look around for an inn to purchase. I could not afford anything grand, but eventually bought a place on the outskirts of town. It was very small but on the corner of two busy roads and I believed I'd fare well. They say it is bad luck to change the name of an inn but I couldn't help myself: it became The Red Lion.

The place was so small that I could run it alone, though the hours were long. As I'd always hoped, the job suited me well; I enjoyed socializing with my patrons, who were always a disparate mix of regulars and those passing through.

I read a newspaper when I could and this was how I learned that Princess Sophia Christine had recently given birth to her third child. I felt no jealousy and no regret; my only hope was that her husband treated her well, that she was happy. And though I did not wear my ring, I kept it safe.

It was on one September afternoon when I found a pair of merchants at my counter. As I washed mugs, I heard one tell a remarkable account: the story of The King of Thieves. There were several inaccuracies and exaggerations but the fundamentals were correct: the gifted thief who could steal anything from anyone; the hero of the people who gave to the poor; the king's spy who double-crossed both sides and escaped Prague.

When the merchant had finished, his companion slapped him on the shoulder. 'Very entertaining but what far-fetched nonsense. Who would believe all that?'

The End

